ALEKSANDR SERGEYEEVICH PUSHKIN Born in 1799 in Moscow. He was mortally wounded in a duel with Baron George Heckeren d'Anthès, 1837.

NIKOLAI VASILIEVICH GOGOL Born in 1809 in Sorochintsky. Lived abroad, mainly in Rome, 1836–48. Died in 1852.

LEO NIKOLAEVITCH TOLSTOY Born in 1828 in Yasnaya Polyana, where he spent most of his life. Served in the army 1851–5. In 1857 and 1860 he travelled in Europe. Died in Astapovo, 1910.

VLADIMIR GALEKTIONOVICH KOROLENKO Born in 1853 in Zhitomir. Spent six years (1879–85) in exile in Siberia. Died in 1921.

ANTON PAVLOVICH CHEHOV Born in 1860 in Taganrog. Adopted literature as a career after practising for some time as a doctor. Died in 1904.

EVGENY NIKOLAEVICH CHIRIKOV Born in 1864 in Kazan. Died in Prague, 1932.

LEONID NIKOLAEVICH ANDREYEV Born in 1871 in Orel. His writings earned him a fortune, which he lost when he fled to Finland on the outbreak of the Revolution. Died in 1919.

ALEKSANDR IVANOVICH KUPRIN Born in 1870 in Narovchat. Served with the White Army during the Revolution; lived in exile at Paris 1920–37, when he returned to Russia. Died in 1938.

MAXIM GORKY (real name Alexey Maximovich Peshkov) Born in 1868 at Nizhniy-Novgorod. After working at many trades he became a journalist and a world-famous author. In 1922 he visited Germany, then settled in Sorrento, but returned to Russia in 1928. Died in 1932.

FEDOR SOLOGUB (real name Fedor Kuzmich Teternikov) Born in 1863 in St Petersburg. Died in 1927.

JOHN BAYLEY, who is Thomas Warton Professor of English at the University of Oxford, has written important studies of Tolstoy and Pushkin (*Tolstoy and the Novel*, 1966; *Pushkin: A Comparative Commentary*, 1971) and many essays and articles on modern poetry and the novel in Russia. He is married to the novelist Iris Murdoch.

Russian Short Stories

Translated by R. S. Townsend
Introduction by John Bayley

J.M. Dent & Sons Ltd
London
Charles E. Tuttle Co. Inc.,
Rutland, Vermont
EVERYMAN'S LIBRARY

Introduction © J.M. Dent 1992

First published in Everyman's Library in 1924
Reissued 1992

Made in Great Britain by
The Guernsey Press Co. Ltd., Guernsey, C.I. for
J.M. Dent & Sons Ltd.
91 Clapham High Street, London SW4 7TA
and
Charles E. Tuttle Co., Inc.
28, South Main Street,
Rutland, Vermont 05701,
U.S.A.

ISBN 0 460 87164 1

Everyman's Library
Reg U.S. Patent Office

CONTENTS

INTRODUCTION

Russian literature came late in the day; then it made up for lost time. None in the world is richer. From Pushkin at the beginning of the nineteenth century to Pasternak and Solzhenitsyn in our own time, it has produced poets and novelists of varied genius, but always with a strong sense of identity and continuity. Generalisations about such a wonderful body of work are bound to be misleading, but one or two may be risked none the less. Russian writers are never detached. They are always in the thick of things, grasping life – *zhivaya zhizn*, 'living life' as Dostoevsky spoke of it – with both hands. And, explicitly or implicitly, the question they ask is that of Tolstoy – 'How should we live?', and 'What must be done?'

The reason for this is at least partly historical. Although Pushkin grew up on the French classic authors of the eighteenth century, he was the child of an epoch that had produced Rousseau and Hegel, the great romantic poets and the idealistic philosophers. Modern Russian literature came to flower in an age in which human aspiration and social improvement were everywhere talked and argued about (and Russian writers were also prodigious talkers), while reform, rebirth, spiritual and scientific progress were matters whose burning importance were taken for granted. Chekhov is the least didactic and polemical of Russian authors, but Chekhov too believed devoutly in human progress and the advance of science and enlightenment. He was a doctor by profession and thus he used to say, a servant of humanity: he was a writer in his spare time. He made an arduous journey across Siberia to Sakhalin island to see and report at first hand on the conditions in the convict settlements. And all the time he was writing stories, and later plays, which, when they travelled to Europe and to England, were greeted as beautiful and melancholy demonstrations of the Russian 'soul', with its humour and sadness, its hopelessness and inconsequentiality.

As is shown by a masterpiece like 'The Kiss', this impression was not entirely wrong. Chekhov's stories do indeed reveal the pathos of life, and, above all, the sense the Russians have of the world of beauty the soul yearns for, whilst, at the same time, recognising the way we have to plod on daily and boringly in the same old habits and routines. Like the harp string at the end of *The Cherry Orchard*, the pathos of this contrast in life underlies all Chekhov's art. But so – and just as important – does the humour, the touching and absurd aspects of such an incongruity. In his quiet and unobtrusive way Chekhov is one of the funniest of writers, and, as Samuel Beckett observed, there is always something funny about unhappiness. In another famous story, 'The Lady with the Little Dog', which has been made into a film, the couple in love sit silently in a hotel room together while the man consumes a water-melon. But they also sit by the seashore, hearing the waves breaking, and feeling both the timeless indifference of the sea, and the sense that for them something great and joyful is at hand.

It is this sense of mysterious ecstasy that Chekhov conveys so well in 'The Kiss', which is perhaps an even more touching and more unobtrusively artful tale. Lieutenant Riabovitch has an experience, in the midst of the dull or pompous military routines of his daily existence which is in an unconsequential, yet intoxicating way, the best that life can offer. It doesn't last, but perhaps it – or something similar – will come to him again. Everyone has known experiences of this sort, commoner no doubt in youth than in age, but Chekhov's art manages to create a unique impression of total newness so that we as readers share in the experience in a marvellously surprised apprehension of what is both lyrical and comical in life.

Other stories in this collection display the same genius of comedy, and no doubt a particularly Russian form of comedy. Evgeny Chirikov, who was also a doctor, is not in the same class as Chekhov or Gogol in their unique mastery of the short story form; but he is an interesting writer, never well known and now almost forgotten in the west, who nonetheless deserves commemoration in a selection of tales like this one. More inadvertently, he also reveals how the greater writer Chekhov always avoids the sentimental, or what the Russians term *poshlost*. Chirikov is not sentimental, but he verges upon it in his best stories, and one of the charms of 'Faust' is to see how near to it he can come while just managing to evade its facile embrace! A characteristically and spontaneously Russian moment in 'Faust' is when the little girl with her serious blue eyes asks her mother if the fairy-tale witch Babi Yaga snores, as she has heard her father doing so often.

Aldous Huxley once pointed out that the great Russian novelists and story-tellers were never vague or sentimental, in the way that Dickens for example can be, because they always conveyed so well the sheer clutter of contingency in which we spend our lives, and among which our finer emotions have to find their place. In 'The Cloak' (usually but less accurately translated as 'The Overcoat') Gogol is quite explicit in enlisting our pity for the poor clerk Akaky, in pointing out the isolation in which he lives, and in drawing out all the pathos with which he sometimes says to his fellow clerks, 'Why do you bother me? Please leave me alone'. Gogol is also the satirist and in a sense the reformer (as in his play *The Government Inspector*) when he criticises the manners and behaviour of the great and powerful, and points out the unfeeling tyranny of their ways. But all this goes with and is transformed by his extraordinary sense of detail – his absorbing description of just how and of what materials the new cloak is made, the thumbnail of the tailor, the anxious financial calculations of Akaky, the ecstasy with which he handles and puts on the new coat.

Vladimir Nabokov, author of *Lolita* and other brilliant novels on the border-line between Russian and English fiction, used to say that Gogol's story was the finest one in the world. (Incidentally, he always referred to it as 'The Carrick', a somewhat perverse piece of accuracy, although this then rare and now obsolete English word does signify a voluminous caped garment worn either with or without sleeves. The Russian word is *shinel* – itself derived from French 'chenille', a thick material – Gogol himself would have enjoyed all such details no doubt.) Nabokov has a poor opinion of Dostoevsky, but it was Dostoevsky who said that he and all the other Russian novelists of his generation had come out from under Gogol's *shinel*.

The literalness and forceful detail of all Russian tales does not preclude the presence in them of complex meanings and a deeper resonance. Nothing could seem more like a brilliant tale of graphic action and suspense than Pushkin's 'The Queen of Spades', one of his most masterly pieces of narration, and he was equally good at narrating in prose or in verse. But the story also has dense and even symbolic overtones. The old Countess is representative of the ancient aristocratic Russia of Catherine's time: Hermann of the new age. The confrontation is never emphasised, but it certainly exists. In a similarly oblique fashion Gogol makes his overcoat stand for all the poetry, the love, the sense of romance which has been missing from poor Akaky's tranquil but monotonous existence. When he puts the new coat on and goes off to the party, he becomes aware for the first time of the allurements of the opposite sex: a seductive poster in a shop window, the shapely limbs of a street-walker. (Russian literature is traditionally reticent about sex, but Gogol's skills make all this perfectly apparent.) His new cloak in fact is romance for Akaky, the only romance he has ever known; but Gogol does not do the facile thing that Dickens might have done, and portray him as one of the wretched and downtrodden of the earth. On the contrary, Akaky loves his work, and is happy and content in it: when romance does suddenly arrive in his life, it is the prelude to total misfortune, and agitation, and death.

Such queries and equivocations in his narrative's method and meaning are typical of Gogol, and a great contrast to the brilliant straightforwardness of Pushkin, who read Gogol's tales in the last months of his short life (he died in a duel in St Petersburg at the age of 37) and praised them highly. It is also typical of Gogol that the pathos and homely poetry of the story is so intermixed with farce that the two cannot be separated. Akaky's pathetic death is not the end of it. The absurd business with the ghost who snatches the cloaks off the backs of passers-by then takes over, and even the discomfiture of the 'great personage' in his sleigh does not end it. Indeed the narration ends on a joke which recalls poor Akaky's agony when the new cloak was taken from him. The last policeman to see the 'ghost' before he vanished for ever in the darkness reports that he was a tall fellow with huge whiskers; but no one takes the policeman seriously because he was once knocked off his feet by a pig – just a young one – suddenly rushing out of someone's front door. Who but Gogol would have introduced that piglet at that moment of the story? asked

Nabokov, and what is a piglet doing anyway in a town house in the capital? And why does the ghost have such big fists and whiskers? – if indeed he does have them. It is all part of Gogol's peculiarly dishevelled and yet wonderfully effective narrative manner, the same manner he was to use in *Dead Souls*, the novel that made him famous, and whose subject was probably suggested by Pushkin. 'How sad is life in Russia', Pushkin is supposed to have said on reading it.

But his own stories are not sad: they are as full of animation and gaiety as a Mozart sonata. The continuity of Russian literature, the impression we often get that every author knows every other author, is illustrated by the fact that Varlaam Shalamov, a writer sent to the far eastern *gulag* under Stalin, begins one of his *Kolyma Tales* with a version of the opening sentence of 'The Queen of Spades': 'They were playing cards at Narumov's, the Guards Lieutenant'. Every Russian reader would catch the allusion, and the grim contrast between the gay young bachelors of St Petersburg in 1830, and the miserable plight of Stalin's political prisoners a hundred years later. Tolstoy particularly admired the brisk, plain opening of Pushkin's tales, and was originally inspired to begin his great novel *Anna Karenina* in the same way.

'Korney Vasiliev' is one of Tolstoy's later stories, and one of the most simple and moving that he wrote at that time. In such a story Tolstoy knows how to move us without any tricks at all: there is no apparent narrative device, just as there seems neither style nor method. And yet the story is a masterpiece of art. This fact was not lost on Tolstoy's successor and admirer, Maxim Gorky, who wrote many tales that were strongly influenced by Tolstoyan simplicity and his strong moral viewpoint. 'In the Steppes' is one of his best, and it has something in common with Alexander Kuprin's haunting 'In the Swamp'. Kuprin had been an army officer and achieved great fame with a controversial tale of military life called 'The Duel', which delighted the radicals and infuriated the Tsarist establishment. Both he and his friend Andreyev belonged in a sense to the social realist school of Gorky. When Andreyev was a young man, his powerful and sensational manner impressed the aged Tolstoy, who none the less remarked that he wrote too much for effect. 'A Grand Slam' is one of the most characteristic of his tales.

Unlike most of the writers represented here, Feodor Sologub, whose real name was Teternikov, came from a humble background; but his mother's employer – she was a domestic servant – provided him with an education, and he made a sensation in 1907 with his novel *Melky Bes* (*The Little Demon*.) He was a strange and mystical writer, who had enormous influence in Russia's 'Silver Age' of literature, the period between the 1890s and the beginning of the First World War. 'The White Mother' is an excellent example of his dreamy, masochistic poetic temperament, which struck a chord in the atmosphere of mystical despair and foreboding prevalent among many writers and poets of the period. In an odd way he has something in common with a writer of a previous generation, Vladimir Korolenko, whose story 'The Murmuring Forest' is both poetic and sinister. Korolenko came from the Polish Ukraine and was one of the forerunners of Chekhov, not only in the way he wrote, but in the deep interest he took in social questions and practical reform.

It is an admirable thing to have such stories, all dating from the period before the Russian Revolution, collected here in a single volume. We are familiar today with post-revolutionary Russian literature, so much of which has been translated and become well known to Western readers. But the writers who lived before the modern epoch are in most cases less well known, as well as being less accessible. Even Russian readers today are not so likely to have read examples of the art of Korolenko and Kuprin, Chirikov and Sologub, whose tales are all highly characteristic of their time, and deserve to be rediscovered and remembered. So too with the greatest writer of them all, Pushkin, whose stories and poems have never been well known in the West, except in the form of opera, film or ballet. These stories are a fine introduction to what is best and most significant in Russian literature.

1992   John Bayley

RUSSIAN
SHORT STORIES

The Queen of Spades

BY A. S. PUSHKIN

1799–1837

A card party was in progress at the house of Narumov, a lieutenant of the Guards. The long winter's night passed unobserved, and it was five o'clock in the morning when supper was served. The winners ate ravenously, the rest sat listless by their empty places. With the appearance of the champagne the conversation grew animated and general.

'How did you fare, Surin?' the host asked.

'Lost, as usual. I have no luck at all. I play *mirandole*, always keep cool, am never flustered, yet I always lose.'

'Do you mean you have not once been tempted to back the red? Your strength of mind amazes me.'

'And what do you think of Hermann?' one of the guests remarked, indicating a young officer of the Engineers. 'He has never touched a card in his life, never made a bet; yet he sits watching us play till five in the morning!'

'Cards attract me greatly,' Hermann observed, 'but my position is such that I cannot sacrifice a necessity for a doubtful luxury.'

'Hermann is German and careful; he does not surprise me,' Tomsky remarked. 'The person who is a wonder is my grandmother, the Princess Anna Fedorovna.'

'How? Why?' the guests all cried.

'I can never understand,' Tomsky continued, 'why she never plays.'

'There is nothing extraordinary in that,' Narumov said; 'you must remember she is an old lady of eighty.'

'Do you know anything about her?'

'No, nothing at all.'

3

'Oh, then I must tell you. Sixty years ago my grandmother went to Paris and became the rage there. The people ran after her carriage to get a glimpse of the Muscovite Venus. Richelieu made love to her, and my grandmother assures us that he nearly shot himself because she treated him coldly. In those days the women used to play faro. One evening at the Court, she lost a considerable sum to the Duke d'Orléans. When she reached home, grandmother removed the beauty-spots from her face, took off her hoops, informed grandfather of her loss and insisted that he must pay her debt. My grandfather, who is dead now, was, as far as I can remember, almost like a steward to his wife and was mortally afraid of her. Nevertheless, when he heard of her loss he was furious; he produced a packet of bills showing that they had spent more than half a million in six months. In Paris their Moscow and Saratov estates were not available for sale, he pointed out; the end of it was that he absolutely refused to pay. My grandmother boxed his ears and slept apart from him that night to show her displeasure. In the morning she sent for her husband hoping that the conjugal deprivation would have had some effect on him, but she found him obdurate. For the first time in her life she condescended to arguments and explanations. There were differences between debts and debts, she told him, and a prince could not be treated like a coachman. But all her eloquence failed to move him, and grandmother did not know what to do. She happened to be slightly acquainted with a most remarkable man. You may have heard of Count St Germain, of whom so many wonderful stories are told. He was reputed to be a kind of wandering Jew, and was supposed to possess the elixir of life and the philosopher's stone. Some people looked upon him as a charlatan and Kazanov, in his *Memoirs*, says that he was a spy. Be that as it may, St Germain, for all his mysteriousness, was a man of a very venerable appearance and possessed a highly-polished society manner. Grandmother likes to think of him to this day, and gets angry whenever anyone says a disrespectful word about him. Grandmother knew that St Germain could lay his hand on large sums of money and resolved to appeal to him. She sent a note asking him to come and see her immediately. The strange old man came and found her in great grief. Grandmother described her husband's barbarity in the very blackest of colours, and told him at last that all her hopes were placed on his friendship and kindness only. St Germain reflected. "I could lend you the money," he said, "but I know that you would not rest contented until you had paid me, and I do not wish to plunge you into further worries. There is another way; you can win the money back again." "But, my dear count," grandmother objected, "don't you understand that we have no money at all?" "You have no need of money," St Germain replied. "Listen to me." And he told her a secret which each of us would pay dearly to possess.'

The young players listened with increased attention. Tomsky lighted his pipe, took a pull or two, and continued:

'That same evening, grandmother appeared at Versailles, *au jeu de la reine*. The Duke d'Orléans kept the bank. Grandmother excused herself, inventing some tale for not having brought the money to pay her debt, and sat down to play. She chose three cards, which she placed one after another; they won each time, and grandmother was quite freed of her debt.'

'Pure chance!' one of the guests remarked.

'A fairy tale,' Hermann observed.

'The cards may have been marked,' put in a third.

'I do not think so,' Tomsky replied gravely.

'Do you mean to say that you have a grandmother who can divine three consecutive winning cards and you have never got her to tell you how it is done?' Narumov asked.

'Yes, the deuce!' Tomsky replied. 'She had four sons of whom my father was one, and all were confirmed gamblers, but she never disclosed her secret to one of them, though it would have been useful to them and to me too. But my uncle Count Ivan Ilitch, told me, on his word of honour – mind – that the late Chaplitsky, who died in want after having squandered millions, once lost three hundred thousand roubles to Zoritch, I think it was. Grandmother, who was generally severe on the escapades of young men, for some reason took pity on Chaplitsky. She gave him three cards which he was to place one after another, exacting a promise from him that he would never play again in his life. Chaplitsky appeared at Zoritch's, and they sat down to play. On the first card Chaplitsky staked fifty thousand and won, then again, until he had won more than he had lost . . . However, we must get to bed; it is nearly six.'

The dawn was beginning to break. The young men finished their glasses and departed, each his own way.

II

The old Countess —— was seated in her dressing-room in front of a looking-glass. Three maids were in attendance. One held a pot of rouge, another a box of pins, the third a night-cap trimmed with flame-coloured ribbons. The countess had not the smallest pretensions to beauty; it had long since faded, but she retained all the habits of her younger days, assiduously followed the fashions of the 'seventies, and spent as much time over her toilet as she had done sixty years ago. Her companion sat at the window at an embroidering-frame.

'Good morning, Grand'maman,' said a young man entering the room. '*Bonjour*, Mademoiselle Lise. Grand'maman, I have come to ask something of you.'

'What is it, Paul?'

'May I introduce a friend of mine to you, and bring him to your ball on Friday?'

'Bring him to the ball and introduce me to him there. Did you go to —— yesterday?'

'I should think I did! It was jolly; we danced till five o'clock. Mademoiselle Eletskaya looked charming.'

'Charming, my dear! You are easy to please. You should have seen her grandmother, the Princess Daria Petrovna. That reminds me, she must be very old, the Princess Daria Petrovna.'

'But she died seven years ago, Grand'maman,' Tomsky said absently.

The young girl raised her head and made a sign to the young man. He recollected that it was an understood thing the countess was not to be told about the death of her contemporaries and bit his lip. The countess greeted the intelligence with extreme indifference.

'Dead?' she asked. 'And I did not know. She and I were maids-of-honour in the same year, and when we were presented, Her Majesty . . .'

For the hundredth time the countess repeated to her nephew the same tale.

'Help me up, Paul, please,' she said later. 'Lizanka, where is my snuff-box?'

And accompanied by her maids the countess withdrew behind the screens. Tomsky remained with the girl.

'Who is your friend whom you wish to introduce?' Lizaveta Ivanovna asked softly.

'Narumov. Do you know him?'

'No. Is he a soldier or a civilian?'

'A soldier.'

'In the Engineers?'

'No, in the Cavalry. What made you think he was in the Engineers?'

The girl laughed, but made no reply.

'Paul!' the countess called from behind the screen; 'try and send me a new novel, only not of the modern kind, please.'

'Then how can I send you a new one, Grand'maman?'

'I meant a novel where the hero did not strangle his father or mother, and where there were no drowned bodies. I cannot stand drowned bodies. Is there such a novel nowadays?'

'Would you like a Russian one?'

'Are there Russian novels? Send one by all means, Paul.'

'I am sorry, Grand'maman; I must go. I am sorry Lizaveta Ivanovna. What made you think that Narumov was in the Engineers?'

And Tomsky took his leave.

Lizaveta Ivanovna remained alone. She left her work and gazed out of the window. A little later a young officer appeared round the street corner. A flush spread over Lizaveta's cheeks; she resumed her work, bending her head low over the canvas. At this moment the countess entered, fully dressed.

'Order the carriage, Lizanka,' she said. 'We will go for a drive.'

Lizanka rose from the frame and began to put away her work.

'Are you deaf, my dear?' the countess cried. 'Order the carriage at once!'

'Just going,' the girl answered quietly, and ran out of the room.

A servant entered and handed the countess a book sent by Prince Paul Alexandrovitch.

'Thank the prince for me. Lizanka, Lizanka, where are you off to?'

'To put on my things.'

'There is plenty of time, my dear. Sit down here. Open the first volume and read aloud.'

The girl took the book and began to read.

'Can't you read louder?' the countess asked. 'Are you asleep, my dear? Wait a moment. Bring me a footstool. A little nearer, please.'

Lizaveta Ivanovna read a couple of pages; the countess yawned.

'Put down the book,' she said, 'what nonsense it is, to be sure! Have it sent back to Prince Paul with my thanks. Is the carriage ready?'

'Yes,' Lizaveta Ivanovna said, looking out into the street.

'Why are you not dressed?' the countess asked. 'I have always to wait for you. You are impossible, my dear.'

Liza ran away to her room. Two minutes had scarcely passed when the countess rang violently. Three maids ran in at one door, a footman at another.

'How is it I cannot make you hear?' the countess demanded. 'Tell Lizaveta Ivanovna that I am waiting for her.'

Lizaveta Ivanovna entered in a cloak and hat.

'At last, my dear!' the countess greeted her. 'What finery to be sure! Quite superfluous, my dear. There is no one to captivate! ... What is the weather like? I believe there is a wind.'

'No, your Highness, there is no wind,' the footman replied.

'Are you sure? Open the window. You see, there is a wind, and a cold one, too. I shall not want the carriage Lizanka, we will not go for our drive today. I am afraid your finery was all put on for nothing.'

'What a life!' Lizaveta Ivanovna thought.

And truly, Lizaveta Ivanovna was the most unhappy of beings. The bread of others is bitter, says Dante, and the steps leading to a stranger's doors are difficult to tread. And who should know the bitterness of dependence more than the companion and dependent of a celebrated old society woman? The countess had not a bad heart, but she had been spoiled by the world, and had become capricious, mean and egotistical, with the cold egotism of all old people who have loved in their own day and are out of place in the present. She still participated in all society functions, dragged herself to balls where she sat in corners painted and powdered and attired in the fashion of her own day, a formidable, hideous presence. The guests on their arrival came and bowed to her ceremoniously, but no one took the least notice of her afterwards. At her own house she entertained the whole town, but could not recognise a single face. Her numerous menials growing fat and grey in her corridors and servants' hall, did what they liked, vying with each other to rob her. Lizaveta Ivanovna was the household martyr. Did she pour out the tea, she had to account for every lump of sugar used; did she read aloud, she was responsible for the author's shortcomings; did she accompany the countess in her drives, she had to answer for the weather and the paving of the roads. She was supposed to have a fixed salary, but she never received it, yet she was expected to dress like all other girls; that is to say, like a selected few. Her position in society was a very miserable one. Everyone knew her, yet no one paid the least attention to her; at balls she danced only when there were not enough men, and the women took her by the arm whenever they wished to retire to the dressing-room to rearrange their toilets. She was extremely sensitive and felt her position cruelly, looking around eagerly for a deliverer; but the young men she met were calculating, frivolous and conceited, and did not deem her worthy of attention, though Lizaveta Ivanovna was a hundred times prettier than the brazen indifferent girls around whom they hovered. How often, escaping from the gorgeous, dull drawing-room, had she run away to weep bitterly in her own humble room in which stood a screen, a chest of drawers, a painted bed, a mirror, and a tallow candle burned dimly in a brass candlestick.

One day – it happened two days after the evening mentioned at the opening of this story and a week before the scene just described – Lizaveta Ivanovna was seated at her embroidering-frame by the window, when she happened to look out into the street and saw a young officer standing motionless, gazing up at her window. She dropped her head and busied herself with her work; when she looked up again five minutes later, the officer was still there, in the same spot. It was not her way to pay attention to passing officers, so she turned away from the window and sewed steadily for two hours without raising her head. Dinner was announced. She rose and put away her embroidery material and gazing by chance into the street she saw the officer still standing there. The fact struck her as uncommonly strange, but looking out again when she returned from dinner with a certain amount of trepidation, the officer had gone and she soon forgot all about him. Two days later, however, when accompanying the countess to the carriage she saw him again. He was standing by the steps leading to the door, his face hidden in a large beaver collar and his back eyes gleaming beneath his hat. Lizaveta Ivanovna was afraid, without knowing why, and took her seat in the carriage with an inexplicable flutter.

As soon as she returned home she flew to the window – there was the officer in the same spot – his eyes fixed on her. She stepped back from the window hastily, torn by curiosity and agitated by a feeling quite new to her.

Since then not a day passed but the young man appeared at a regular hour beneath the windows of the house. An unconditional relationship was established between them. Sitting at her work she felt his approach and raised her head, and each day she looked at him longer than the last. The young man seemed very grateful for her favours. With the sharp-sightedness of youth she saw a quick flush spread over his face every time their eyes met. In a week she smiled to him . . .

When Tomsky had asked permission to introduce his friend, the poor girl's heart gave a bound, but learning that Narumov was in the Cavalry, not the Engineers, she regretted having betrayed her secret to the light-hearted Tomsky.

Hermann was the son of a Russianised German who had left him a small fortune. Obsessed with the idea of insuring his independence, Hermann would not touch even the interest of his capital, and lived entirely on his salary, not permitting himself the least indulgence. He was reserved and ambitious, and his fellow-officers rarely had an opportunity of making fun of his extreme carefulness. He was passionate and had a fiery imagination, but his strength of character saved him from the usual pitfalls of youth. For instance, by nature a gambler, he never touched cards, considering that he could not afford to, as he himself said, 'My position is not such that I sacrifice a necessity for a doubtful luxury.' For all that, he sat through the nights at the card-tables, following the various turns of the game with a feverish interest.

The story of the three cards fired his imagination and did not go out of his mind the whole of that night. 'Supposing,' thought he, wandering about the streets of St Petersburg the following evening, 'supposing the old countess discloses her secret to me, or tells me the three sure cards? Why shouldn't I try my luck? I must get to know her, worm myself into her favour, become her lover if need be – but all this will take time and she is eighty-seven years old and might be dead in a week; in a day, perhaps! I wonder if the story itself is true, though? It may be fiction. Prudence, temperance, industry – these are the three sure cards that will treble my capital; nay, increase it seven-fold, and ensure me peace and independence!' Reasoning in this manner he found himself in one of the principal St Petersburg streets in front of a beautiful old house. The street was lined with carriages rolling up one after another to a brilliantly lighted porch. From the carriages there stepped now the light elegant foot of a young beauty, now a crunching top-boot, now a striped stocking, now a diplomatic shoe; fur coats and cloaks flashed past the tall handsome footman.

'Whose house is that?' he asked a policeman at the corner.

'The Countess of —— ' the policeman replied.

Hermann started. The extraordinary story again took possession of his mind. He paced up and down before the house thinking of its mistress and her wonderful powers. It was late when he returned to his humble quarters. For a long time he lay awake, but when sleep at last overcame him, in his dreams he saw himself seated at a green table piled with notes and gold. He played card after card, turned the corners resolutely and kept on winning and winning, stuffing the notes and gold into his pockets. He awoke late and sighed over the loss of his phantom wealth. Again he went strolling about the city; again he found himself before the countess's house. An invisible power seemed to draw him towards it. He stopped and gazed up at the windows. A dark head bending, probably, over a book or some work, met his gaze at one of them. The head looked up. Hermann ws confronted by a sweet face and a pair of black eyes. The moment decided his fate.

III

Lizaveta Ivanovna had only just removed her cloak and hat when the countess sent for her once more and again ordered the carriage. They went out. At the moment when two footmen were assisting the countess into the carriage, Lizaveta Ivanovna caught sight of her officer standing by the wheel. He seized her hand. She could scarcely collect herself in her terror. The young man vanished, leaving a note in her hand. She thrust it into her glove. The whole way she sat as in a dream and heard and saw nothing. The countess usually overwhelmed her with questions during their drives. 'Who was that we met?' she asked. 'What is the name of this bridge? What is written on that sign-board?' Lizaveta Ivanovna replied listlessly, without thinking, often irrelevantly. The countess became angry.

'What is the matter with you, my dear? You seem like a

wooden image to-day! Can't you hear me, or don't you understand? I can still speak clearly, thank God, and what is more, to the point!'

Lizaveta Ivanovna did not hear her. She escaped to her own room as soon as she reached home, and pulled the note out of her glove. It was not sealed. She began to read. It contained a declaration of love, tender and respectful, taken word for word from some German novel. Lizaveta Ivanovna could not read German and was therefore satisfied. For all that, the letter caused her much anxiety. In the first place, she had entered into an intimate, clandestine correspondence with a young man. His boldness horrified her. She reproached herself for her irregular conduct and did not know what to do. Should she give up working by the window and by her neglect cool the young man's ardour? Should she return the letter, or reply coldly and resolutely? There was no one whose advice she could ask; she had no girl friend, no preceptress. Lizaveta Ivanovna decided to reply.

She sat down by her little writing-table, took a pen, paper and tried to write. She began, sheet after sheet, tearing one after another, for the tone of one seemed to her too patronising, the tone of another too unkind. At last she managed to write a few lines that satisfied her, more or less. 'I am sure,' she wrote, 'that your intentions are honourable, and that you did not mean to insult me by your thoughtless act, but our acquaintance should not have begun in this way. I return your letter, hoping that in the future I shall have no cause to complain of your disrespect, so completely undeserved on my part.'

Catching sight of Hermann in the street on the following day, Lizaveta Ivanovna rose from her embroidery-frame and went into the drawing-room where she opened a window and dropped her note out of it, relying on the young man's quickness and agility. Hermann ran over, picked up the note and went into a confectioner's shop. Tearing the envelope, he found his own letter and Lizaveta Ivanovna's reply. He had expected such a reply and returned home engrossed in his intrigue.

Three days later a sharp-eyed girl from a milliner's shop brought Lizaveta Ivanovna a note. Lizaveta Ivanovna opened the envelope, taking it to be a bill, when she suddenly recognised Hermann's handwriting.

'You have made a mistake, my dear,' she said, 'this note is not for me.'

'It is for you!' the impudent girl replied, not hiding her roguish smile. 'Will you be good enough to read it?'

Lizaveta Ivanovna glanced at the note. Hermann asked for a meeting.

'Impossible,' she said, terrified at the suddenness of the demand and the means employed. 'This was certainly not written to me.' And she tore the note into a hundred pieces.

'If it was not for you, then why have you torn it?' the girl asked. 'I should have returned it to the person who sent it.'

'My dear,' Lizaveta Ivanovna burst out at the girl's rebuke, 'please do not bring me any more notes in future. And tell the person who sent you that he ought to be ashamed.'

But Hermann was not to be refused. By some means or another Lizaveta Ivanovna received a letter from him every day. They were no longer translations from the German. Hermann wrote them himself. Inspired by his passion he spoke in a tongue peculiarly his own, expressing the fierceness of his desire, the disorder of an unbridled imagination. Lizaveta Ivanovna no longer dreamt of returning these letters; she revelled in them and her replies grew longer and more tender day by day. At last she threw the following letter out of the window to him: 'To-night there is a hall at the —— Ambassador's; the countess will be there. We shall stay until two o'clock. I give you an opportunity of seeing me alone. As soon as the countess departs, the servants will probably go to their own quarters. The hall-footman only will remain, and he generally sits in a little room off the ball. Come here at half-past eleven and walk straight upstairs. If you should happen to meet someone, ask if the countess is at home. She will not be, of course, and in that case you will have to go away, but most likely you will see no one. The maids are generally all together in the servants' hall. When you get upstairs turn to the left and go straight down till you come to the countess's bedroom and there, behind two screens are two doors; the one to the right leads to a little study the countess never uses; the one to the left, into a corridor where you will see a winding staircase leading to my room.'

Hermann walked about restless as a tiger until the appointed hour. At ten o'clock he was already at the countess's house. The weather was terrible; the wind howled, and soft, wet snow fell in large flakes; the street-lamps burned dimly; the streets were deserted. Now and again a sledge-driver went past with his sorry hack, peering about for a belated fare. Hermann stood in his coat only, indifferent alike to the wind and the snow. At last the countess's carriage drove up. Hermann saw two footmen, supporting the countess under the arms as she came out, wrapped in a sable coat; following her, in a thin cloak and fresh flowers in her hair came her companion. The carriage-doors were shut; the wheels rolled over the soft snow. A footman shut the doors; the lights in the windows went out; Hermann began to pace up and down in front of the deserted house. He went up to a street-lamp to look at his watch – it was ten minutes past eleven. He remained by the lamp, his eyes fixed on the hands, waiting impatiently for the minutes to pass. On the stroke of half-past eleven Hermann walked up the steps leading to the countess's door and entered the brightly lighted hall. There was no one there. He ran up the stairs, and on the landing he saw a servant asleep in a battered old arm-chair. With light, firm tread, Hermann passed him. The ball-room and drawing-room were in darkness, except for a faint light from a little lamp on the landing. Hermann went into the countess's bedroom. In front of an altar, decorated with old ikons, a golden ikon lamp was burning. The faded, upholstered arm-chairs and couches with their down, gold-embroidered cushions, stood in solemn array against the walls, papered with a Chinese wall-paper. Two portraits, painted in Paris by Madame Lebrun, hung on a wall – one was of a stout, ruddy-cheeked man of about forty in a bright-green uniform, decorated with a star, the other a young beauty with an aquiline nose, and a rose in her powdered hair, drawn tightly over her temples. In every corner were porcelain shepherdesses, clocks by the famous Leroy, little boxes, roulettes, fans, various feminine playthings, acquired at the end of the last century, together with a globe and a mesmerising magnet. Hermann went behind the screens. In front of him was a little iron bedstead; to the right a door, leading into the study; to the left, another door, leading into a corridor. Hermann opened it and saw the narrow, winding staircase leading to poor Lizaveta's room. He turned back, however, and went into the study.

The time passed slowly. All was still. A clock in the drawing-room struck twelve; one after another the clocks in the other rooms struck the hour and all grew quiet once more. Hermann stood leaning against the cold stove. He was calm; his heart beat evenly like the heart of a man who had embarked on a perilous, but a non-essential enterprise. The clock struck one and two, and he caught the sound of a distant carriage. An involuntary excitement came over him. The carriage drew up at the door. He heard how a carpet was spread in the snow. There was a bustling in the house; the servants rushed out; a sound of voices; the lights went up. Three maids came into the bedroom supporting the countess, who dropped half-dead into a chair. Hermann looked through a crack in the door. Lizaveta Ivanovna passed near him; Hermann heard her hurried footsteps up the winding stairs. A faint pang shot through him, but he paid no heed to it. Suddenly he was petrified.

The countess began to undress before the looking-glass. The maids removed her cap, ornamented with roses, then her powdered wig, exposing her grey, closely-cropped hair. The pins rained around. Her yellow gown, embroidered in silver, dropped to her swollen feet. Hermann witnessed the disgusting details of her toilet. At last the countess put on a light dressing-jacket and a night-cap, and in this guise, more fitting for her years, she seemed less formidable and hideous. Like most old people, the countess suffered from insomnia. She dismissed the maids and sat down in an armchair. The candles were gone; the room was illumined only by the ikon lamp.

Yellow and sickly the countess sat twitching her nerveless lips and rocking herself to and fro. Her lustreless eyes reflected a complete absence of thought. Gazing at her one would have thought that the rocking motion was automatic, and came through no will of her own.

Suddenly an inexplicable change came over her impassive face. Her lips ceased moving, her eyes started – a strange man was standing before her.

'Fear not! In God's name, fear not!' he said in a quiet impressive voice. 'I do not want to harm you; I came only to ask a favour.'

The old woman stared at him in silence, seeming not to hear. Thinking that she was deaf, Hermann bent down and whispered the same words into her very ear. Still the countess was silent.

'You can make my fortune,' Hermann continued; 'you can make me happy with no cost to yourself. I know that you know three successive cards . . .'

Hermann stopped; the countess, it seemed, had realised what was demanded of her and was trying to frame the words for her reply.

'It was a jest!' she said at last. 'I assure you it was a jest!'

'It was no jest at all!' Hermann rejoined angrily. 'Have you forgotten Chaplitsky whom you helped to win back his losses?'

The countess was taken aback, evidently. Her features expressed strong emotion, but she soon lapsed again into an apathetic state.

'Can you tell me what these three winning cards are?' Hermann demanded.

The countess was silent; Hermann continued:

'For whom do you guard your secret? For your grandsons? They are rich enough as it is; they do not understand the value of money. Your three cards will not help a spendthrift. A man who squanders his father's inheritance will die in poverty, black magic or no. I am not a spendthrift; I know the value of money; your three cards will not be wasted on me. Well? . . .'

He stopped and waited in anguish for her reply. The countess was silent. Hermann went down on his knees.

'If your heart has ever loved,' he implored, 'if you remember your triumphs, if you have ever smiled at the cry of your new-born babe, if any human feeling has ever touched your heart, then I implore you in its name, in the name of your feelings as a wife, a mistress, a mother, everything that is sacred in life, not to refuse my request; tell me your secret . . . Perhaps it is bound up with some horrible sin, with the loss of salvation – perhaps you have made as compact with the devil . . . Remember you are old and have not long to live – I will take your sin upon myself; only tell me your secret. Don't you see? You hold a man's happiness in your hand; not only I, but my children and grandchildren and great-grandchildren will bless your memory and hold it sacred . . .'

Not a word did the countess reply.

Hermann rose.

'You old witch!' he said, grinding his teeth; 'I will compel you to speak!'

With these words he drew a revolver out of his pocket.

At sight of the revolver, for a second time the countess betrayed emotion. She threw back her head and raised her arm to shield herself, then fell backwards insensible.

'Stop your infantile play,' Hermann said, taking her hand. 'I ask you for the last time: Will you or will you not, tell me the three winning cards?'

The countess did not reply. Hermann saw that she was dead.

IV

Lizaveta Ivanovna, still in her ball-dress, was sitting in her room wrapt in thought. When she came home she hastily dismissed her sleepy maid who reluctantly offered her services, and saying that she would undress without her aid, she ran up to her own room, expecting to find Hermann, yet hoping that he would not be there. At a glance she was assured of his absence and thanked her stars for the accident that had prevented their meeting. She dropped into a chair and tried to recall all the circumstances that had occurred in such a short time, yet had carried her so far. Three weeks had scarcely gone by since, for the first time, she had seen the young man from the window, and they were already in correspondence with each other and he had prevailed upon her to grant him a nocturnal meeting. She only knew his name from the signature of his letters; had not spoken to him once; had never heard his voice; never heard anyone speak of him until this very evening. What a strange coincidence! That very same evening at the ball, Tomsky, annoyed with the Princess Paulina who was flirting with someone else, to spite her, danced an endless mazurka with Lizaveta Ivanovna. As they danced he chaffed her about her partiality for Engineer officers, and assured her that he knew more than she suspected. Several of his sallies were so well aimed that Lizaveta Ivanovna thought once or twice that he must know her secret.

'Who told you all that?' she asked with a laugh.

'A friend of someone you know,' Tomsky replied. 'A very remarkable man!'

'Who is this remarkable man?'

'His name is Hermann.'

Lizaveta Ivanovna made no reply; her hands and feet grew cold.

'Hermann,' Tomsky continued, 'is a truly romantic person. He has a profile like Napoleon, and a soul like Mephistopheles. He must have three crimes on his conscience at least! How pale you have grown!'

'My head aches . . . What did Hermann . . . or whatever his name . . . tell you?'

'Hermann is not at all pleased with his friend. He maintains that in his place he would have behaved differently. I imagine Herman himself has his own plans about you; at any rate, he listens with extreme indifference to the love-lorn confidences of his friend.'

'But where could he have seen me?'

'In church, in the street, God knows! In your own room, perhaps, when you were asleep.'

Three ladies came up and cut short the conversation that had become painfully interesting to Lisaveta Ivanovna. One of them was the Princess Paulina herself. She managed to explain things to Tomsky and when he returned to Lizaveta Ivanovna he was no longer thinking either of her or of Hermann. She desired to renew their conversation, but the mazurka was over and soon after the old countess took her leave.

Tomsky's words may have been no more than idle ball-room gossip, but they sank deeply into the young dreamer's soul. The portrait conjured up by Tomsky's words fell in with the one in her own imagination. The commonplace face held her terrified. Her bare arms crossed, she sat with head drooping over her bare breast, the flowers still in her hair. Suddenly the door opened and Hermann entered. She started.

'Where you have been?' she asked in a terrified whisper.

'In the countess's bedroom,' Hermann replied. 'I have just come from there. The countess is dead.'

'Dead! My God! what are you saying?'

'And I am the cause of her death, it seems,' Hermann added.

Lizaveta Ivanovna looked at him and Tomsky's words struck at her heart, 'He must have three crimes on his conscience at least!'

Hermann sat down on the window-sill beside her and told her everything.

Lizaveta Ivanovna listened to him in horror. So all his passionate letters, all his ardent requests, his insolent, stub-born persecution had not been love at all. It was money that his soul had thirsted for! She could not have appeased his desires or have made him happy. She had been nothing but a blind tool of a robber, the murderer of her benefactress! Lizaveta Ivanovna shed bitter, painful tears; Hermann looked at her in silence; his heart, too, was torn, only not by the poor girl's tears; he was not touched by her grief; he felt not the smallest touch of remorse about the old woman's death; the only thing that horrified him was the complete loss of the secret with the aid of which he had hoped for wealth.

'You monster!' Lizaveta Ivanovna said at last.

'I did not desire her death,' Hermann replied; 'my revolver was not loaded.'

Both were silent.

The dawn broke. Lizaveta Ivanovna extinguished the

flickering candle; a pale light penetrated through the window into the room. She wiped her tear-stained eyes and raised them to Hermann's; he was seated on the window-sill with folded arms and a heavy frown on his face. In this position he bore a striking resemblance to the portraits of Napoleon; Lizaveta Ivanovna could not help seeing it.

'How will you leave the house?' she asked at last. 'I would have taken you down a secret staircase, only I dare not pass the countess's bedroom.'

'Tell me where the staircase is and I will find the way myself.'

Lizaveta Ivanovna rose, took a key out of a drawer and gave it to Hermann with detailed instructions about the way to the staircase. Hermann pressed her cold, unresponsive hand, kissed her bent head and went out.

He descended the winding staircase and once more entered the countess's bedroom. The old woman sat stiff and straight in her chair; her face absolutely peaceful. Hermann stopped to look at her, though desirous of convincing himself of the horrible truth; at last he went into the study, fumbled about by the door, and disturbed by strange thoughts and sensations he began to descend a dark staircase. 'Down this very staircase,' thought he, 'sixty years ago, perhaps, a happy lover was stealing from the very same room at this very same hour. A handsome lover, no doubt, in a rich embroidered coat, hair dressed *à l'oiseau royal*, his three-cornered hat pressed to his breast. And now his bones are rotting in the grave and the heart of his aged mistress has ceased to beat.'

v

On the third day after the fatal night, at nine in the morning, Hermann set off for —— Monastery, where the countess's funeral service was to take place. Though he felt no remorse at what had happened, he could not quite drown the voice of his conscience that kept on telling him, 'It was you who killed the old woman!' Possessed of little faith, he was nevertheless superstitious, and fearing that the dead countess might be a bad influence in his life, he resolved to attend her funeral and beg her forgiveness.

The church was full of people; Hermann, with difficulty, pushed his way through the crowd. The coffin was placed on a gorgeous catafalque beneath a velvet canopy. The dead woman lay attired in a white satin gown and lace cap, her hands crossed over her breast. Surrounding her were her own people and menials, the latter in black liveries and candles in their hands; her relations were in deep mourning – children, grandchildren, and great-grandchildren. No one shed a tear, for no one regretted her death; the countess was very old and her relations had long looked upon her as one who had outlived her day. A young priest preached the funeral sermon. In simple, touching words he spoke of the saintly woman's peaceful death, saying that the whole of her long life had been one humble preparation for a Christian end. 'The Angel of Death,' the orator concluded, 'discovered her in blessed vigil for the nocturnal bridegroom.' The service was conducted with solemn decorum. Relatives were the first to bid the body farewell; then came the numerous acquaintances who had once bowed to her in the whirl of their social amusements. After them came the domestics, among them the two young girls who used to support the countess when she walked about the house; one had not the strength to prostrate herself, the other shed a tear or two as she kissed the cold hand of her mistress. It was then Hermann resolved to approach the coffin. He prostrated himself to the ground and lay for several moments on the cold floor strewn with twigs of pine; at last he rose, pale as the dead woman herself, and walking up the steps of the catafalque he bent over her. It seemed to him that the countess gave him a mocking look and winked an eye. Hermann stepped away hastily and crashed backwards on to the floor. Someone helped him to rise. At the same moment Lizaveta Ivanovna was carried out unconscious. The incident for a moment disturbed the sombre, solemn service. A murmur arose among the crowd, a gaunt chamberlain, closely related to the dead woman, whispered to an Englishman standing near him that the young officer was an illegitimate son of the countess, to which the Englishman responded coldly 'Oh!'

The whole day Hermann went about distraught. He dined in a secluded inn, and contrary to his usual habit, drank a great deal of wine in the hopes of drowning his inner tumult, but the wine merely quickened his imagination. When he returned home he threw himself on his bed without undressing and fell fast asleep.

He awoke in the night; the moon shone in at his window. He looked at his watch; it was a quarter to three. He sat up in bed and began thinking of the old countess's funeral. At this moment someone from without peeped in at his window and instantly drew back. Hermann paid no need. In a minute or so someone opened the door of the outer room. Hermann took it to be his orderly who had returned home drunk in his usual manner after a night's carouse. But his ear caught the sound of an unfamiliar footstep, a soft shuffling gait. The door opened and there entered a woman in a white dress. Hermann thought it was his nurse, and wondered what had brought her there at such a late hour. The woman glided softly over the floor, and stood before him. Hermann recognised the countess!

'I have come to you against my will,' she said in a steady voice, 'but I have been commanded to grant your request. The three, seven and ace are the winning cards, only you must never stake more than one at a time and never play again in your life. I will forgive you my death if you marry my ward Lizaveta Ivanovna.'

With these words she turned quietly and disappeared through the door with her shuffling gait. Hermann heard the door bang in the passage and again someone looked in at the window.

It was some time before he recovered. He went into the next room. His orderly was asleep on the floor; Hermann had some difficulty in rousing him. The man was drunk as usual, and was able to give no sensible information. The door in the passage was locked. Hermann returned to his room, lit a candle and wrote down his vision.

VI

Two fixed ideas cannot exist together in the world of mind any more than two bodies can occupy the same space in the world of matter. The three, seven and ace soon obscured the image of the dead countess in Hermann's imagination. The three, seven and ace were for ever in his mind and on his lips. When meeting a young girl he would say, 'How graceful she is! just like the three of hearts!' Should anyone ask him the time, he replied unvariably, 'Five minutes to seven.' Every portly, round-bellied man reminded him of the ace. The three, seven and ace followed him about in his sleep, assuming every possible shape and form. Sometimes the three blossomed before him as some tropical plant, the seven appeared as a Gothic archway, and the ace as a huge spider. He was obsessed by one thought only – to make use of the secret that had cost him so dearly. He began to dream of retirement and travel. In the public gambling-houses of Paris did he desire to wrest from enchanted fortune the treasure that he coveted. An occasion arose that delivered him from his troubles.

In Moscow, a society was formed of wealthy gamblers, under the presidency of the famous Chekalinsky, who had spent his whole life at card-tables and had acquired millions at one time, winning bills of exchange and losing solid money. His lengthy experience gained him the confidence of his friends, and an open house, a good cook, gaiety and good humour obtained for him the respect of the public. This man came to visit St Petersburg. The young men rushed to him, neglecting the dance for the cards, preferring the charms of faro to the seductions of the fair sex. Narumov took Hermann to visit him.

They passed through a line of gorgeous rooms full of polite, attentive footmen. Many people were there; a few generals and privy councillors were playing whist; several young men were lounging on couches and smoking. At a long table in the drawing-room, around which sat about twenty players, was the host, who kept the bank. He was a man of sixty, of a most venerable appearance; his hair was silver-white; good-nature was expressed in his full round face; his eyes sparkled with a constant smile. Narumov introduced Hermann to him. Chekalinsky gave him a friendly hand-shake and asked him to make himself at home. The game proceeded. The deal took a long time. There were about thirty cards on the table. Chekalinsky paused before each throw to give the players time to settle their losses, listening attentively to their requests, still more attentively straightening an odd corner accidentally bent by some careless hand. At last the deal was over. Chekalinsky shuffled the cards and made ready to throw again.

'Allow me to play a card,' Hermann said, extending his hand over the shoulder of a stout man near him.

Chekalinsky smiled and bowed silently in token of consent. Narumov laughingly congratulated Hermann over this break in his long fast and wished him a happy beginning.

'I shall win!' Hermann said, marking the stake above his card with a piece of chalk.

'How much?' asked Chekalinsky with a frown; 'I can't see very well.'

'Forty-seven thousand,' Hermann replied.

At these words all heads turned and all eyes were fixed on Hermann.

Has he gone mad? Narumov thought.

'Your stake is high, if you will allow me to say so,' Chekalinsky observed with his never-failing smile. 'No one here has ever staked more than two hundred and seventy-five.'

'Well, will you take my card or not?' Hermann asked.

Chekalinsky nodded submissively.

'There is one thing I must tell you, though,' he said; 'as I enjoy the confidence of my friends I cannot throw otherwise than on ready money. For my own part your word alone is enough, but to maintain the regularity of the game and accounts, I must ask you to put your money on your card.'

Hermann took a bank-note out of his pocket and handed it to Chekalinsky, who glanced at it and placed it on Hermann's card.

He began to throw. To the right lay a nine, to the left a three.

'I have won!' Hermann exclaimed, holding up his card.

A murmur arose among the players; Chekalinsky frowned, but his smile instantly returned to his face.

'Will you pay, please?' Hermann asked.

'With pleasure.'

Chekalinsky pulled some bank-notes out of his pocket and settled the amount. Hermann took the money and walked away from the table. Narumov could not collect himself. Hermann drank a glass of lemonade and departed for home.

The following evening once more he appeared at Chekalinsky's. The host kept the bank. Hermann approached the table; the players made room for him. Chekalinsky gave him a friendly nod.

Hermann waited for a new deal. He put down his card, laying on it his forty-seven thousand, together with the money he had won yesterday.

Chekalinsky began to throw; a knave fell to the right, a seven to the left. Hermann disclosed a seven.

There was a general murmur of surprise. Chekalinsky was agitated. He counted out ninety-four thousand and gave them to Hermann who received the money coolly and walked away.

The next evening again Hermann appeared at the table. All were expecting him. Generals and privy councillors abandoned their whist to watch the extraordinary play; the young officers sprang up from their couches, the footmen gathered in the drawing-room. All made way for Hermann. The other players did not put down their cards, waiting to see the end of Hermann's play. Hermann stood by the table preparing to play alone against Chekalinsky, who was still smiling, though the colour had gone from his face. Each cut the pack of cards; Chekalinsky shuffled them. Hermann took his card and put it on the table placing a pile of bank-notes on top of it. The scene was like a duel. Perfect silence reigned.

Chekalinsky began to throw; his hands trembled. To the right lay a queen, to the left an ace.

'The ace has won!' Hermann exclaimed, uncovering his card.

'Your queen is beaten,' Chekalinsky said affably.

Hermann started; and truly, in place of the ace there lay the queen of spades. He could scarcely believe his own eyes, failing to comprehend how he had come to draw it.

The queen of spades seemed to wink and smile at him mockingly. He was struck by the extraordinary likeness . . .

'The old woman!' he cried in horror.

Chekalinsky drew the notes towards him. Hermann stood motionless. When he retired from the table a loud murmur arose. 'A capital throw!' the players said. Once more Chekalinsky shuffled the cards, and the play proceeded.

Hermann went mad, and is now in the Obuhovsky Asylum, in ward seventeen. He does not answer questions, but keeps on mumbling incessantly. 'Three, seven, ace! Three, seven, queen!'

Lizaveta Ivanovna married a most excellent young man who has a good post somewhere and possesses a respectable estate of his own. He is a son of the old countess's late steward. In Lizaveta Ivanovna's house a poor young kinswoman finds a home.

Tomsky was promoted and married the Princess Paulina.

The Cloak

BY N. V. GOGOL
1809–1852

In the department of ——, but it is better not to give its name; it is dangerous to offend an official body, be it department, regiment, or chancery. Every private individual in these days offends against society by his very existence. It is said that a short time ago a complaint was lodged by a certain chief-of- police – I cannot remember of what town – in which he proved irrefutably that the ordinance of the State was undermined, and that its sacred name was for ever being taken in vain, and in proof of his theory he enclosed a long novel in which on every tenth page or so there figured a certain chief-of-police, frequently in anything but a sober condition. Thus, for the sake of avoiding all possible unpleasantness, it is better that we call the department in question *a certain department*. Now we can proceed. *In a certain department* there worked *a certain clerk*. He was not remarkable in any way – short of stature, red-haired, short-sighted, with a bald patch on his forehead and wrinkled cheeks; his complexion was what we call hemorrhoidal. Who was to blame? The St Petersburg climate, no doubt. As regards his rank (for it is, above all, essential to give a man's rank) he was what is known as a perpetual titular councillor – a rank that has been the sport of many writers who possess the praiseworthy habitude of attacking those who cannot retaliate.

The clerk's surname was Bashmatchkin,[1] a name that had obviously originated from the word 'shoe,' but when, where and how, no one knew. His father and grandfather, even his brother-in-law – indeed, all connected with the Bashmatch-

[1]Bashmak in Russian means shoe.

kins wore boots and had them re-soled but three times in the year. His name and patronymic was Akaky Akakievitch, an unusual, artificial name, the reader may think, but he may rest assured that it had been in no way sought after and had come about most naturally; in fact, owing to a peculiar circumstance he could not have been given any other name. Akaky Akakievitch was born on the night of March 23, if my memory does not deceive me. His late mother, a good woman, the wife of a civil servant, arranged for the christening in due course. She lay on the bed, facing the door; on her right-hand stood the godfather, a most excellent man, Ivan Ivanovitch Egorshkin by name, head-clerk in the senate, and the godmother, Arina Semionovna Belobruhkova, a woman of the rarest virtues and the wife of a quarter-master. The mother was given a choice of three names – Mokia, Sosia or Hosdazata – after the martyr.

'What awful names!' she thought.

To please her the calendar was opened at another place giving the three names of Trifily, Dula and Varahasy.

'What awful names! They seem to come as though on purpose!' the mother exclaimed. 'I have never heard the like. Varadat or Varuh would have been bad enough, but Trifily and Varahasy!'

Again a page of the calendar was turned over, happening on the names of Pavsikahy and Vahtisy.

'There seems to be a fate about it,' the mother said. 'Rather than any of those names, let him be called after his father – Akaky. What is good enough for the father is good enough for the son.'

So Akaky Akakievitch he was called. At the christening the infant cried and pulled a wry face; he seemed to have a presentiment that he would one day be a titular councillor. This is how it all came about. We mention the incident so that the reader may see for himself that it was impossible to give the child any other name.

When and how he had entered the department, and who had appointed him, no one could remember. Directors and heads might come and go, but he was always found in the same place, and the same position, with the same duties, the same style of writing; so that people came to believe that he had been born into the world, ready-made, as he was – uniform, bald patch and all. The porters not only did not rise from their seats when he came into the hall, but paid no more heed than if he had been a common fly. The heads treated him with a calm despotism. Some head-clerk's assistant would thrust a bundle of papers beneath his very nose without so much as a 'copy these, if you please,' or 'here's an interesting bit of business,' or any pleasant word such as one hears in well-conducted offices. And he would take the papers without a glance at the person who handed them to him, or a question of his right, and instantly settle down to copy them out. The younger clerks laughed at him and sharpened their wits on him, as far as the office wit would go; they invented stories about him which they repeated in his very presence, saying, for instance, that his landlady, an old woman of seventy, used to beat him. They would chaff him unmercifully about her, ask when the wedding was to take place and throw bits of paper on his head, meant for rice. But Akaky Akakievitch answered not a word as though the talk did not concern him at all. It never even interfered with his work; the whole time the chaff would go on he made not a single mistake in his writing. It was only when some practical joker jogged his elbow that his patience gave out, and he flared up with a 'Leave me alone! Why will you worry me?' And there was a strange quality both in the words and the tone in which they were uttered; a quality that aroused pity. One newly-appointed young man, imitating the others, began to make fun of him, but he pulled himself up suddenly as though touched to the quick, and since then, everything was changed for him, and he saw Akaky Akakievitch in new light. Some supernatural power drew him away from his comrades, whom he had taken for decent well-bred fellows. Long afterwards, in the merriest of moments, he recalled the little clerk with the bald patch on his head and his touching words, 'Leave me alone! Why will you worry me?' And beneath these words he seemed to hear the refrain, 'Am I not your brother?' And the poor young man would cover his face with his hands and shudder at the age he lived in, when a man was so inhuman and there was so much senseless brutality in his so-called refined good-breeding – oh, God! even a man whom the world regarded as upright and honourable.

No man was as absorbed in his work as Akaky Akakievitch. It is little to say that he worked with zeal – he worked with love. The act of copying papers opened up to him a world of his own – a pleasant world, full of variety. An expression of pleasure fitted across his face when he settled down to his task, and when he came to his favourite letters he smiled and blinked his eyes and moved his lips so that one could almost tell from his face what letters his pen was forming. Had he been promoted in proportion to his zeal, he would have been a state councillor by now, but as his fellow-clerks said of him, he was always glued to his work and the only reward he reaped was piles. However, it would be unfair to say that no notice was taken of him. A certain director – a worthy man – desiring to reward him for his long service, arranged that he should be given more important work than copying, and the first thing that fell to his lot was a finished document in which he merely had to alter the title page, and in places change some of the verbs from the first to the third person. This caused Akaky Akakievitch so much trouble that he perspired and panted and at last said:

'Please give me something to copy instead.'

From that day he was left to copy papers.

Besides copying, nothing else existed for him. He never gave a thought to his dress, and his uniform was no longer green, but of a rusty, mealy hue. His collar was low and narrow, and though he had not a long neck it seemed unnaturally long, like the necks of the plaster kittens foreign venders carry on trays on their heads. And something was always sticking to his coat, such as a piece of straw, or thread; and he possessed a wonderful knack of passing a window at the exact moment when the inmate was pitching some rubbish into the street, so that he invariably went about with bits of melon and pumpkin rind lodged in the brim of his hat. He never paid the least heed to what went on daily in the street; unlike his fellow-clerks, whose penetrating eyes never failed to detect a loose brace, a hanging trouser on the opposite side, an incident which always brought a knowing smile to their lips. Akaky Akakievitch, however, if he looked at anything at all, saw nothing but his clear, carefully written documents; it was only when some horse's head knocked against his shoulder and its nostrils breathed violently into his very face that he realised he was in the middle of the street, and not in the middle of a document. When he reached home he would sit down to the table and eat his soup, and a piece of mutton and onion, scarcely aware of their taste, together with the flies and anything the Lord cared to send at the time. His stomach filled, he would rise from the table, take out an ink-pot and begin copying the papers he had brought home. If there chanced to be no papers to copy for the office, he would copy one for himself, particularly if the document happened to be remarkable, not so much by its contents as by the fact of its being addressed to some personage of importance.

Even in the hour when the grey St Petersburg sky had quite faded and the whole of the civil service world had dined as best it could, each according to his means and individual taste; when all were resting from the departmental pen-scratching and the hurry and scurry of one's own and others' occupations; when every energetic man abandoned himself freely to the enjoyment of his leisure, and some, the more venturesome among them, hastened to a theatre; others into the street to inspect the hat-shops; others to an evening party to flirt with some pretty girl – the star of a small civil service set – still others to spend the evening with some fellow-clerk, who lived on the third or fourth floor of some house in two tiny rooms with a passage and perhaps a kitchen, furnished with certain pretensions to modern taste, in the shape of a lamp or some other object which had cost the family many sacrifices in the form of dinners and little outings; in a word, when all civil service clerks settled down to a game of whist in the cramped abodes of their friends, sipping their glasses of tea, eating cheap biscuits, smoking long pipes, and varying the proceedings during the deal by indulging in high society gossip, so beloved by every Russian, or repeating the everlasting story of the commandant who was informed that the horse of the Falconet Monument had had its tail clipped; when all were trying their hardest to amuse themselves, Akaky Akakievitch did not indulge in the least distraction. No one could remember ever having seen him at an evening party. Having written to his heart's content he would go to bed with a smile on his face at the prospect of the morrow. What would he be given to copy to-morrow? Thus flowed the life of a man with a wretched salary who was contented with his lot, and would have flowed on perhaps to a good old age had it not been for certain misfortunes that are strewn on the path of life not only of titular councillors, but of privy councillors, and aulic councillors, and all manner of councillors, and even of those who neither give nor take counsel.

In St Petersburg every man with an income of not more than four hundred roubles a year has a great enemy in the northern frost though some people will persist in maintaining that it is healthy. At nine in the morning, the very hour when the streets are filled with civil service clerks hurrying to their work, the frost is so keen and biting that the poor fellows do not know what to do with their noses. At the hour when the foreheads of even the highest officials ache from the frost and the tears come into their eyes, poor titular councillors are oftentimes quite unprotected. The only salvation is to cover the five or six streets they have to traverse as quickly as possible, wrapped in their thin cloaks, and then to warm their feet well in the porter's room, thus thawing the energy and working capacity lost on the way. Akaky Akakievitch observed that for some time past his back and shoulders were unusually affected by the frost, notwithstanding the fact that he ran to the office as fast as he could. It occurred to him at last that his cloak might be at fault. Examining it carefully at home he discovered that in two or three places, particularly on the back and shoulders, it was quite threadbare and the lining was torn away from the cloth. The reader must be told that Akaky Akakievitch's cloak, too, had been a subject of derision and laughter among his fellow-clerks; it was not called by the dignified name of cloak, it was talked of as a dressing-gown. And, indeed, it was of a most unusual cut; the collar grew smaller and smaller as the years went on, since bits of it were used for patching other parts. The patches did not boast the skill of a tailor's needle; they were clumsily made and unsightly to look it. Realising the state of the case, Akaky Akakievitch decided to take the cloak to the tailor, Petrovitch. He lived on the fourth floor of some back staircase, and, notwithstanding his one eye and pock-marked face, carried on a comparatively profitable business repairing the coats and trousers of civil service clerks and other people; that is to say, when he was in a sober enough condition, and when his head was not occupied with some other enterprise. We ought not to have mentioned this Petrovitch at all, but having done so, custom has it that we must say something about him, since every person introduced into a story must be accounted for. Years ago he used to be known simply as Gregory; that was in the days when he was serf to some landowner. It was after his emancipation that he began to call himself Petrovitch, at the same time as he began drinking heavily, too, on every holiday and festival; at first on the more important ones, and then without discrimination on every day in the Church calendar that was marked with a cross. In this respect he upheld the habits of his forefathers, and when he quarrelled with his wife he called her a worldly woman and a German. As we have mentioned his wife, we must just say a word or two about her, though, unfortunately, little is known of her, except the fact that Petrovitch had a wife and that she even wore a cap, not a kerchief. She could not, however, have boasted of beauty, for only the soldiers of the guard were known to peep beneath her cap when they met her in the streets; but they always made wry faces and uttered strange exclamations.

Mounting the stairs leading to Petrovitch's abode, which, in justice be it said, had recently been washed down with slops and was saturated with that spirituous odour so hurtful to the eyes, with which one is familiar on all the back staircases of St Petersburg – mounting the stairs, we repeat again, Akaky Akakievitch was wondering what Petrovitch would ask for the work, inwardly resolving to give no more than two roubles.

Petrovich's door was open, for his wife was cooking some fish and the kitchen was so filled with fumes that even the cockroaches were not visible. Akaky Akakievitch passed through the kitchen, unobserved by Petrovitch's wife, and entered a room where Petrovitch himself was seated on a broad, plain deal table cross-legged like a Turk. The first thing that met the eye of Akaky Akakievitch was a big familiar thumb with a deformed nail, strong and thick as a tortoise shell. Skeins of silk and thread hung round Petrovitch's neck, and some ragged garment lay on his knees. For the last three minutes he had been trying to thread a needle, and at last he grew angry with the darkness and the thread, and muttered to himself, 'It won't go in, curse, damn.' Akaky Akakievitch was annoyed that he had arrived at a moment when Petrovitch was out of humour; he liked to deal with Petrovich best when he was not so quarrelsome, 'when the drink had got the better of the one-eyed devil,' as his wife used to say. On those occasions he came down in his price more readily, and even bowed to his customer and thanked him. It is true that his wife never failed to appear on the scene at such moments and lament that her husband had agreed on the low price because he was drunk, but that would only mean an additional twenty kopeks and the matter was settled. On this day, it seemed, Petrovitch was in a sober mood and, consequently, silent and greedy. Akaky Akakievitch would have turned back, but it was too late. Petrovitch had fixed his one eye upon him and Akaky Akakievitch involuntarily said, 'Good evening, Petrovitch.'

'Good evening, sir,' Petrovitch replied with a squint at Akaky Akakievitch's hands to see what manner of prey the latter was bringing.

'I've come to you, Petrovitch, for . . .'

It must be observed that Akaky Akakievitch expressed himself mostly by the use of prepositions and adverbs and those parts of speech that have the least meaning. If the matter in question happened to be a complex one, he would never finish his sentence; often beginning with the words: 'It is true, quite – that . . .' with nothing to follow on, Akaky Akakievitch thinking that he had sufficiently explained himself.

'Let us see what it is,' Petrovitch said, examining the cloak with his one eye from the collar to the sleeves, from the skirt to the buttonholes, though it was the work of his own hand, and he was familiar with every stitch in it. But that is the custom with tailors, the first thing they do when a client brings them a piece of work.

'I came to . . . Petrovitch . . . the cloak . . . the cloth . . . you see, it is quite good in most places . . . A little dusty . . . makes it look old, but it's quite good, really . . . only here and there, you see . . . on the back and on one shoulder it is a little worn, and on this shoulder a little . . . do you see? But there is not much to do to it . . .'

Petrovitch laid the cloak on the table and examined it for a long time, shaking his head; then he reached over to the window-sill and took up a round snuff-box, the lid of which was painted with the portrait of a general, but what general it was no one could tell, for the paint on the place where the face should have been was rubbed off and had been pasted over with a piece of paper. Petrovitch took a pinch of snuff and held the cloak up against the light with another shake of the head; then he examined the lining and shook his head once more; again he took a pinch of snuff and snapping the lid with the general's portrait and piece of paper, he spoke at last:

'It can't be mended; the cloth is rotten.'

Akaky Akakievitch's heart sank at the words.

'But why not, Petrovitch?' he asked in a pleading, childlike voice. 'It's only a little worn on the shoulders; I daresay you could find a piece or two . . .'

'I have pieces enough,' Petrovich said, 'We are not hard up for pieces, but the cloth is too rotten to hold them. You have only to touch it with a needle and it will fall away.'

'But you can patch parts.'

'There is no substance for the patches to hold on to; the cloth is so rotten that a strong wind will blow it away.'

'Then you must strengthen it. Surely it is . . .'

'Impossible,' Petrovitch said firmly. 'The cloak is too bad to repair. When the winter comes, you can cut it up and make foot-cloths out of it. Socks have no warmth; the Germans invented them to get more money out of us (Petrovitch jibed at the Germans on every possible occasion). And as for the cloak, I am afraid you have got to have a new one.'

At the word 'new' a mist rose before Akaky Akakievitch's eyes and everything in the room swam before him. The only thing he saw clearly was Petrovitch's snuff-box with the general and piece of paper pasted on the lid.

'New?' he queried, as though in a dream. 'But I have no money at all.'

'New, I fear,' Petrovitch repeated with callous calmness.

'And if I must, what would it . . .'

'Cost, you mean?'

'Yes.'

'A hundred and fifty would be a small figure to mention,' Petrovitch said with a significant bite of the lip. He liked to produce an effect, to bewilder his client, then to take a sly look to see how his words had been taken.

'A hundred and fifty roubles for a cloak!' cried poor Akaky Akakievitch, crying out for the first time, perhaps, in his life; he was always distinguished for the quietness of his speech.

'Yes,' Petrovitch replied. 'And not much of a cloak at that. With a marten collar and the hood lined with silk, it would cost you two hundred.'

'Petrovitch, please,' Akaky Akakievitch pleaded, disregarding Petrovitch's words and paying no heed to his effects, 'try to mend the cloak so that it can last for a little while at least.'

'It's no good; work and money spent for nothing,' Petrovitch said, and Akaky Akakievitch went out at these words, absolutely crushed. And Petrovitch stood still for a long while after his departure, lips firmly pressed, pleased that he had not cheapened himself or the dignity of his craft.

Akaky Akakievitch walked out into the street as in a dream. 'A fine business, to be sure!' he said to himself. 'Really, I did not think it would . . .' and after a pause, he added: 'So that's how it is; I had no idea it would end like that! dear me!' A long silence ensued, after which he again said: 'Dear me . . . who would have thought? . . . What an event!' And after these words, instead of turning home, he turned unwittingly in the opposite direction. He had not gone far when a dirty chimney-sweep barged into him and blackened his shoulder; a little further on, a trowelful of lime was dropped on him from the top of a half-built house. But he was quite oblivious to everything; it was only when he barged into a policeman who, with a bayonet at his side, was shaking some tobacco out of a box on to his horny hand that he roused himself somewhat, and then because the policeman said to him:

'Where the devil are you going to? Why don't you keep on the pavement?'

This caused him to look about him and to turn home. Only then did he collect his thoughts and see his position in a proper light. He began to talk to himself, not in abrupt broken sentences, but clearly and reasonably as one talks to a sensible friend to whom one has appealed for personal advice. 'No,' said Akaky Akakievitch; 'it's no use tackling Petrovitch today. He is so . . . He must have got a beating from his wife. I had better go to him on Sunday morning. After the effects of Saturday night he'll be half-asleep, and then he's sure to want money for drink and his wife won't give him any. I shall only have to slip a twenty-kopek piece into his hand, and he'll grow more amenable, and then the cloak . . .' Thus Akaky Akakievitch reasoned with himself, trying to keep up his courage, and the very first Sunday when he saw Petrovitch's wife leave the house, he went straight in to the tailor. Petrovitch, be it said, after the effects of Saturday night, was half-asleep; he rolled his one eye and hung his head, but he no sooner realised what was wanted of him than he said, as though possessed of the very devil:

'Can't. You must order a new one.'

Akaky Akakievitch slipped twenty kopeks into his hand.

'Thank you, sir,' Petrovitch said. 'I'll drink a glass to your health. And don't you worry about your cloak; it is no use for anything whatever. I shall have to make you a new one, that's certain.'

Again Akaky Akakievitch began to talk of mending, but Petrovitch would not hear him.

'I shall have to make you a new one,' he said; 'you can rely

on me; I'll try to do my best. I can make it in the new fashion –
the collar to fasten with silver-plated buckles.'

Akaky Akakievitch's spirits fell, for he realised that there
was no other way out than to order a new cloak. But how
could he? Where would he get the money to pay for it? There
would, of course, be the bonus at the next holiday, but the
money had long been apportioned and disposed of. He needed
new trousers and the shoemaker must be paid an old debt for
boot repairs, and he must order three new shirts and two
unmentionable under-garments. In a word, the money would
all be spent, and even if the chief was gracious enough to give
him forty-five or even fifty roubles instead of the usual forty,
there would remain but a paltry sum that would be as a drop in
the ocean as far as the cloak was concerned. Though he knew
full well that Petrovich liked to quote a price that astonished
his wife even, and made her exclaim: 'Are you mad, you fool?
One day you work for nothing and the next you ask a price
that you're not worth yourself!' and that Petrovitch would
make the cloak for eighty roubles; still, where was he to get
even eighty roubles? He might manage half the sum; a little
more, perhaps, but where would the other half come from?
The reader must first learn where the first half was to come
from. Out of every rouble he spent, Akaky Akakievitch made a
habit of saving two kopecks, which he put into a large money-
box, changing them at the end of each half-year into silver. In
this manner, after many years, he had managed to save about
forty roubles. But where would he get the rest of the sum
needed? Akaky Akakievitch puzzled over the dilemma and
resolved to cut down his ordinary expenses for at least a year.
He could forgo his evening tea, do without candles; if he had to
work in the evening he could always go in to his landlady's; he
would have to step lightly over the stones in the street, walk
almost on tip-toe, thus to save shoe-leather; he would send his
linen to the wash less often; and, in order to keep it clean as
long as possible, he could take his under-clothes off in the
evening and sit in his old, worn cotton dressing-gown.

It must honestly be said that he found it difficult to accustom
himself to these privations at first, but by degrees he grew used

to them and all went well; he even resigned himself to evenings of hunger, having in consolation a certain spiritual satisfaction in the contemplation of his future cloak. During those days his life seemed to have grown richer; he might have become married; it seemed as though some other person was always with him, some dear friend with whom he trod the path of life, and this friend was none other than his future cloak, padded with thick wadding and lined with a strong lasting lining. He was more animated, more resolute, like a man with a definite purpose in view. Doubt and uncertainty disappeared from his face and his manner; a fire was occasionally seen in his eye, and the most daring, audacious thoughts floated about in his brain. Could he not rise to a marten collar? The very thought reduced him to a state of blankness, once nearly causing him to make a mistake in his writing, but he recovered himself with an 'Oh, dear!' and made the sign of the cross. At least once a month he paid a visit to Petrovitch to talk about his new cloak, asking where he should buy the stuff, what colour it should be, what price he should pay, and though somewhat preoccupied, he always returned home reflecting that some day, soon, he would actually buy the stuff and the cloak would be made. The time passed sooner than he had expected. Beyond Akaky Akakievitch's wildest dreams the chief had given him a sum of sixty roubles; not forty, or forty-five, as he had supposed. Did the man realise that Akakievitch needed a new cloak, or was it pure coincidence? Be that as it may, Akaky Akakievitch found himself with twenty extra roubles. This circumstance hastened the matter. But two or three months more of semi-starvation and Akaky Akakievitch would possess eighty roubles. His heart, usually so calm, began to beat fast. The very next day he and Petrovitch set out to shop. They bought some very good cloth, having decided on it some six months beforehand and gone every month to inquire about the price; Petrovitch himself said that a better cloth could not be found. For a lining they chose a good stout sateen which, according to Petrovitch's words, was better than silk and richer and more shiny. Marten was out of the question, it being too dear, but, instead, a cat-skin was chosen – the best in the shop – at a

distance it might have been taken for marten. Petrovitch took
two weeks to make the cloak; he would have taken less time
had there not been so many fastenings. For the work he
charged twenty roubles; he could not take less, for the cloak
was sewn throughout with silk in close double seams which
Petrovitch had bitten into various patterns with his own teeth.
It was on –the day is hard to recall – but it was probably the
happiest day of Akaky Akakievitch's life, when Petrovitch at
last brought home his cloak. He brought it in the morning, a
little before the hour when Akaky Akakievitch usually set out
for the office. It could not have arrived at a more opportune
moment, for that very day there was a hard frost and the
weather showed every sign of turning colder. Petrovitch
himself appeared with the cloak, as a good tailor should.
Akaky Akakievitch had never seen such an air of importance
about him. He seemed fully conscious of the dignity of the
work that had raised him from a tailor who repaired old
clothes to a tailor who made new ones. He took the cloak out
of the handkerchief in which it was wrapped, which had just
come back the from wash, and then put it into his pocket for
private use. He shook out the cloak and looked at it proudly;
then holding it in both hands he threw it skilfully over Akaky
Akakievitch's shoulders, smoothed it down at the back and
draped it artistically about Akaky Akakievitch's figure. Akaky
Akakievitch, in consideration of his years, insisted on trying it
on with the sleeves. Petrovitch helped him get into the sleeves,
and even then the effect was perfect. Admiring his handiwork,
Petrovitch did not let slip the opportunity to say that he had
charged a low price because he had known Akaky Akakievitch
for so long, and because he lived in a back street without a
sign-board; a tailor on the Nevsky Prospect would have
charged him eighty-five roubles for the work alone. Akaky
Akakievitch had no desire to go into the matter; even the
mention of the large sums Petrovitch was so fond of talking
about frightened him. He paid him, thanked him, and
departed for his office in his new cloak. Petrovitch followed
him and stopped in the street to admire the cloak; then he
rushed up a little alley and ran round the other side in order to

meet the cloak full-face. Meanwhile, Akaky Akakievitch walked along in the happiest of moods. Every moment he was conscious of the new cloak on his shoulders, and now and again he smiled with inner satisfaction. Two advantages had come with the cloak – in the first place it kept him warm; in the second, it gave him such a pleasant feeling to wear it. He arrived at the office without having noticed the way he had come, and taking off the cloak he examined it, then handed it to the porter, cautioning him to take great care of it. Naturally, everyone in the office soon heard of Akaky Akakievitch's cloak and of the disappearance of the 'dressing-gown,' and everyone rushed out into the hall to see it. Akaky Akakievitch was complimented and congratulated on all hands. At first he smiled, then became embarrassed; and when all insisted that he must give a party to celebrate the occasion, Akaky Akakievitch quite lost his head and did not know what to say, nor how to excuse himself. He flushed red and was about to explain that it was not a new cloak at all, but one he had had for some time, when one of the men, an assistant of one of the heads, to show that he was not a snob, no doubt, said: 'All right, you fellows, Akaky Akakievitch and I will give a party to-night; come to my place all of you to tea. It happens to be my Saint's day.'

The other clerks immediately congratulated the man and accepted the invitation readily. Akaky Akakievitch was about to decline, but the rest assured him that it would be rude and a shame and so on, so there was nothing to be done but to accept the invitation, too. Soon he experienced a sense of satisfaction that he would be able to wear his cloak in the evening. The day was a memorable one for Akaky Akakievitch. He came home in the best of spirits, took off his cloak, hung it carefully on the wall, once more examined the cloth and the lining; he brought out his old cloak and compared the two. He could not help smiling – the difference was so great! And even during dinner he smiled now and again when he remembered the condition of his 'dressing-gown.' Dinner over, he did not sit down to copy papers, but lay down on the bed waiting for the evening. At the appointed hour he dressed, put on his cloak and went out into the street. Unfortunately, we cannot say where the clerk who was giving the party lived, our memory fails us in this respect – the streets and houses of St Petersburg are so confusing – however, we have no doubt that he lived in the better part of the town, a long way from the abode of Akaky Akakievitch. At first Akaky Akakievitch passed through several dark and deserted streets, but as he neared the clerk's home the streets grew brighter and livelier; there were many pedestrians, pretty, fashionably dressed women among them, and men with beaver collars on their coats; not a single cheap hack was about; smart drivers in red velvet caps with varnished sleighs and bear rugs flew over the snow, and the crunching wheels of carriages with ornamental box-seats. Akaky Akakievitch stared at everything in wonder; for some years he had not been out of the house at night. He stopped before a brightly illuminated shop window in which was the picture of a pretty woman throwing off her shoe and exposing a pretty leg; behind her in a doorway stood a man with side whiskers and a tuft of hair beneath his lower lip. Akaky Akakievitch shook his head with a smile, then went on his way. Why did he smile? Had he seen something that to him was strange and unfamiliar, something that every man carries a knowledge of deep down in his heart? Or had he said to himself, like most civil service clerks, 'These Frenchmen to be sure! What can you expect of them? What won't they do?' But perhaps he thought nothing at all; you cannot probe deeply into another man's soul. At last he reached the house. The clerk lived in grand style; there was a light on the stairs; the flat was on the second floor. Entering the hall, Akaky Akakievitch was confronted with rows of goloshes. Among them, in the middle of the floor, stood a *samovar* boiling and bubbling. From the next room issued a hubbub of voices, which grew more distinct when the door opened and a servant came out with a trayful of empty glasses, cream-jug and sugar-basin. The company had evidently arrived and partaken of their first glasses of tea. Hanging up his coat, Akaky Akakievitch entered the room; men, pipes, candles, card-tables flashed before his eyes and his ear was struck by the sound of voices on all sides and the noise of moving chairs. He stopped awkwardly in the middle of the room, wondering what to do next, but the company had already seen him. He was greeted loudly; everyone immediately went into the hall once more to inspect his cloak. Soon, however, Akaky Akakievitch and his cloak were forgotten for the greater attraction of the card-tables. The noise, the crowd, the conversation, all seemed wonderful to Akaky Akakievitch. He was at a loss to know waht to do with his hands, with his feet, with himself generally. He sat down at a card-table, stared at the cards, at the faces of the players, and soon he began to yawn; he was beginning to feel bored, for the hour had long come when he usually retired to rest. He wanted to take leave of his host, but the others would not let him go, saying that they must drink champagne in honour of the new cloak. An hour later supper was served, cold mutton, pasties, pies and champagne. Akaky Akakievitch was compelled to drink two glasses, after which everything in the room began to take on a brighter hue. Still he did not forget that twelve o'clock had come and that he ought to have been at home long ago. Fearing that his host might detain him, he slipped quietly out of the room and went in search of his cloak, which, unfortunately, he found on the floor. He shook it, removed every particle of dust, put it on, and walked down the stairs and out into the street. It was still light without. A few little shops were still open – the haunts of all kinds of low people – and those that were closed still showed lights within, where men-servants and maid-servants were doubtless busy discussing their masters and mistresses who were blissfully ignorant of their whereabouts. Akaky Akakievitch walked along in the very best of spirits; he was about to set off at a trot when a woman dashed out from somewhere and flashed past him as quick as lightning; every part of the woman's body seemed to be alive. Akaky Akakievitch stopped, then went quietly on his way, wondering how he had managed to walk so fast. Soon he reached the deserted streets that were lonely even by day. Now they seemed darker and more deserted than ever; the street-lamps were few and far between, and the oil in them had evidently burned out; wooden houses and fences were seen, but not a soul was in sight, only snow sparkled on the ground, throwing into relief the dark, silent little houses. He came to a big square where the houses on the opposite side were hardly visible; it was terribly lonely and deserted; a light in a sentry-box glimmering in the distance, seemed far, far away as though at the other end of the world. Akaky Akakievitch's spirits fell. He began to cross the square with a feeling of apprehension and a foreboding of ill in his heart. He glanced from side to side as though in the middle of the ocean. 'No, it is better to shut it out,' he thought and walked on with eyes closed, and when at last he opened them to see if he had reached the end of the square, he was confronted by some whiskered men whom he could not see distinctly. A mist rose before his eyes and his heart beat fast.

'The cloak is mine!' thundered a voice, and he was seized by the collar.

Akaky Akakievitch opened his mouth to cry for help when a big fist was thrust into it and a voice said, threateningly:

'You just dare!'

Akaky Akakievitch felt his cloak taken from him, then he felt a kick that sent him sprawling backwards in the snow, and then he felt no more. When he regained consciousness a few minutes later, he got up and looked about him, but no one was in sight. He was cold, and realising that his cloak was gone, he cried aloud for help, but his voice was not loud enough to reach the other end of the square. Desperate and crying out wildly, he ran across the square straight to the sentry-box, where a policeman stood leaning on his rifle, wondering who the devil was the man coming towards him. Akaky Akakievitch rushed up to him and, panting, began to abuse him for sleeping in his sentry-box instead of doing his duty. The policeman declared that he had seen nothing more than that two men had stopped him in the middle of the square, but believing them to be friends of his, he had taken no further notice, and that instead of abusing him for nothing whatever he had much better go to the superintendent to-morrow; the superintendent might help him to recover his cloak. Akaky Akakievitch reached home in a miserable state; his hair – what little there was left of it on the temples and nape of the neck — was dishevelled; his clothes were covered with snow. At his loud knock his landlady hurried from her bed to open the door leaving one slipper behind in her haste and holding her night-dress over her bosom modestly; at the sight of Akaky Akakievitch she stepped back in horror. When he explained what had happened to him she threw up her hands and advised him to go to a certain inspector she knew — the policeman at the sentry-box would probably do nothing at all — Anna, her late cook, was now nurse in this inspector's family and she saw him often herself as he rode past the house, and she saw him too, at church each Sunday, where he kept a kindly eye on everybody as he said his prayers and must, to all appearances, be a respectable person. Having heard her solution of the problem, Akaky Akakievitch went sadly into his own room. Only those who can feel for others can judge how he spent the rest of that night. He set out early next morning to the inspector's house, and was informed that he was still in bed; he went there again at eleven o'clock, to find that the inspector was not at home, and again at dinner-time, but the clerks would not admit him without knowing on what business he had come, till at last, his patience exhausted, Akaky Akakievitch asserted himself and spoke sharply for once in his life, saying that he must see the inspector for himself, that he had come from the department on some government business and would not be denied admittance, and that any one who dared to interfere with him would have to reckon with him, and words to that effect. To this the clerks had nothing further to say and one of them went in to the inspector. The latter received the story of the stolen cloak sceptically. Instead of devoting his attention to the main issue of the case, he put all manner of questions to Akaky Akakievitch — Why had he returned home so late? Had been he to a house of ill-fame? — until Akaky Akakievitch was so embarrassed that he took his leave, not knowing whether he had advanced the matter of the cloak or no. For the first time in his life he did not go to the office, appearing there next day white as a ghost in his old cloak, which looked more wretched and older than ever.

The story of the stolen cloak touched the hearts of nearly all his fellow clerks, though some were not wanting who made sport of it, too. It was decided to collect subscriptions for a new cloak, but the sum raised was a small one as the clerks had many demands upon their pockets; there was the director's portrait to be subscribed for, and that book written by a friend of the director's and so on. One man, at any rate, moved by pity, resolved to give Akaky Akakievitch sound advice. He told him not to go to the police-superintendent at all, because even if the police found the cloak merely from a desire to please the department, he would not be able to claim it unless he could produce irrefutable proofs that it belonged to him; instead he advised him to appeal to a particular *great person*, which *great person* would write to or see the proper people concerned to expedite the case. Since there was nothing else to be done, Akaky Akakievitch resolved to go to this great person. Who he was and what position he occupied remains a mystery to this day, but it must be said that the particular great person had only recently become a *great person*, and that he had previously been quite a small person. However, even now his position is not so very great compared to others greater than his, but some people imagine that to seem great in the eyes of others is to be great. Moreover, this particular great person did his best to enhance his greatness in different ways, such as making his subordinates greet him on the stairs when he came to the office or not to permit any report to be made direct to him; the strictest regularity had to be observed before a report reached him; a collegiate registrar had to report to a district secretary, a district secretary to a titular councillor, and so on, until, in due course, the matter came to him. It is thus our holy mother Russia becomes infected with a spirit of imitation; every subordinate imitates his chief and does what he does.

It is said that a certain titular councillor who had been promoted to the headship of a small department immediately partitioned off a part of the room for himself which he called 'the audience-chamber'; he had two porters in uniform placed at the door to admit anyone who desired to enter 'the audience-chamber,' which was hardly big enough to hold an ordinary writing-desk. The rules and customs of the *great person* were imposing, though somewhat involved. Severity was the mainspring of his system.

'Severity, severity and severity,' he used to say, looking gravely into the face of the person he addressed, though, in truth, there was little need of severity – the ten clerks or so composing the staff of his office were, in any case, in a constant state of terror, and when they heard him at a distance, would throw down their work and stand erect until he had passed through the room. There was an atmosphere of severity in his daily intercourse with his subordinates, and his remarks usually consisted of the three sentences, 'How dare you? Do you know whom you are speaking to? Do you realise who is before you?' At heart he was a kindly man, always ready to do a good deed for a friend, but the rank of general had made him lose his head. When among people of his own rank he was quite tolerable and sensible, but when he happened to be in the company of people who were but one degree below him in rank, he would not say a word and became quite impossible. His condition was one to arouse pity, particularly as he himself realised that he might have been enjoying himself if he chose. A strong desire to participate in some interesting conversation or to join some group would sometimes be seen in his eye, but invariably he was held back by the thought that it might be lowering to his dignity. As a result he remained for ever silent, occasionally perhaps uttering some monosyllabic sound. Thus he gained the reputation of being a bore.

It was to a *great person* of this description that our Akaky Akakievitch appeared at an unpropitious and inconvenient moment. The great person was in his private room talking to an old friend of his who had just arrived from the country and whom he had not seen for many years, when a certain Bashmatchkin was announced.

'Who is he?' he asked curtly.

'A civil service clerk,' was the reply.

'Oh, let him wait! I don't receive people at this hour.'

Now it must be said that the *great person* had told a lie. This was the hour in which he received people; he had long finished what he had had to say to his friend, the conversation had long been interspersed with lengthy pauses, slappings of thighs with a 'Well, Ivan Abramovitch!' or, 'Well, Stefan Varlamovitch!' only he wished to impress his friend with the fact that he had the power to keep a man waiting in his ante-room. At last, after much more talk and more pauses, having finished their cigars in their comfortable upholstered arm-chairs, he said to his secretary who came in with some papers:

'Some clerk is waiting there, I believe; tell him to come in.'

At sight of humble Akaky Akakievitch and his old cloak he turned to him abruptly, asking 'What is your business?' in a harsh severe tone practised at some pains in his own private room at home before the looking-glass a week before he had been promoted to the rank of general and had taken up his present position. Timid Akaky Akakievitch grew more timid, still; as far as his tongue would allow him he explained that he had been robbed of a new cloak; that he had come in the hope that the general would do something for him, write to the police-superintendent or to whomever else it was necessary to try and recover the cloak. The general, for some reason or another, considered his conduct as disrespectful.

'Sir,' he began severely, 'don't you know the usual procedure in these matters? Why did you come to me direct? You ought to have lodged a petition in the department to be passed on to the head-clerk, then to the head of the department, then to my secretary and then to me.'

'But, your excellency,' Akaky Akakievitch said, trying to summon up the little courage that was left to him, 'I took the liberty of coming to you direct, your excellency, because secretaries are . . . such hopeless people.'

'What? What? What?' demanded the great person. 'Is this the spirit in which you have come? Where did you pick up such ideas? Is this the way you young men regard your elders and betters?'

The *great person* could hardly have observed that Akaky Akakievitch was over fifty, and that he could only be regarded as a young man in relation to men of eighty.

'Do you know whom you are speaking to? Do you realise who is standing before you? Do you, I ask?'

At this point he stamped his foot with rage, and raised his voice to such a high pitch that a less timid man than Akaky Akakievitch would have quaked with fear. Akaky Akakievitch was quite stunned; he swayed backwards and forwards; if a porter had not caught him in time he would have fallen on the floor. He was carried out insensible. And the *great person*, pleased at the effect he had produced, an effect which had exceeded his utmost expectation, and quite intoxicated with the thought that a word from him could cause a man to lose his senses, looked askance at his friend to see how the latter had taken the scene; he noticed, not without a feeling of satisfaction, that his friend, too, seemed almost to fear him.

Akaky Akakievitch did not remember how he managed to walk down the stairs and out into the street; there was no sensation in his arms or legs; never in his life had he been so severely reprimanded by a general, and a strange general at that. He fought his way through the howling wind, open-mouthed. The wind, in the usual St Petersburg way, blew from every side, from every street and alley. He caught a severe cold, which developed into quinsy; when he reached home he was unable to speak a word, and went straight to bed. A reprimand may sometimes produce an effect so terrible! On the following day he was in a raging fever. With the aid of the St Petersburg climate the malady developed more quickly than one would have expected, and when the doctor came and felt his pulse, there was nothing that could be done, so he ordered fomentations, for no other purpose apparently than that it should not be said that the patient had died without medical aid. For all that, in a few hours, he pronounced his condition as hopeless, and turning to the landlady said, 'You had better order a pine-coffin for him as quickly as you can; he cannot afford an oak one.'

Did Akaky Akakievitch hear these fateful words? And if so, what effect did they produce on him? Did he regret his wretched life? No one could tell, for Akaky Akakievitch was delirious. Apparitions, each more terrible than the last, appeared before him continuously; now he could see Petrovitch from whom he was ordering a cloak to be made with some wonderful trap for thieves; the thieves were under the bed, and Akaky Akakievitch kept calling to the landlady to come and pull one out from the very bed-clothes; now he asked why his old cloak was hanging there when he had a new one; now he imagined himself before the general, hearing his abuse and muttering 'I am sorry, your excellency!' and then followed oaths such as caused the old landlady to cross herself hurriedly; she had never heard Akaky Akakievitch use such language, particularly in connection with words such as 'your excellency.' Later, no sense at all could be made of what he said, the only clear thing being that his disordered brain centred round the cloak. Soon poor Akaky Akakievitch breathed his last. Neither his room nor his belongings were sealed, for, in the first place he had no successors to inherit them, and in the second he had little to leave. His property consisted of a bundle of quill-pens, a quire of government paper, three pairs of socks, and two or three buttons that had come off his trousers, and the familiar 'dressing-gown.' God knows who inherited them. I confess that the person who told me the story was not even interested in the question. Akaky Akakievitch was buried, and St Petersburg was left without Akaky Akakievitch, as though he had never existed. Thus there disappeared a creature, uncherished and unloved, who failed to arouse so much as the curiosity of a natural scientist, who is more interested in the anatomy of a common fly – a creature who had humbly submitted to the jeers of his fellow workers and to whom no eventful thing had ever happened until the very end, when, for a brief space, his life was brightened by the possession of a cloak that had brought down on his head misfortune of such magnitude as though he might have been one of the mighty of the world.

Four days later a porter from the office called at his lodging to say that the chief insisted on his returning to work, but the porter went back without Akaky Akakievitch, announcing that the latter could not come.

To the question 'Why?' he replied simply:

'Because he is dead; he was buried four days ago.'

This is how the news of Akaky Akakievitch's death reached the office and on the following day a new clerk was installed in his place, a man taller of stature than Akaky Akakievitch; his writing was not straight and even as that of Akaky Akakievitch; he wrote a sloping, crooked hand.

Who would have believed that this was not the last of Akaky Akakievitch and that for a few days he was destined to become famous after his death, as though to compensate him for the shadowy, colourless life he had led? But that is what actually happened, and our poor story unexpectedly assumes a fantastic ending. A rumour suddenly spread throughout St Petersburg that Kalinkin Bridge and the neighbourhood was haunted at night by a ghost in the garb of a civil service clerk, looking for a stolen cloak. Under this pretext he snatched the cloaks from the shoulders of any passers-by, irrespective of their rank and station – cloaks lined with cat, cloaks lined with beaver, wadding, and raccoon, cloaks lined with bear or any sort of skin man uses for the protection of his own. One of the office clerks had seen the ghost with his own eyes and recognised Akaky Akakievitch. He was so terrified that he bolted as fast as he could, and was unable consequently, to get a good look at the ghost; having observed from a distance only that the ghost shook a finger at him threateningly. There were endless complaints on all sides, not only on the part of titular councillors but of others whose backs went bare owing to the ghost. The police resolved to catch him at all costs, dead or alive, and mete him out such a punishment that he would act as an example to others. They very nearly succeeded. It fell to the lot of a certain constable in Kirushkin Street to seize the ghost by the collar in the very act of his crime, just as he was snatching a cloak from the shoulders of some retired musician, a flute-player in his day. The constable's cries brought along two other constables. He ordered them to hold the prisoner while he dived down into the leg of his boot for his snuff-box in order to revive his frozen nose with a pinch, but the snuff was so strong evidently that it was too much for a ghost, even. The constable had hardly covered his right nostril with his thumb than the ghost sneezed so violently as to send the snuff into the eyes of the three of them. When they raised their fists to rub their eyes the ghost had vanished so completely that they began to doubt if they had really held him at all. From that night the whole of the police were in such terror of ghosts that they feared to arrest even the living and cried to an offender from a distance, 'Go thy way in peace!' Then the ghost of the civil service clerk began to walk beyond the Kalinkin Bridge, bringing terror to the hearts of timid people. But we must not forget a *certain great person* who was more or less the cause of the fantastic turn this perfectly true story has taken. A sense of justice forces me to say that *the certain great person* experienced a feeling of pity after the departure of poor, crushed Akaky Akakievitch. Pity was not foreign to his nature; his heart was susceptible to many kindly emotions, but his rank prevented him from showing them. As soon as his friend had left him his thoughts recurred to poor Akaky Akakievitch, and almost every day since he visualised the poor man who had collapsed at a reprimand from him. The thought of him so worried the general that a week later he sent one of his clerks to inquire who he was, and to find out if nothing could be done to help him, but learning of Akaky Akakievitch's death he was so astounded that he was filled with remorse for the rest of the day. Desiring to distract his mind and to rid himself of the unpleasant impression, he set out that evening to the house of a friend where he found an agreeable company gathered, consisting of men of the same rank as himself, so that he was quite free to enjoy himself. This produced a wonderful effect on his spirits. He was quite affable and pleasant in conversation and spent a most delightful evening. At supper he drank two glasses of champagne, and champagne, we know, conduces cheerfulness and disposed him to other indulgences. He resolved to pay a visit to a lady of his acquaintance – Karoline Ivanovna, by name – a lady of German origin, to whom he entertained feelings of pure friendliness. It must be said that our great person was a man well on in years, a good husband and the respected father of a family. He had two sons who already worked in the department, and a pretty sixteen-year-old daughter with an attractive little tilted nose, who came to kiss his hand each morning with a '*Bonjour*, Papa!' His wife, still young and attractive, would give him her own hand first, and then kiss his in turn. The great person, however, quite contented, apparently, with the affections of his family, considered it proper to have a lady-friend in another part of the town, the lady-friend being neither younger nor better-looking than his own wife; but these are some of the incongruities to be met with in the world, which one cannot account for. Thus our great person walked down the stairs and, seating himself in his sleigh, ordered the coachman to drive to Karoline Ivanovna. He wrapped his warm rich cloak closely around him and abandoned himself to a condition very pleasant to a Russian; a condition in which without any effort thoughts, each more agreeable than the last, come into the head unbidden, and one has not the trouble even of following them up. In perfect contentment he recalled the pleasant evening spent, the jokes that had amused the small circle. Some of these he repeated to himself in a whisper and found them just as amusing as before and laughed with pure enjoyment. He was bothered now and again by a biting wind that seemed to come from nowhere and cut his face, raising lumps of snow or blowing out the cape of his cloak like a sail, or dashing it suddenly with force over his head, so that he had no little trouble in disentangling himself. All at once the great person felt someone seize him violently by the collar, and, turning, he saw a little man in a shabby old cloak, whom in terror he recognised as Akaky Akakievitch. The great person's face turned as white as snow. He too, seemed like a ghost. His terror reached a maximum when he saw the ghost's mouth open and he felt his sepulchral breath and heard him speak the words, 'Ha, ha, I've got you at last! At last I've got you by the collar! It's your cloak that I want! You refused to help me recover mine and abused me into the bargain, now you can give me yours!' The poor *great person* nearly died of fright. At the office he was a strong man, strong generally in relation to his inferiors, and, glancing at his manly form, any one would have said, 'What a fine strong-looking man!' At the present moment, like many people of a valiant exterior only, he was in such a condition of fright, that he apprehended a heart attack. He threw the cloak from his shoulders, and cried to the coachman in an unnatural voice:

'Whip up home as fast as you can!'

The coachman, hearing the voice that was terrifying enough at ordinary times, hastily drew his head into the collar of his coat and, lashing his whip, flew away like the wind. In five or six minutes the great person was at the door of his own house. Pale and distraught, he dragged himself to his own room and spent a most miserable night there instead of at Karoline Ivanovna's, and at tea the following morning his daughter remarked, 'How pale you are to-day, Papa!'

But papa was silent, he did not say a word of what had happened to him, nor where he had been, nor where he had intended to go. The incident made a great impression on his mind. Less often did his subordinates hear the expressions, 'How dare you? Do you realise who is standing before you?' On the rare occasions when he used them it was not until after he had made himself acquainted with the matter in hand. But the most remarkable thing of all was that the ghost disappeared from that night; the general's cloak must have fitted him perfectly; at any rate, no more cloaks were snatched from the shoulders of men. There were still some busy-bodies whose fears would not be allayed, and who persisted in saying that the ghost still haunted the distant parts of the town. One policeman declared that with his own eyes he had seen an apparition come out of a house, and that he did not stop him because he was physically unable to do so. He was in such a condition of weakness that on one occasion a sucking-pig rushing out of a house had bowled him off his feet, much to the amusement of the *isvoschicks* standing near, who had afterwards to pay for their merriment by tipping him two kopecks each for tobacco. While unable to stop the ghost, the policeman had followed him, nevertheless, until at last the ghost had turned and demanded what he wanted, shaking such a formidable fist at him as one rarely meets with among the living. The poor policeman turned back as fast as he could. This apparition, however, was taller and had a long moustache. After the incident with the policeman he had quickened his pace in the direction of the Obukhov Bridge, and had disappeared into the darkness of the night.

Korney Vasiliev

BY LEO N. TOLSTOY

1828–1910

Korney Vasiliev was fifty-four years old when he had last been in the country. Not a single grey hair was visible in his thick curly crop; only his black beard near the cheek-bones contained a touch of white. His face was smooth and ruddy, the nape of his neck broad and strong, and the whole of his body was covered with the fat of a comfortable city life.

Twenty years ago he had finished his military service and returned home with money. At first he opened a shop, then he abandoned the shop and took to dealing in cattle. He would go to Chekas for 'goods' (cattle), and drive them to Moscow.

In the village of Gayi, in his stone house covered with an iron roof, lived his old mother, his wife and two children (a girl and a boy), as well as an orphan nephew, a dumb boy of fifteen, and a labourer.

Korney had been married twice. His first wife, a weak, ailing woman, had died without bearing any children, and when a widower, getting on in years, he had married for the second time a strong, handsome girl, the daughter of a poor widow of a neighbouring village.

Korney had sold his last batch of goods so well that he possessed about three thousand roubles in money, and hearing from a countryman that a ruined landowner was selling a piece of woodland cheap, he resolved to deal in timber, for he knew the business well, having served as assistant to a timber-merchant's clerk before his soldiering days.

At the railway station – the railway did not go by Gayi – he met a fellow countryman, Kusma the lame. Kusma came out from Gayi to meet every train in the hope of picking up a fare

57

for his sorry pair of shaggy hacks. Kusma was a poor man, and in consequence disliked rich men, and Korney in particular; he called him Kornushka.

Korney, in a short coat, a long sheep-skin coat and a bag in his hand, came out on to the station steps, his round belly protruding in front of him. He stopped, blew out his cheeks and looked round. It was morning; the weather was clouded, with a slight touch of frost.

'No fare, Uncle Kusma?' asked he. 'Won't you take me, eh?'

'If you like – for a rouble.'

'Seventy kopeks is enough, eh?'

'A man with a full stomach ready to deprive a poor man of his thirty kopeks.'

'Very well, come along then,' said Korney, and putting his bag and his bundle into the sleigh, he spread himself out on the back seat.

Kusma remained on the box.

'Well, you can start now.'

They left the holes and ruts near the station and drove out on to the smooth road.

'Well, how is it with you – not with us, but with you – in the country?' asked Korney.

'There is little good, to be sure.'

'How is that? Is my old woman alive?'

'Oh, yes, she is alive; I saw her in church the other day. Your old woman is alive. And so is your young wife. She has nothing to worry about. She has taken a new labourer.'

And Kusma laughed, in a curious way, it seemed to Korney.

'A labourer? And what has happened to Peter?'

'Peter is ill. She has taken Evstigny Bely from Kamenka,' said Kusma, 'from her own village, that is.'

'Indeed!' said Korney.

When he became engaged to Marfa there had been some gossip among the women about Evstigny.

'That's how it is, Korney Vasilievitch,' said Kusma; 'the women have too much freedom nowadays.'

'So they say,' said Korney. 'Your grey is getting old,' he added, anxious to change the subject.

'I am not young myself. The horse is like the master,' said Kusma in reply to Korney's words, with a lash of the whip at the shaggy bow-legged gelding.

About half-way they came to a posting inn; Korney ordered Kusma to stop and went in. Kusma led the horses to the empty trough and rearranged the harness, not glancing at Korney, yet hoping that the latter would ask him in for a drink.

'Won't you come in and have a glass, Uncle Kusma?' asked Korney, coming out on to the step.

'Thank you,' replied Kusma, pretending to be in no hurry.

Korney asked for a bottle of vodka and took it to Kusma. The latter, having eaten nothing since morning, got drunk with the first glass, and drawing near to Korney began telling him in a whisper what was being said in the village. And the talk went that Marfa, his wife, had engaged her former lover as labourer, and was living with him.

'I am sorry for you,' said the drunken Kusma; 'it is not well; the people are laughing at you. Wait, I tell them, wait till he comes home himself. That is how it is, Korney Vasilievitch.'

Korney listened in silence to Kusma's words, his bushy brows lowering over his sparkling black eyes.

'Do you want to water the horses?' he only asked when the bottle was finished. 'If not, let us start.'

He paid the innkeeper and went out into the street.

He reached home at dusk. The first person he met was Evstigny Bely himself, of whom he could not help thinking the whole way. Korney greeted him. Looking at the haggard face and white lashes of Evstigny as he hurried up, Korney shook his head in perplexity. 'The old dog lied,' he thought, recalling Kusma's words. 'But who knows? I must find out.'

Kusma winked at Evstigny as he stood by the horses.

'So you live with us, it seems?' Korney began.

'One must work somewhere,' Evstigney replied.

'Is the room heated?'

'Of course it is. Matvaeva is there,' replied Evstigney.

Korney walked up the steps. Marfa, hearing his voice, came out into the passage, and catching sight of her husband flushed red and hastened to greet him with unusual affection.

'Mother and I gave up expecting you,' said she, following Korney into the room.

'Well, how have you been getting on without me?'

'We live just as we used to do,' said she, and seizing her two-year-old daughter in her arms, who was tugging at her skirt and begging for milk, she walked out into the passage with long resolute strides.

Korney's mother, black-eyed like himself, shuffled into the room in low felt boots.

'Thank you for having come to see me,' said she, shaking her quivering head.

Korney told his mother on what business he had come home, and remembering Kusma, he went out to pay him. As soon as he opened the door into the passage, confronting him, in the yard door, stood Marfa and Evstigny. They were talking very near to each other. Catching sight of Korney, Evstigny slipped across the yard and Marfa went up to refix the chimney on the singing *samover*.

Korney passed her silently, and taking up his bundle invited Kusma to tea in the large room. Before tea Korney distributed the presents he had brought home from Moscow for his family – a woollen shawl for his mother, a picture book for Fedka, a waistcoat for his dumb nephew and a print material for a dress for his wife.

At tea Korney sat frowning and silent; only now and again he smiled involuntarily when he looked at the dumb boy, who amused everyone with his joy over the waistcoat. He folded and unfolded it, put it on, kissed Korney's hand and looked at him with laughing eyes.

Tea and supper over, Korney went into the room where he slept with Marfa and the little girl. Marfa remained in the large room to clear away the dishes. Korney sat alone, his elbows resting on the table, waiting. His anger against his wife grew and grew. He took some bills from the wall, a note-book from his pocket, and to distract his thoughts, began to add up accounts, glancing at the door now and again, and listening to the voices in the large room.

Several times he heard the door of the room open and

someone come out into the passage, but it was not his wife. At last he heard her footsteps; there was a pull at the door and it opened, and she came in, rosy, handsome, in a red kerchief, carrying her little girl in her arms.

'You must be tired with the journey,' said she smiling, as though not observing his sulky mood.

Korney looked at her but made no reply, and went on with his counting, though there was nothing further to count.

'It is getting late,' said she, and putting down the little girl she went behind the partition.

He heard her making the bed and putting the child to sleep.

'People are laughing,' he recalled Kusma's words.

'You wait!' thought he, breathing with difficulty, and he rose slowly, put his scrap of pencil into his waistcoat pocket, hung the bills on a nail, and went up to the partition door. His wife stood with her face to the ikon, praying. He stopped and waited. For a long time she bowed and crossed herself and murmured her prayers. It seemed to him that she had long finished them all, and was repeating them over again on purpose. At last she prostrated herself to the ground, rose, and muttering a few words of a prayer quickly, she turned to him.

'Agasha is sleeping,' said she, pointing to the little girl, and, without a smile, she sat down on the creaking bed.

'Has Evstigny been here long?' asked Korney, coming through the door. With a calm movement she threw one of her thick plaits across her shoulders on to her breast, and with quick fingers began unplaiting it. She looked him straight in the face, her eyes laughing.

'Evstigny? I can't remember – about two or three weeks, I suppose.'

'Do you live with him?' asked Korney.

She dropped the plait, then caught it up again, and began replaiting the coarse thick hair.

'Live with Evstigny! What an idea, indeed!' said she, pronouncing the word 'Evstigny' in a peculiar ringing voice. 'What lies people tell! Who said so?'

'I ask you, is it true or not?' demanded Korney, clenching his strong hands, thrust into his pockets.

'Don't talk nonsense! Shall I take off your boots?'

'I ask you,' repeated Korney.

'What a compliment for Evstigny, to be sure!' said she. 'Who told you such a lie?'

'What did you say to him in the passage?'

'What did I say? I told him to put a new hoop on the barrel. Why will you worry me?'

'Tell me the truth, or I'll kill you, you dirty hussy!'

He seized her by her plait. She pulled it away from him, her face contorted by pain.

'You only want a fight! What kindness have I known from you? What am I to do with such a life?'

'What are you to do?' he repeated, moving towards her.

'Why do you pull out my hair? Why do you call me names? Why do you worry me? It is true that . . .'

She had no time to finish. He seized her by the arm, pulled her off the bed and began raining blows on her head, her sides, her breast. The more he beat her the stronger his anger grew. She screamed, defended herself, tried to escape from him, but he would not let her. The little girl awoke and rushed to her mother.

'Mamka!' cried she.

Korney seized the child's arm, tore her away from the mother, and threw her into a corner like a kitten. The child screamed for a moment or two, and then no further sound came from her.

'Murderer! You have killed the child!' Marfa cried, and tried to raise herself to go to her daughter, but again he seized her and gave her such a violent blow on the breast that she fell backwards and also ceased her cries.

The child resumed her cries and screamed and screamed without stopping to take breath.

The old woman, without a shawl, with dishevelled grey hair and quivering head, came in, swaying as she walked; taking no notice of Korney or Marfa, she went up to her grandchild, whose hot tears were streaming down her cheeks, and picked her up.

Korney stood breathing heavily and looking around as

though he had just awakened from sleep, not comprehending where he was nor what had happened to him.

Marfa raised her head, groaning, and wiped the blood from her face with her sleeve.

'You horrible villain!' said she. 'I do live with Evstigny and always did! Kill me if you like! Agashka is his daughter, not yours,' she blurted out quickly, covering her face with her arm to shield it from a further blow.

But Korney seemed not to understand anything and looked about him vacantly.

'See what you've done to the child! You've broken her arm!' said the old woman, pointing to the child's dislocated arm hanging limply by her side. Korney turned and walked silently into the passage and out at the door.

Outside it was still frosty and clouded. The snowflakes fell on his hot cheeks and forehead. He sat down on the steps and began eating handfuls of snow which he picked up from the rails. From the other side of the door came Marfa's groans and the child's pitiful cries. The door opened and he heard his mother walk across the passage into the large room with the little girl. He rose and went into the room. The lamp was turned down, casting a faint light on the table. Marfa's groans grew louder as she heard him enter. He dressed silently, pulled a bag from beneath the bench, into which he packed his clothes, and afterwards bound it with a piece of cord.

'You've nearly killed me. What have I done to you?' Marfa said in a plaintive voice.

Without replying, Korney took up his bag and carried it to the door.

'Jailbird! murderer! You just wait! There are laws for the likes of you!' changing her tone she cried spitefully.

Korney, without a word, pushed the door open with his foot, then banged it so violently that the walls shook.

Going into the large room, Korney woke the dumb boy and ordered him to harness the horse. The latter, only half awake, looked wonderingly at his uncle and scratched his head with both hands. Comprehending at last what was required of him, he put on his felt boots and ragged sheepskin coat, took a lantern and went out into the yard.

It was quite light when Korney and the dumb boy came out of the gate in the little sledge, and drove along the road he had come the day before with Kusma.

He reached the station five minutes before the departure of the train. The dumb boy saw him take a ticket, get into a carriage with his bag, and nod to him as the carriage rolled away out of sight.

Besides the injuries to her face, Marfa had two broken ribs and a wound in the head. But the strong, healthy woman recovered, and in about six months no trace of her injuries remained. The little girl, however, remained a cripple for life. Two bones in her arm were broken and the arm remained permanently crooked.

From that day nothing was heard of Korney and no one knew if he were living or dead.

II

Seventeen years passed. It was late in the autumn. The sun set low in the sky and at four it was already dark. The Andreyev flock was returning to the village. One shepherd, having served his term, had left before the festival and the cattle was driven in turn by the women and children.

The flock had just come out of the stubble-fields on to the dirty churned ruts of the gravel road, muddy and hoof-trodden, and with an incessant lowing and bleating moved towards the village. Along the road, ahead of the flock, in a large cap and patched peasant coat, black from wind and weather, a large leathern bag on his bent back, walked an old man with a grey beard and grey curly hair; his bushy eyebrows only were black. He walked, moving with difficulty over the mud in his soaked, torn, heavy boots, and at each step he leant on his wooden staff. When the flock caught him up he stopped, leaning on his staff. Driving the flock came a young woman, her skirt tucked up, with a coarse shawl on her head, a man's pair of boots on her feet, running quickly from side to side of the road, and urging on the lagging sheep and swine. When she came abreast of the old man she stopped and looked him up and down.

'Good evening, grandfather,' she said in a soft ringing young voice.

'Good evening, bright child,' replied the old man.

'Do you want a bed for the night, eh?'

'It seems so. I'm tired out,' the old man replied hoarsely.

'Don't you go to the elder's man, grandfather,' the young woman said kindly. 'Go straight to our place, the third hut from the end. My mother-in-law takes in wanderers like you.'

'The third hut? That must be the Zinovyevs',' said the old man, puckering his black brows.

'How do you know?'

'I have been there.'

'Fedushka, how can you be so careless! The lame one has been left behind!' cried the young woman, pointing to a limping, three-legged sheep which had lagged behind the rest of the flock, and switching the stick in her left hand, in a curious way, she rearranged her kerchief with her crooked right arm and ran back for the lame sheep.

The old man was Korney, the young woman Agasha, whose arm he had broken seventeen years ago. She had married into a rich family in Andreyevka, four versts from Gayi.

From the strong, rich, proud man he was, Korney Vasiliev became what he is now – an old mendicant who possessed nothing but the ragged clothes on his body, a soldier's ticket and two shirts in his bundle. The change took place so gradually that he could not have said when it began and how it had come about. The only thing he knew, the only thing he was sure of, was that his misfortune had been brought about by his wicked wife. It was both strange and painful to him to recall what he had been formerly. Whenever he thought of it he remembered the person whom he considered to be the cause of all the evil he had suffered for the past seventeen years.

On the night when he had beaten his wife he went to the

landowner who had the piece of woodland to sell, but could not buy it, as it had already been sold. Then he returned to Moscow, where he began to drink. He always drank more or less, but now he drank without stopping for a whole fortnight, and when at last he came to himself, he went down to buy cattle. The deal proved unfortunate, and he lost money over it. Then he bought some more cattle, and again he was unfortunate. In a year, from three thousand roubles he was left with twenty-five, and was compelled to find a job. And he began to drink the more.

For the first year he served as a clerk to a dealer in cattle, but once when on the road he got so drunk that the merchant dismissed him. Then, through the aid of a man he knew, he obtained a place at a wine merchant's, but here, too, he did not stay long – he entangled his accounts and was sent away. He was too ashamed and too angry to return home.

'They live quite well without me. Perhaps the boy, too, is not mine,' thought he.

Things went from bad to worse. He could no longer take a place as a clerk, but had to go as a cattle-driver, and later they refused to employ him even for this work.

The worse things grew, the more he blamed his wife, and the stronger became his wrath.

For the last time Korney got a place as cattle-driver with a strange employer. The cattle were attacked by some disease; it was not Korney's fault, but the master was angry and dismissed both him and the clerk. Korney could obtain no other place and resolved to tramp. He made himself a pair of boots, a good bag, took some tea and sugar with him and eight roubles in money and set off for Kiev. He did not like Kiev and went on to the Caucasus to Novy Afon. On the way he was seized by a fever and grew suddenly weak. The only money he had was a rouble and seventy kopeks. He had no friends anywhere, so he decided to go home to his son. 'Perhaps the wicked creature is dead by now,' thought he. 'And if she isn't, then I will tell her before she dies, damn her! What she has done to me.' With this thought he set off for home.

In two days he was in full grip of a fever. He grew weaker

and weaker and could not walk more than ten or fifteen versts a day. Two hundred versts from home his money had all gone and he was compelled to beg for food in Christ's name, and sleep in the night where the elder's man in each village put him. 'Rejoice, see what you have brought me to!' he said in thought to his wife, and by old habit he clenched his aged feeble hands, but there was no one to strike at and the strength with which to strike had gone from his fists.

It took him two weeks to walk the two hundred versts, and ailing and weak he had reached the place, four miles from home, where he had met Agasha, without recognising her or being recognised – Agasha, who was considered but was not his daughter, and whose arm he had broken seventeen years ago.

III

He did as Agasha had told him. Going into the Zinovyev yard, he asked if he could stay the night there, and they took him in.

Entering the hut, he crossed himself in his usual manner before the ikon, and then greeted the hosts.

'Frozen, grandfather? Here, come to the stove!' said the jolly wrinkled old mistress, clearing the table.

Agasha's husband, a youngish peasant, was sitting on a bench by the table, trimming the lamp.

'How wet you are!' said he; 'dear, dear, come and dry yourself.'

Korney undressed, took off his boots and hanging his leg wrappings against the stove, he climbed on to it.

Agasha came into the hut, carrying a pitcher. She had already driven in the cattle and come back from the sheds.

'Did an old man come here?' asked she. 'I told him to look in.'

'There he is,' said the host, pointing to the stove where Korney sat rubbing his rough bony hands.

At tea the hosts called to Korney to come and join them. He climbed down from the stove and seated himself on the edge of the bench. He was given a cup of tea and a piece of sugar.

They talked of the weather, crops, saying that the land-owners' corn could not be gathered in because of the rain; the peasants had taken in all theirs, but the corn of the gentry was rotting in the fields, and the mice, too, were terrible.

Korney related how he had seen a field full of corn sheaves on his way.

The young woman poured him out a fifth cup of weak tea and handed it to him.

'Never mind, grandfather, drink; it is good for you,' said she when he refused it.

'What is wrong with your arm?' he asked, taking the cup from her carefully and puckering his brows.

'It was broken when she was quite little; her father wanted to kill our Agasha,' said the talkative old mother-in-law.

'But why?' asked Korney. And looking at the young woman's face he suddenly recalled Evstigny Bely with his blue eyes, and the hand holding the cup shook so violently that he upset half his tea before he could put it down on the table.

'There was a man in Gayi, her father he was – Korney Vasiliev he was called. A rich man he was and proud of his wife. He beat her one day and crippled the child.'

Korney was silent, looking up from beneath his quivering black brows, now at his hosts, now at Agasha.

'Why did he do it?' he asked, biting off a piece of sugar.

'Who knows? There is always gossip about us women,' said the old mistress. 'It was because of a labourer they had – a fellow from our village. He died in their house.'

'Died?' asked Korney, coughing.

'A long time ago. Our young woman comes from their family. They lived well, the good people. The first in the village they were when the master was alive.'

'Is he dead, too, then?' asked Korney.

'We suppose so. He disappeared about fifteen years ago.'

'It was longer than that. Mamushka told me that she had only just left off nursing me.'

'Are you angry with him for having broken . . .' began Korney, but his voice broke.

'He is no stranger, you see, after all he is my father. Have some more tea; it will make you warm. Shall I pour you out some?'

Korney did not reply, but sobbed aloud.

'What is the matter?'

'Nothing; Christ save us!'

And Korney, with trembling hands, supporting himself by pillar and wall, climbed on to the stove with his long emaciated legs.

'There now!' said the old woman to her son with a wink in the direction of the old man.

IV

The next day Korney rose earlier than the rest. He climbed down from the stove, straightened out the creases in the dried crumpled leg-wrappings, put on his boots, shrivelled with heat, and slung his bag over his back.

'Why not stay to breakfast, grandfather?' said the old woman.

'God save you! I must go.'

'Then take some of yesterday's *lepeshka* with you. I will put some in your bag.'

Korney thanked her and took his leave.

'Come in on your way back; we shall still be alive, I suppose.'

Outside a heavy autumn fog enveloped everything, but Korney knew the way well; every slope and every rise of the ground, every bush and every willow on the road, to the right and the left, were familiar to him, though during the last seventeen years some had been cut down and in place of the old there were young trees and the young had turned to old ones.

The village of Gayi was just the same; there were a few new houses on the outskirts, and some of the old wooden houses had given place to brick ones. His own stone house was the same, only a little aged by time. The roof had not been painted for a long time, a few bricks were missing from the corners, and the steps leading to the door were crooked.

As he approached his one-time home the gates creaked and

out came a mare and a foal, an old gelding roan and a three-year-old. The old roan resembled the mare Korney had bought home from the fair a year before his departure.

'It must be the one she was carrying at the time,' thought he. 'It has the same hanging hind-quarters, the same broad breast and shaggy legs.'

The horses were being driven to water by a dark-eyed boy in new bast shoes. 'My grandson, no doubt, Fedka's boy. He is dark-eyed like him,' thought Korney.

The boy looked at the strange old man, then ran after a young stallion frisking about in the mud. Following the boy came a dog just as black as the former Volchok.

'Can it be Volchok?' thought Korney, and recalled that Volchok would now have been twenty years old.

With difficulty he mounted the steps on which he had sat that night eating the snow from the rails, and opened the door into the passage.

'Why do you poke your nose in here without asking?' a woman's voice called to him from the hut. He recognised his wife's voice. And there she was herself, a withered, stringy, wrinkled old woman, coming out at the door. Korney had expected to see the young and handsome Marfa who had wronged him, whom he hated and wanted to upbraid, but instead here was some strange old woman. 'If you've come begging you can eat at the window,' she said in a harsh grating voice.

'I have not come to beg,' said Korney.

'What do you want, then?'

She stopped suddenly, and by her face he could see that she recognised him.

'There are many of the likes of you who come prowling about the house. Go away, go away in God's name!'

Korney swayed against the wall, and supporting himself on his staff, he gazed at her intently, feeling in wonder that the anger he had nursed against her for so many years had suddenly vanished. His emotion made him feel faint.

'Marfa, we shall soon be dead.'

'Go, go in God's name!' she said quickly and viciously.

'Have you nothing more to say?'

'There is nothing for me to say,' said she. 'Go in God's name, go, go! There are many tramps like you prowling about the place!'

With quick steps she re-entered the hut and banged the door behind her.

'Why do you abuse him?' A man's voice was heard, and a dark peasant appeared at the door with an axe at his girdle. He was the same as Korney had been forty years ago, only shorter and thinner, but he had the same black, sparkling eyes.

It was no other than Fedka, whom seventeen years ago he had presented with a picture book. He was remonstrating with his mother for her unkindness to the beggar. Following him, also with an axe at his girdle, came the dumb nephew. He was now a grown peasant with a thin beard, wrinkled and wiry, with a long neck and a resolute, penetrating gaze. The two peasants had only just finished their breakfast and were going out into the wood.

'In a moment, grandfather,' said Fedor, and pointing to the old man and then to the room, he made a gesture to the dumb man as of cutting bread.

Fedor walked out into the street; the dumb nephew re-entered the hut. Korney stood with bent head, leaning against the wall and supporting himself on his staff. A great weakness had come over him; he restrained his sobs with difficulty. The dumb man came out of the hut with a large hunk of new fragrant black bread and handed it to Korney. When Korney, crossing himself, took the bread, the dumb man turned to the door of the hut, passed both his hands over his face, and made a motion as though of spitting; in this way he expressed his disapproval of his aunt. Suddenly he was petrified and stared open-mouthed at Korney in recognition. Korney could contain his tears no longer, and wiping his eyes, nose and grey beard with the skirts of his coat, he turned from the dumb man and walked down the steps. He experienced a strange, gentle, exalted feeling of submission – of humility before mankind, before his wife, before every one; the feeling tore at his heart with a painful sweetness.

Marfa gazed out of the window and sighed with relief only when she saw the old man disappear round the corner of the house. When she was convinced that her man had really gone, she sat down by the loom and went on with her weaving. Ten times she struck the comb, but her hands refused to work. She stopped and tried to recall Korney as she had just seen him; she knew that it was he – the man who had loved and beaten her, and she was terrified at what she had done. She had done something she ought not to have done. But how ought she to have treated him? He did not say he was Korney and that he had come home again. And again she took up the shuttle and went on with her weaving until evening.

v

With difficulty Korney reached Andreyevka by nightfall and the Zinovyevs again took him in.

'You didn't go far, grandfather.'

'I couldn't; I was too weak. I must go back the way I came, it seems. Can I stay the night?'

'You won't hurt the place, you know. Come and dry yourself.'

The whole night Korney was racked by fever. Towards morning he dozed off, and when he awoke the house folk had all departed to their work, and Agasha alone remained in the hut.

He was lying on a dry coat the old woman had given him.

Agasha was taking the bread out of the oven.

'Come here, clever child,' Korney called to her in a feeble voice.

'In a minute, grandfather,' she replied, putting down the bread. 'Would you like something to drink? Some kvas?'

He made no reply.

When she put down the last loaf, she went to him with a jug of kvas. He did not turn to her or take the kvas, but lay on his back, his face turned upwards, and spoke without moving.

'Gasha,' he said in a soft voice. 'My time has come. I want to die; forgive me, for Christ's sake.'

'God will forgive. You have never done me any harm.'

He was silent.

'There is something more, my child. Go to your mother and tell her ... that the stranger, tell her ... the stranger of yesterday, tell her ...'

He began to sob.

'Have you been to our place, then?'

'Yes, yesterday. Tell her that the stranger of yesterday ... the stranger, say ...' Again his sobs choked him, and at last, pulling himself together, he went on, 'came to say goodbye to her,' he said, and began fumbling for something in his bosom.

'I'll tell her grandfather; I'll tell her. What are you looking for?' asked Agasha.

The old man was silent; convulsed with the effort, he pulled a piece of paper out of his bosom with his emaciated hairy hand and held it up to her.

'There; give this to whoever asks for it – my soldier's ticket. Thank God I have unburdened myself of my sins.' His face assumed an expression of ecstasy. He raised his brows, fixed his eyes on the ceiling and became still.

'A candle,' he said without moving his lips.

Agasha understood. She took a small piece of wax candle from the ikon and gave it to him. He seized it with his thumb.

Agasha went to put away his ticket in a box, and when she returned, the candle had fallen out of his hand and the light had gone out of his stony eyes and the breath from his bosom. Agasha crossed herself, blew out the candle, took a clean towel and covered his face ...

The whole of that night Marfa could not sleep and lay thinking of Korney. In the morning she put on her coat, covered her head with a shawl and went out to learn what had become of the stranger of yesterday. She had not gone far when she learned that the old man was in Andreyvka. Marfa took a stick and set off for Andreyvka. The farther she walked the greater her fears grew. 'We will forgive each other; I will bring him home and we will free ourselves of sin. Let him at least die in his own home, near his son,' she thought.

When Marfa neared her daughter's house a large crowd was gathered outside. Some stood in the passage, others by the window. Every one knew that the rich, famous Korney Vasiliev, who forty years ago had cut a figure in the place, had died as a poor wanderer in the house of his daughter. The hut, too, was full of people. The women whispered among themselves, sighing and shaking their heads.

When Marfa entered the hut they made way for her. Beneath the ikon she saw the body washed and laid out and covered with a towel, and Philip Konovitch, who could read, was chanting the Slavonic words of the psalter in the manner of the deacon.

It was too late to forgive or to beg forgiveness, and from Korney's impassive, dignified old face it was impossible to know whether he had forgiven or was still nursing his wrongs.

The Murmuring Forest

A Polish Legend

BY V. KOROLENKO

1833–1921

I

The forest murmured.

There was always a murmur in this forest, a prolonged, measured murmur, like the echo of distant bells, tranquil and mellow, like a soft song without words, like a hazy recollection of the past. There was always a murmur in this forest, for it was an old dreamy pine forest still untouched by woodcutter's axe or saw. The tall hundred-year-old pines stood in solemn array, their green tops pressed closely together. Below, it was still; there was a smell of resin; brightly coloured ferns peeped out from the carpet of pine needles covering the earth, and their gorgeous rugged leaves were motionless; tall blades of grass sprouted in damp corners and the white clover-blossoms bent their heavy little heads in gentle weariness. And above, ever and without a break, was the noise of the forest, as though it were the muffled sighs of the old pines.

How the sighs grew deeper and stronger! I was riding through a track in the forest, and though the sky was not visible, I could yet feel by the way the trees frowned that a heavy cloud was rising above them. It was not early in the day. In places, the slanting rays of the setting sun pierced through the trunks of the trees, while in the thickets a misty dusk was already creeping. By the evening a storm had gathered.

Ideas of shooting for that day had to be abandoned; I had to hasten back to shelter before the storm broke. My horse beat his hoofs against the bare roots of the trees, snorting and pricking up his ears, listening to the reverberating forest echoes. Of his own accord he quickened his pace along the familiar forest path.

A dog barked, the trunks of the trees grew less dense, a painted wall gleamed through them, a column of blue smoke rose beneath the over-hanging greenery, a sloping hut with a thatched roof nestled against the wall of red trunks. It seemed to rise out of the ground while the proud, majestic pines were shaking their heads above it. In the middle of the clearing, standing close together, was a clump of young oaks.

Here lived the constant companions of my shooting expeditions, the foresters Zakhar and Maxim. Evidently neither of them was at home, for no one appeared at the bark of the big sheep-dog. Only the old grandfather, bald-headed, grey-whiskered, was sitting upon the earthen seat, cobbling a bast shoe. Grandfather's whiskers reached almost to his waist; his eyes peered dimly, as though he were trying to recall something which had always eluded his memory . . .

'Good evening, grandfather. Is any one at home?'

'Eh?' Grandfather shook his head. 'Zakhar and Maxim and Motria have gone into the wood after the cow . . . the cow's gone off somewhere. I daresay the beasts have devoured it. That's how it is . . . There is no one at home.'

'It doesn't matter. I'll sit here with you and wait.'

'Wait, wait,' grandfather nodded, and as I fastened my horse to the branch of an oak, peered at me with his weak, dim eyes. Feeble was old grandfather; his eyes could not see and his hands trembled.

'And who are you, boy?' he asked, when I sat down on the earthen seat.

This query I heard at every visit.

'Ah, I know now, I know,' said the old man, resuming his work on the bast shoe. 'It's an old head I have, and it holds nothing – like a sieve. The people who have long been dead I can remember, oh, very well, but new faces I always forget. I've lived too long in this world.'

'Have you lived long in this forest, grandfather?'

'Aye, very long. I was here when the Frenchman came to the Tsar's land.'

'I expect you've seen plenty of things in your time and have lots of tales to tell.'

Grandfather looked at me in wonder.

'What could I see, boy? I've seen the forest . . . It murmurs, murmurs, day and night; summer and winter it murmurs . . . And I, like that old tree, have lived a hundred years in the forest and they have passed unobserved. It is time for the grave now, and sometimes it seems to me, boy, that I do not know whether I have lived in the world or not . . . Aye, that's how it is! Perhaps, I've not lived at all . . .'

The edge of a dense cloud moved from the tops of the trees over the little clearing; the branches of the surrounding pines shook in the gusts of wind, and the roar of the forest was borne along in a deep, rising chord.

'A storm is gathering,' he said in a little whine. 'This is what I do know. How the storm will rage at night, to be sure, breaking and tearing and pulling up the pines by the roots! . . . The master of the forest is going to enjoy himself . . .' he added in a whisper.

'How do you know, grandfather?'

'Oh, I know, I know well what the trees say . . . a tree, boy, is also afraid . . . Yonder now is an aspen, a cursed tree, it is always cracking, and shaking even when there is no wind. A pine in the forest on a clear day plays and murmurs to itself, but no sooner does the wind rise than it begins to roar and to moan. But that is nothing . . . Listen now . . . Though I see badly with my eyes, I can hear with my ears. The oak has begun to rustle, the wind has touched the oak in the clearing. That signifies a storm.'

And truly, the low clump of gnarled oaks that stood in the middle of the clearing, protected by the high wall of pines, were shaking their powerful branches, emitting a dull sound, easily distinguishable from the resounding peal of the pines.

'Aye, do you hear, boy?' grandfather asked with a childishly subtle smile. 'I know if the oak is touched like that it means that *the master* will walk in the night and root up . . . But no, he will not break it! the oak is a powerful tree, too powerful even for the master's strength.'

'What master, grandfather? Didn't you say yourself that the storm uprooted trees?'

Grandfather shook his head with a cunning air.

'Aye, I know. Nowadays I hear there are some people who believe in nothing. That is what we have come to! But I have seen him as I see you now, and better perhaps, for my eyes are old now and they were young then. Welladay! How well my eyes could see in those days!'

'But how did you see him, grandfather? Tell me.'

'It happened just as now; at first the pines began to moan in the forest, and then they roared and moaned again . . . o-oh . . . o-oh . . . o-oh-o! and grew quiet, then again and again the moans came, faster and more pitiful. Aye, that was because many of them were uprooted in the night. And then the oak began to speak. And in the evening it grew worse, and at night *he* rushed and tore about the forest, laughing and crying and dancing. And he kept on attacking the oak which he wished to pull up . . . Once in the autumn I looked out of the window, *he* did not like that; he rushed up to the window and crash! A pine root came through, nearly disfiguring my face, the devil take him! But I was no fool; I jumped away quickly. Aye, boy, that's how vicious he is!'

'What does he look like?'

'To look at he is like the old willow that stands by the bog. Very like that . . . And his hair is like mistletoe that creeps up the trees, and his beard too, and his jaw is overgrown with lichen . . . Faugh, how ugly he is! God forbid that any Christian should look like him! . . . Another time I saw him by the bog, quite close . . . If you want to, come in the winter, then you will see *him* for yourself. You should walk up there on the hill – the forest has covered that too – and climb on to the topmost branch of the highest tree. From there he can be seen some days; like a white pillar he walks over the forest and whirls and rushes from hill to valley, from valley to hill, and then he disappears into the forest . . . Aye, and wherever he goes the white snow covers up his tracks . . . If you don't believe an old man, then come and see for yourself some day.'

The old man was stirred. It seemed that the exciting talk about the forest and the storm pending in the air had quickened his aged blood. Grandfather shook his head with a smile and blinked his lustreless eyes.

Suddenly a shadow seemed to flit across his high forehead, furrowed with wrinkles. He touched me with his elbow and said with a mysterious air:

'And do you know what I will tell you, boy? The master of the forest is an abominable creature, to be sure; it is disgusting for a Christian to behold such an ugly face as his. But one must give him his due; he never does any harm . . . He'll make sport of a man, amuse himself at his expense, but he never does any harm.'

'How can that be, grandfather, when you have just said that he tried to strike you with a root?'

'Aye, he tried to. He was angry because I looked at him through the window, that was why. But if a man never pokes his nose into his affairs, he never does any harm. That is what he is like, the master of the forest! Do you know? Men have done worse things in the forest than he, by God they have!'

Grandfather drooped his head and sat for a while in silence, then when he looked at me, in his eyes, through the cloudy film that covered them, a spark of awakening seemed to glimmer.

'I will tell you, boy, an event that happened here in the forest . . . on this very spot, long ago . . . I remember . . . like a dream, only when the forest roars loudly it comes back to me . . . Would you like to hear it, eh?'

'O yes, I would, grandfather! Tell me!'

'I will tell you, aye. Listen then.'

II

'My father and mother both died long ago when I was still a little boy . . . they left me in the world alone. That is how it was with me, aye! And the elder thought, "What shall we do with the boy?" and the Pan too . . . That day the forester Roman came out of the forest and said to the elder, "Give me the boy to take to the forest. I will look after him . . . It will be less lonely for me in the forest and the boy will be fed." Thus he spoke and the elder said, "Take him!" So he took me and I've remained in the forest ever since. It was here that Roman brought me up. But he was a terrible man! God forbid such another. Tall and black-haired and black-eyed; his dark soul gazed out of his eyes, because all his life the man had lived alone in the forest; a bear, people said, was like a brother to him, and a wolf, like a nephew. He knew every kind of beast and did not fear them, but people he avoided, and would not look their way . . . That is what he was like, aye! Sometimes when he looked at me it seemed as though a cat swished her tail down my back . . . But he was a good man nevertheless, and fed me well, I must say; there was always buckwheat porridge and fat, and when he killed a duck there was duck, too. What is true, is true, he fed me well . . . Thus we lived alone together, he and I. Roman would go into the forest and lock me into the hut so that the beasts should not get me. And later they gave him Oksana for a wife.

'The Pan it was who gave him a wife. He summoned him to the village, and said to him, "Well now, Romasiu," he said, "you must get married." And Roman at first said to Pan, "What the devil do I want with a wife? What could I do with a woman in the forest when I already have a boy on my hands? I don't want to get married," he said. He was not used to courting the girls, that is how it was! Well, and the Pan, too, was cunning . . . When I recall the Pan, boy, then I think to myself that there are no more like him left – there are no more Pans like that – They've disappeared . . . Take yourself, for instance, you too are a Pan, they say . . . It may be true, only there is nothing of the genuine Pan about you . . . A sorry bachelor, no more . . .

'But he was a genuine Pan of the olden days . . . Things are so arranged in this world, I tell you, that a hundred men may fear one man and fear him horribly, too! For instance, take a hawk and a chicken, boy; both birds are hatched out of eggs, but a hawk instantly watches its opportunities from above, aye. It has only to cry out in the sky and not only the chickens, but the old cocks run away . . . The hawk is a bird like the Pan; the hen, like a common peasant . . .

'I remember one day when a small boy, I saw some peasants moving heavy timber out of the forest, about thirty of them, perhaps. And the Pan came up alone on his horse, twirling his mustachios. The horse frisked beneath him as he looked about. No sooner did the peasants catch sight of him, when, oh dear, they rushed forward and moved the horses into the snow and took off the caps. And afterwards what trouble they had to get the horses out of the snow! and the Pan galloped away; though alone, the path was too small for him, you see! The Pan had only to raise his brows and the peasants trembled, he had only to laugh and all grew gay; frown and all were sad. And no one dared to thwart him.

'Well, Roman, as you know, was brought up in the forest and had no manners, but the Pan was not angry with him.

' "I want you to get married," the Pan said, "I have my own reasons why. You must take Oksana."

' "I won't," Roman replied. "I don't want a wife even though it be Oksana. Let the devil marry her, I don't want her . . . so there!"

'The Pan ordered the whip to be brought. Roman was stretched out and the Pan asked:

' "Will you marry, Roman?"

' "No," he replied, "I will not."

' "Take off his clothes and belabour him as much as you can," the Pan said.

'And they belaboured him not a little; and though Roman was a strong man, he grew tired of it.

' "Leave off," he said, "it is enough. Let all the devils in hell take her rather than that I should suffer such tortures for a woman. Bring her here. I will marry her."

'There lived in the Pan's yard a whipper-in, Opanas Shvedsky. He came up from the fields just as Roman had made up his mind to marry. Learning the cause of Roman's plight, he threw himself at the Pan's feet and began to kiss them . . .

' "Gracious Pan," he said, "why force another man? I would gladly marry Oksana without a word!"

'Aye, and so he wanted to marry her. That was the kind of man he was!

'Roman was overjoyed. He got up, tied up his trousers and said:

' "That is good," he said, "only why didn't you come before, man? And the Pan too . . . is always like that. Instead of trying to find out who wants to marry, he instantly seizes a man and has him whipped. Is that as a Christian should act? Faugh!"

'Aye, sometimes he would not give way, even to the Pan; that's the kind of man Roman was! When he grew angry no one dared to go near him, not even the Pan himself. But the Pan was cunning! He had other aims in view. Again he ordered Roman to be stretched out on the grass.

' "I want to make you happy, you fool," he said, "and you complain. Now you live alone like a bear in his den and it's anything but gay to come to you . . . Belabour the fool until he cries enough! . . . And you, Opanas, go to the devil's own mother. Nobody," he said, "invited you to the feast, so don't sit down to the table, for you see what fare Roman is getting. Take care you do not get the same."

'And Roman grew angry in earnest, aye. And they whipped him well, for the men in those days, you know, understood how to handle the whip, and he lay there and would not cry, "Enough!" For a long time he bore it, then he spat on the ground.

' "Enough! Her father shall not live to see the day when a Christian shall be whipped thus for a woman! May your hands rot off, you lackeys of the devil! The devil himself taught you to use the whip! I am not a sheaf upon the threshing floor that you should thrash me like this. I will marry her since there is no way out."

'And the Pan laughed.

' "That is good," he said, "for now that you will not be able to sit at the wedding, you will dance the more . . ."

'A merry man was the Pan, by God, a merry man, aye! But should some disagreeable thing happen to him, God forbid that a Christian should cross his path. He pitied no one, truly.

Not even a Jew should be plagued with a man like him. That's what I think . . .

'Thus they married Roman. He brought the young wife to the forest hut and at first he did nothing but abuse her and taunt her because of the whipping.

' "You are not worthy that a man should suffer so much for you," he would say.

'Sometimes, it happened, he would come home from the forest and order her out of the hut.

' "Begone with you! I don't want a woman here! Take yourself off, bag and baggage! I hate a woman to sleep in my house! It makes the air foul!"

'Aye!

'As time went on he became reconciled. Oksana would clean and scrub the hut, place the dishes about so that everything shone to gladden the heart. And Roman saw that she was a good woman, and little by little he got used to her. And not only that, boy; he even grew to love her. By God, I do not lie! That was what happened to Roman; as soon as he really got to know her, he said:

' "All thanks to the Pan for having shown me what is good. I was a foolish man to have suffered the whip now that I see nothing bad was intended for me – only good. That is how it is."

And the time passed – I do not know how long. One day Oksana lay down on the bench and began to groan; in the evening she was quite ill, and the next morning when I awoke I heard a little voice crying. Aye, thought I, a baby has been born. And I was right; it had really happened.

'Not long did the baby live in this world, only from morning till evening. In the evening it ceased its crying . . . Oksana wept and Roman said:

' "The baby is gone, and now that it is dead, there is no need to bring the priest. We will bury it beneath a pine."

'Thus spoke Roman, and no sooner had he spoken than he dug a little grave and buried the child. Yonder is an old stump that was struck down by lightning – it was beneath that pine that Roman's child was buried. Do you know, boy, what I am going to tell you? To this day when the sun sets and the stars shine brightly over the forest, a bird comes flying here and cries and beats its little wings so as to make the heart ache to watch it. It is the unchristened soul of that child begging a cross for itself. If a learned man, taught by books, they say, were to give it a cross it would not rise again and come flying here . . . But we who live in the forest here know nothing . . . It comes begging and begging and all we can say is:

' "Poor soul, we can do nothing for you."

'And it cries and flies away and comes back again. Ah, boy, I am sorry for the poor little soul!

'As soon as Oksana grew well she would go to the grave and sit down and weep, so loudly sometimes that her voice could be heard throughout the forest. Thus she mourned for her child; Roman was not sorry it had died, but Oksana was. Some days he would come home from the forest and stand by Oksana and say:

' "Be quiet, you silly woman! What is there to cry about? One child has died and another will be born, perhaps. And it may be a better one too, aye! And perhaps that child was not mine. I don't know. But the new one will be."

'Oksana did not like him to talk thus. She would stop crying and begin to abuse him. But Roman did not get angry with her.

' "Why will you scold?" he asked. "I did not say that. I only meant I did not know. I do not know because you were not mine always, and did not live in the forest, but in the world among other men. How should I know? Now that you live in the forest it is well. When I went to the village the woman Fedosia said to me, 'It is early days for you to have a child, Roman!' And I said, 'How should I know if it is early or late?' You had better cease your scolding or I may get angry and strike you."

'And Oksana scolded and scolded and then left off. Sometimes she would scold and strike him on the back, but no sooner did Roman show signs of rising anger than she grew quiet, for she feared him. And she would caress him and put her arms about him and kiss him and gaze into his eyes . . . And my Roman would be soothed. Because . . . you see, boy . . .

you may not know, but I, an old man, though I never married, have seen many things in my time; the kisses of a young woman are a dozen times sweeter when she wants to get round an angry peasant. Oh yes . . . I know what the women are! And Oksana was a slim, fine young woman; I never see any like her nowadays. I tell you, boy, even the women nowadays are not what they used to be.

'One day a horn sounded from the forest: Tra-ta, tara-tara, ta-ta-ta. Gaily and merrily the blast echoed through the trees. I was a small boy then and did not know what it was. I saw the birds come flying out of their nests crying and flapping their wings, and hares with their ears flattened back, running as hard as they could. "Perhaps it is some rare beast that has such a sweet call," thought I. But it was no beast; it was the Pan on his horse riding through the forest and blowing a horn, and behind him came the huntsmen on horseback too, and leading the dogs on a leash. The most handsome of all the huntsmen was Opanas Shvedsky, galloping after the Pan in a blue Cossack coat, his gun and mandore strapped across his shoulder. The Pan liked Opanas because he could play the mandore and was a master at singing songs. And handsome was this fellow Opanas, very handsome! The Pan could not compare with him; the Pan was already bald and had a red nose, and though his eyes were merry they were not like the eyes of Opanas. When I, a small boy, used to look at him, it made me want to laugh, anad I was not a girl. Some said that Opanas' father and mother were Cossacks from beyond the rapids in Stechy, and there the people are slim and handsome and graceful. You just picture him, boy. There he was on horseback, with a lance, more goodly to look at than the birds flying in the fields, or an axe felling a tree . . .

'I ran out of the hut and looked; the Pan rode up, and then the huntsmen. Roman came out of the hut and held up the Pan's stirrup while he sprang to the ground. Roman bowed to him

' "How are you?" the Pan asked Roman.

' "Aye," Roman replied, "I am quite well, thank you; what should ail me? And how are you?"

'You see, Roman had no manners, and knew not how to reply to the Pan's words. The huntsmen burst out laughing and the Pan laughed too.

' "Well, thank God that you are well," the Pan said. "And where is your little wife?"

' "Where should she be? She is in the hut, of course."

' "Well, we will go into the hut," the Pan said, "and you boys, spread a carpet on the grass and get everything ready to feast the young couple for the first time."

'And so they went into the hut, the Pan and Opanas, followed by Roman, hatless, and Bogdan, an old huntsman and faithful servant of the Pan's. There are no servants in the world like him nowadays; he was an old man, severe with the other servants, but like yonder dog before the Pan. Bogdan had no one in the world beside the Pan. When his father and mother died, people said he went to the old Pan and asked permission to marry, but the old Pan would not give it; he took him in to his little son and said to him, "Here is your father, mother and wife." And Bogdan carried the young boy in his arms and drove with him and taught him to ride and to shoot, and when the young Pan grew up Bogdan followed him about like a dog. Oh, I tell you truly, many are the people who have cursed Bogdan, and many are the tears that have been shed because of him . . . and because of the Pan. At a word from the Pan Bogdan would have torn his own father to pieces . . .

'And I, like a small boy, ran after them into the hut because I was curious. Wherever the Pan went, I followed him.

'The Pan was standing in the middle of the room, twirling his mustachios and laughing. Roman was shuffling his feet and crushing his cap in his hand. Opanas, his shoulder propped against the wall, stood there, poor fellow, like yonder young oak on a bad day, frowning and sombre.

'And the three of them turned to Oksana. Only old Bogdan sat down on the bench in the corner, hanging his head, awaiting the Pan's commands. And Oksana was standing at the corner of the stove with drooping eyes, blushing red as the poppies yonder among the barley. The poor thing felt that some evil would come because of her. And let me tell you too, boy, that when three men fix their regards upon one woman no good ever comes of it – it generally leads to blows, if not worse. I know, because I have seen it.

' "Well, Romasiu," the Pan said, with a laugh, "have I found you a nice wife?"

' "What would you? For a woman she is not bad," Roman replied.

'Here Opanas shrugged his shoulders, raised his eyes to Oksana and said to himself:

' "Woman! The fool is not satisfied!"

'Roman, catching the words, turned to Opanas and said to him:

' "And why do I seem a fool to you, Opanas, tell me, eh?"

' "Because you don't know how to protect your wife," Opanas said, "that is why you are a fool!" . . .

'Those were the words Opanas said to him! The Pan stamped his foot. Bogdan shook his head . . . Roman thought for a moment, then he raised his head and looked at the Pan.

' "Why should I protect her?" he said to Opanas, while his eyes were fixed on the Pan. "Besides the beasts there are no other devils here, unless the Pan himself sometimes comes to visit us. Against whom should I protect her? You had better take care what you say to me, you Cossack, or you may make me angry and I shall take my gun."

'They would have come to blows had not the Pan intervened. He stamped his foot and they ceased instantly.

' "Quiet!" he said, "you sons of the devil! You did not come here to fight. We must feast the young couple and in the evening set out for the shooting on the swamp. Follow me!"

'The Pan turned and went out of the hut. Beneath the trees the huntsmen had already prepared the repast. Bogdan followed the Pan, and Opanas stayed behind with Roman in the passage.

' "Don't be angry with me, brother," the Cossack said. "Listen to what Opanas has to say to you. You saw, did you not, how I fell at the Pan's feet and begged him to give me Oksana to wife? Well, God be with you, man . . . the priest has bound you together . . . it is fate seemingly. And now my heart cannot bear to see the cruel foe come making sport of you and of her. Ah me! No one knows what is in my heart. It were better that I took my gun and laid both him and her in the damp earth for a bed!"

'Roman looked at the Cossack and asked:

' "Have you gone mad, Cossack?"

'I did not hear Opanas reply, for they began whispering softly in the passage, only I heard Roman clap Opanas on the shoulder:

' "Oh, Opanas, Opanas, what cunning, wicked people there are in the world! And here am I living in the forest and know nothing. Ah, Pan! Pan! How much evil you have raised about your head!"

' "Well," Opanas said, "go and show a good countenance, especially before Bogdan. You are not wise and the dog is cunning. And mind you don't drink much of the Pan's brandy, and if you are sent with the men to the marsh and you want to stay behind, then lead the men to the old oak and show them the roundabout way, and say simply that you are going into the forest . . . then make haste back as quickly as you can."

' "Good," Roman said. "I will make ready for the hunt and load my gun, not for a bird on the wing, but for a bear!"

'And they went out. And the Pan, already seated on the carpet asked for a flask and a goblet, and filling the goblet with brandy, he gave it to Roman. Aye, good was the Pan's flask and his goblet, and his brandy was better still. One goblet you drank and the heart grew glad, another and the heart beat fast in the breast, and if a man were not accustomed to it, with the third goblet he was rolling under the bench, unless his wife had laid him on top of it.

'Aye, cunning was the Pan, I tell you! He wished to make Roman drunk with his brandy, but there never was a brandy that would overcome Roman. From the Pan's hand he drank one goblet, then a second, and a third, but his eyes only began to shine like a wolf's and his dark whiskers trembled a little. The Pan grew angry.

' "See how the cursed wretch gobbles the brandy and does

not blink an eye! Another man would have been crying by now, but look at him, good people, he is laughing still!" . . .

'He knew well, the wicked Pan, that when a man gets to crying, after brandy, his head will soon be lying on the table. But this time they picked the wrong man.

' "And why should I cry?" Roman asked. "It would not be well on my part. Here our gracious Pan comes to feast me and I take to crying like a woman! Thank God, I have nothing to cry about, rather let my enemies cry" . . .

' "You are happy then?" the Pan asked.

' "Aye, why should I not be happy?"

' "Do you remember how we married you with the whip?"

' "Aye, do I remember? And I say now that I was a foolish man then and did not know the bitter from the sweet. A whip is bitter and I preferred it to the woman. I thank you now, gracious Pan, you have taught a fool like me that honey is too good to eat."

' "Very well, then," the Pan said, "for that you must serve me well. Go with the men to the marsh and shoot as much game as you can, and be sure you bring me back some grouse."

' "When does the Pan wish us to go to the marsh?" Roman asked.

' "We will drink a little more, and Opanas shall sing us a song, then you can go, and God be with you."

'Roman looked at the Pan and said:

' "But that is a hard task; the time is not young, there will be a storm to-night. How can we kill such a wily bird at this hour?"

'And the Pan was getting drunk, and when drunk he was terribly fierce. Hearing the huntsmen whisper among themselves that "perhaps Roman was right and there might be a storm," he grew angry. He banged down his goblet, and fixed his eyes upon them. All were silent.

'Only Opanas was not afraid. At the Pan's request he had left the circle to sing a song, and tuning his mandore, he looked askance at the Pan and said to him:

' "But consider, gracious Pan! Can anyone send men for

game in the forest on a night like this with a threatening storm?"

'He was as bold as that. The others, as you know, the Pan's serfs, were afraid, but he was a free man of the Cossack race, brought over as a small boy by a Cossack minstrel from Ukraina. There had been some trouble in the town of Uman; the old Cossack had had his eyes put out, his ears lopped off, and then he had been thrust out into the world. And he wandered from town to village, from village to town until he came to our part, with the young boy Opanas. The old Pan took him in, for he was fond of good songs; then the old man died, and Opanas grew up in the house. The young Pan, too, was fond of him, and sometimes bore a word from him that would have cost another man three whippings.

'Thus it was then. The Pan grew angry at first, and was going to strike the Cossack, but in a little while he said to Opanas:

' "Ah, Opanas, Opanas, you are a smart fellow, yet you cannot see that you must not poke your nose in at a door lest it should shut with a bang!"

'This was the riddle he put to the Cossack! And the Cossack saw his meaning. And he replied to the Pan with a song. Ah! had the Pan understood the Cossack's song, he would not have wept the tears of it that he did.

' "Thank you for your lesson," Opanas said. "In return, listen, and I will sing you a song."

'And he struck the strings of the mandore.

'Then he raised his head and looked up at the sky. And an eagle was swooping down and the wind was chasing the dark clouds. And he pricked up his ears and listened to the tall pines murmuring in the forest.

'And again he struck the strings of the mandore.

'Aye, boy, it never fell to your lot to hear Opanas Shvedsky play, and nowadays no one plays like him. The mandore is a simple instrument, but in the hands of an able man how well it speaks! When his hand passed over it, it would speak to him of everything – the murmur of the forest in foul weather, the howling of the wind in the desolate steppes before a storm, the dry grass rustling over the big Cossack's grave.

'No, boy, you will never hear what real playing is like! All kinds of people come here nowadays who have been not only in Poland, but in other places as well, over the whole of Ukraina, in Chigirin, in Poltava, in Kiev and in Cherkas. They say that the mandorists have disappeared. They no longer play at fairs and in market-places. In the hut yonder hangs my old mandore. Opanas taught me to play it, but no one has learned it from me. When I die – that will not be long now – then nowhere in the wide world will the sound of the mandore be heard again. That is how it is.

'And Opanas began a song in a soft voice. Opanas' voice was not strong, but sweet and plaintive, floating straight to the heart. And the song, boy, the Cossack had composed for the Pan. I never heard it again, and when later I would beg Opanas to sing it, he always refused.

' "The man I sang the song for is no longer in this world," he would say.

'In the song the Cossack told the Pan the truth of what would happen to him, and the Pan wept and the tears rolled down his cheeks, but not a word of the song did the Pan understand.

'Ah, I cannot remember the whole song, only a little of it. The Cossack sang about the Pan, about Ivan:

> "O Pan, O Ivan
> Wise Pan, wise Ivan,
> Knowest that the hawk in the sky is watching
> To pounce upon its prey?
> O Pan, O Ivan,
> But the Pan, he knoweth not
> What indeed is the lot
> Of the hawk at the nest
> Whom the prey destroyeth at his will."

'It seems to me, boy, that I can hear that song now and see them all. Yonder stood the Cossack with his mandore, the Pan sat on the carpet, hanging his head and weeping, the huntsmen crowded together, elbowing each other; old Bogdan shook his head. . . .

'And the forest, as now, was murmuring, and the mandore sounded soft and plaintive as the Cossack sang about his lady, mourning for the Pan, mourning for Ivan:

> "The Pan's lady is mourning, is weeping,
> While the Pan in the cold earth is sleeping,
> And the black crow is croaking overhead."

'Ah, but the Pan did not understand the song. He dried his tears and said:

' "Well, make ready, Roman! Take to your horses, boys! And you Opanas, go with them. I have had enough of your songs. It was a good song that you sang, only nothing ever happens in the world like that."

'And the song had softened the Cossack's heart and bedimmed his eyes with tears.

' "O Pan, Pan," Opanas said, "with us the old people say that there is truth in a fairy-tale and truth in a song; only the truth in fairy-tale is like iron, having passed for many years from hand to hand and got rusted, while the truth in a song is like gold and never rusts . . . That is what the old people say."

'The Pan gave a wave of the hand.

' "That may be in your parts, but with us it is not so . . . Begone, Opanas . . . You have wearied me with your talk."

'The Cossack stood still for a moment, then he suddenly fell on his knees before the Pan.

' "Listen to me, Pan! Mount your horse and ride back to your lady. In my heart there is a foreboding of evil!"

'Then the Pan grew angry in earnest, and kicked the Cossack like a dog.

' "Get away from me! You are more like an old woman than a Cossack! Get away from me or it may be the worse for you . . . And what are you standing there for, you children of slaves? Am I no longer your Pan? I will show you what your forefathers had never seen from mine! . . ."

'Opanas rose like a dark cloud and exchanged glances with Roman. And Roman was standing on one side, leaning on his gun, as though nothing whatever was happening.

'The Cossack struck the mandore against a tree; it broke to atoms, and a heavy groan reverberated throughout the forest.

' "Let the demons in the next world," he said, "teach wisdom to the man who refuses to listen to wise counsel . . . I see you have no need of a faithful servant, Pan."

'The Pan had no time to speak, for Opanas sprang on his horse and was gone. The huntsmen also mounted. Roman shouldered his gun and walked away, calling out to Oksana as he passed the hut, "Put the boy to bed, it is late! And get the Pan's bed ready."

'Soon all had departed into the forest by yonder path; only the Pan's horse remained, tied to a tree. It grew dark; the forest roared, and the rain began to fall, just as now . . .

'Oksana put me to bed in the hay-loft, and made the sign of the cross over me for the night . . . And I heard that my Oksana was crying.

'Ah, I did not understand, small boy that I was, all that was happening around me! I curled up in the hay, listening to the song of the storm in the forest, and began to doze.

'Aye, suddenly I heard someone walking outside around the hut . . . someone went up to the tree and untied the Pan's horse; the horse snorted, gave a kick and galloped off into the forest, and soon the sound of his hoofs grew fainter and ceased. Then again I heard someone galloping along the path towards the hut, and springing to the ground, call through the window:

' "Pan! Pan!" – it was the voice of Bogdan. "Oh, Pan! open quickly! The wicked Cossack has some evil design in view; he has let your horse escape into the forest . . ."

'The old man had scarcely uttered the words when he was seized from behind. I grew frightened and heard something fall. . . .

'The Pan opened the door and rushed out with his gun. In the passage Roman seized him by the hair and knocked him on the ground. . . .

'And the Pan saw that things were bad with him, and he said:

' "Let me go, Romasiu! Is this your gratitude for the good I have done you?"

'And Roman replied:

' "I am grateful, wicked Pan, for the good you have done me and my wife. Now I am going to pay you for it . . ."

'And the Pan spoke again:

' "Help me, Opanas, my faithful servant! I have loved you as my own son."

'And Opanas replied to him:

' "You spurned your faithful servant like a dog. You loved me as the stick loves the back, and now you love me as the back loves the stick . . . I begged and prayed to you, but you would not listen . . ."

'And then the Pan appealed to Oksana:

' "Help me, Oksana, you at least have a kind heart!"

'Oksana ran out and wrung her hands.

' "I begged you, Pan, on my bended knees to spare my maiden purity and not to shame me as a wife. You took no pity on me, and now you beg in your turn . . . Oh, woe is me, what am I to do?"

' "Let me go!" the Pan cried again. "You will all perish in Siberia for me . . ."

' "Don't you worry about us, Pan," said Opanas; "Roman will get to the marsh before your men, and as for me, by your grace, I am all alone in the world and have little need to worry about my head. I will shoulder my gun and walk away into the forest . . . I will gather together some stalwart lads and we will wander together . . . At night we will come out of the forest into the highway, and when we go to the village we will make straight for the Pan's manor. Here, Romasiu, lift the Pan, and let us carry his grace out into the rain."

'And the Pan struggled and screamed, and Roman muttered to himself, and the Cossack laughed. Thus they got outside.

'And in my terror I rushed into the hut straight to Oksana, and my Oksana was sitting on the bench, white as the wall . . .

'And the storm broke out in the forest; the pine trees roared in a hundred voices; the wind howled, and now and again the thunder crashed. Oksana and I were sitting on the bench when suddenly I heard someone moan in the forest, oh, so pitifully that even to this day when I think of it my heart stands still. And it is many, many years ago. . . .

' "Oksana, dear," I said, "who is that moaning in the forest?"

'And she caught me up in her arms and rocked me to and fro.

' "Sleep, little one," she said, "it is nothing; only the trees roaring in the forest . . ."

'And truly the forest roared. Ah, how it roared!

'For a little longer we sat, then I heard a bang as from a gun.

' "Oksana, dear," I said, "who is it firing a gun?"

'And she, poor thing, kept on rocking me, and saying:

' "Be still, be still, little one. It is God's thunder crashing in the forest."

'And she herself was crying, and pressing me tightly to her breast, she began to sing a lullaby:

' "The forest murmurs, the forest murmurs, little one, the forest murmurs . . ."

'Thus I went to sleep in her arms . . .

'And the next morning, boy, I jumped up and looked around. The sun was shining brightly, Oksana was asleep in the hut, fully dressed. I recollected the events of the night before, and wondered whether I had dreamed it all.

'But I had not dreamed it all; oh no, it was really true! I ran out of the hut, out into the forest, and the birds were singing and the dew was sparkling on the leaves. I ran up to the bushes, and there were the Pan and the huntsman, lying side by side. The Pan was white and calm, the huntsman as grey as a dove, and morose as he had been when living. On the breasts of both were the marks of blood . . .'

'Well, and what happened to the others?' I asked, seeing that the old man had finished and drooped his head.

'Aye, it all happened as the Cossack Opanas had said. For a long time he lived in the forest and roamed the highways with the other boys and visited the Pan's estates. It was the Cossack's fate from his very birth; his forefathers had been robbers before him, and it was his fate to be a robber too. Many times, boy, he came to visit us in this very hut, mostly when Roman was not at home. He would come and stand there and sing his songs and play on the mandore. But when he brought his comrades, both Oksana and Roman would always receive them. Aye, and to tell you the truth, boy, it was a sinful thing they did. Maxim and Zahar will soon return from the forest; take a good look at them both. I have never said anything to them, only whoever knew Roman and Opanas can see at a glance which is like which, though they are not the sons but the grandsons of those men . . .

'Such are the things, boy, that I remember happening in the forest . . .

'How the forest does roar, to be sure! There is going to be a storm.'

III

The last words of the story were spoken wearily. The old man's excitement had abated and signs of exhaustion were visible; his tongue grew heavy, his head shook and the water streamed from his eyes.

Evening had descended over the earth; it grew dark in the forest, the angry pine trees roared around the hut like the roar of the sea at high tide; their dark tops rose and fell like waves in stormy weather.

The merry barking of the dogs announced their masters' return. The two foresters walked quickly up to the hut, and behind them, panting, came Motria, driving the lost cow. Our company was all gathered together. ·

In a few moments we were seated in the hut. The fire crackled merrily in the stove and Motria was preparing the supper.

Though I had seen Zahar and Maxim many times, I looked at them now with a new interest. Zahar's face was dark, with bushy brows beneath the severe, low forehead; the expression of the eyes were stern, though the face showed a natural kindliness in the inherent strength. Maxim had grey eyes, frank and gentle; every now and again he would shake his curly locks, and his ringing laugh was hard to resist.

'Did the old man tell you a tale about our grandfather?''
Maxim asked.

'He did,' I replied.

'He is always like that. As soon as the trees begin to roar in
the forest the old times come back to him. He won't go to sleep
the whole night now.'

'Just like a little child,' added Motria, ladling out the old
man's soup.

The old grandfather did not understand that the talk was of
him. He was quite unconscious, smiling senselessly from time
to time, and shaking his head; it was only when a gust of wind,
howling and raging through the forest, blew into the hut, that
he became anxious and seemed to listen for something with a
frightened air.

Soon all was quiet in the forest hut; the flickering wick shone
dimly and the cricket sang his shrill, monotonous song . . . And
in the forest thousands of powerful raucous voices were
speaking, threatening each other in the darkness, preparing
from all sides to strike at the poor little lonely forest hut. From
time to time the confused noise grew stronger and rose with a
rush, and then the door shook as though someone, hissing
angrily, had leaned against it from without, and the night wind
howled mournfully and threateningly in the chimney, making
the heart stand still. At intervals the storm abated, and the
ominous stillness wearied the timid heart, until once more the
rumble began, as though the old pines had suddenly made up
their minds to rise up from their places and fly away into
unknown space with the force of the nocturnal hurricane.

I dozed off for a few moments; not for long, I think. The
storm raged in the forest in many voices and keys. From time to
time the wick flickered, lighting up the hut. The old man was
sitting on the bench, his hand groping about him as though
hoping to find someone near. An expression of fear and almost
childish helplessness was on his poor face.

'Oksana, dear,' I heard his pitiful voice, 'who is that
moaning in the forest?'

He waved his hand about anxiously, and listened intently.

'Aye,' he spoke again, 'no one is moaning. It is the storm

roaring in the forest . . . Nothing more . . . the forest is roaring, roaring . . .'

Several minutes more went by. A flash of blue lightning shot across the window, lighting up the fantastic forms of the tall trees that instantly disappeared again amidst the angry din of the storm. Another bright flash eclipsed the pale gleam of the wick and a crash rolled throughout the forest.

The old man again moved anxiously on the bench.

'Oksana, dear, who is that firing in the forest?'

'Go to sleep, old man, go to sleep,' Motria's calm voice was heard from the stove. 'He is always like that, always calling for Oksana on a stormy night. He forgets that Oksana has long departed to the next world. Oh dear!'

Motria yawned, whispered a prayer, and peace once more descended over the hut, broken only by the roar of the forest and the old man's anxious mumbling:

'The forest roars, and roars . . . Oksana, dear . . .'

Soon a heavy rain came down, the streaming torrents drowning the violence of the wind and the moaning of the old pine-trees.

The Kiss

BY ANTON CHEHOV

1860–1904

At eight o'clock in the evening of 20 May the six batteries of the 'U' reserve artillery on its way to camp stopped for the night in the village of Mestechko. During the bustle, when some officers were busy with the guns and others scattered over the square hearing the reports of the quartermasters, a horseman in civilian clothes appeared from behind the church on a curious, small light bay with a beautiful neck and a clipped tail, which ran sideways rather than straight, and threw out its legs in short frisky movements as though they were being lashed with a whip. The horseman drew up by a group of officers and, raising his hat, said:

'His Excellency General von Rabbek, the squire here, would be glad if you gentlemen would come and take tea with him.'

The horse frisked and backed sideways; the horseman once more raised his hat and, turning, disappeared behind the church with his strange-looking animal.

'Damn!' some of the officers grumbled, departing to their quarters. 'A fellow wants to sleep, and here comes this von Rabbek with his tea! We know what that means!'

And every officer in the six batteries vivdly recalled an incident that had happened to them last year during manœuvres when, together with the officers of a certain Cossack regiment, they were invited to tea in this manner by a certain count and retired officer, and how the cordial, hospitable count had entertained them royally and insisted on their spending the night in his house instead of at their quarters. It was all very nice, of course, and nothing better could have been desired, only the count was overmuch pleased with the society of the young men. Until daybreak he wearied them with episodes of his own happy past, led them from room to room to show them his costly pictures, old engravings and rare pieces of armour; he even read them letters he had received from various celebrities, and the tired officers listened and looked, inwardly longing for their beds and yawning cautiously behind their palms; when at last their host released them it was too late to go to bed.

Was von Rabbek by any chance such another? However, there was nothing to be done. The officers washed and dressed and set off together to find the squire's house. In the square by the church they were told that they could cut down to the river by a path behind the church, and then along the bank till they came to the squire's own garden, and the avenue would bring them to the door, or they could ride along the road that turned off half a verst up by the squire's barns. The officers chose the latter.

'Who is this von Rabbek?' they asked each other on the way. 'Is he the man who commanded the "U" cavalry division in Plevna?'

'No, that was not von Rabbek, but simply Rabbe, without the von.'

'What lovely weather it is!'

At the first barn the road divided in two – the one straight ahead vanished into the evening darkness, the other to the right led to the squire's house. The officers turned to the right and lowered their voices. On either side of the road stretched the stone barns with red roofs, massive and sombre, like the barracks of a provincial town.

'A good sign, gentlemen,' one of the officers remarked. 'Our setter is in front, which means that he scents game!'

Ahead of us all was Lieutenant Lobitko, tall and broad-shouldered, with clean upper lip. He was twenty-five, though his full round face did not show it. He was famous in the brigade for his knack of sensing the presence of women in a place, even at a distance. He turned round and said:

'Yes, I am sure there are women here; I feel it by instinct.'

At the door of the house the officers were met by von

Rabbek himself, a handsome old man of sixty, in civilian clothes. Shaking hands with his guests, he said that he was pleased and happy to see them, but begged them to excuse him for not having invited them to stay the night; his two sisters and their children had come, as well as his brothers and some neighbours, and in consequence he had not a single spare room.

The general was affability itself, but from the expression of his face it was obvious that he was not quite as overjoyed with his guests as the count of last year, and that he had invited them merely out of a sense of politeness. And this was made quite clear to them as they walked up the carpeted stairs, listening to their host, and saw the footmen hurrying to light the lamps in the hall and on the staircase. They felt that they were a nuisance in the house. Under a roof where two sisters and brothers and neighbours had gathered together, perhaps for the celebration of some family event, how could the family be pleased with the presence of nineteen strangers?

At the drawing-room door the guests were received by a tall, graceful old lady with an oval-shaped face and dark brows, who resembled the Empress Eugénie. With a gracious smile she welcomed them, apologising for not being able to ask them to stay the night. By the smile that disappeared from her face the moment she turned away, it was plain that the lady had seen many officers in her day and that she had no use for them now, and that if she had invited them to her house and was offering her excuses, it was only because her breeding and position demanded it of her.

When the officers entered the dining-room about a dozen men and women, old and young, were sitting at one end of a long table having tea. Behind their chairs, enveloped in cigar smoke, was a group of men, in the midst of whom a thin young man with red mustachios was speaking in English in a loud voice. Behind the group, through a door, was a view of a brightly lighted room with pale blue furniture.

'Gentlemen, there are so many of you that it is impossible to introduce you all!' the general said aloud with an effort at gaiety. 'Please introduce yourselves in a homely way.'

The officers – some with solemn countenances, others with strained smiles, and all feeling extremely uncomfortable, bowed and seated themselves at the table. There was one among them who felt more uncomfortable than the rest – the staff officer Riabovitch, a round-shouldered little man in spectacles.

At the moment when some of his comrades put on a serious expression and others constrained themselves to smile, his face, lynx-like mustachios, spectacles and all, seemed to say, 'I am the shyest, most modest, most colourless officer in the whole brigade!' When he first entered the room and sat down by the table he could not fix his attention on any one particular object or face – faces, garments, cut-glass decanters of cognac, the steam from the glasses, the stucco cornices – all mingled into a single impression that confused Riabovitch and aroused in him a desire to hide his head. Like a lecturer facing his audience for the first time, he saw the objects before his eyes, but seemed to comprehend nothing. (This condition, when a subject sees without comprehending, is known among physiologists as 'psychological blindness.') Becoming used to his surroundings after a while, Riabovitch began to look about him. Being a shy man unused to society, he was first of all struck by the unusual courage of his new acquaintance – von Rabbek, his wife, two elderly ladies, a girl in a lilac dress, a young man with red whiskers, that turned out to be Rabbek's youngest son, who had very cleverly, as though they had rehearsed the thing beforehand, distributed themselves among the officers and begun an enthusiastic discussion in which the guests could not help but join. The lilac girl maintained warmly that life in the artillery was much easier than in the cavalry or infantry, while Rabbek and one of the old ladies defended an opposite view. A cross-conversation arose. Riabovitch looked at the lilac girl discussing a subject she knew nothing about and that she was not the least interested in, and watched the artificial smiles playing over her face.

Von Rabbek and his wife cleverly drew the officers into the discussion, keeping a careful eye meanwhile on their guests' glasses and plates to see that all were eating and drinking. The more Riabovitch looked and listened, the more he liked this insincere though excellently disciplined family.

After tea the officers went into the drawing-room. Lieutenant Lobitko's instinct had not failed him; there were many girls and young women in the room. The setter lieutenant stood near a fair young girl in a black dress, bending gallantly towards her as though he were leaning on an invisible sword. He smiled and moved his shoulders coquettishly. He must have been talking some interesting nonsense, no doubt, for the fair girl looked condescendingly at his round face and said indifferently, 'Really?' By this apathetic 'really' the setter, had he been wise, might have known that she was not very much entertained.

Someone began to play a melancholy valse on the piano; the sad air floating through the wide-open windows made everyone remember that it was May and that the weather was beautiful, and that the scent of lilac and rose and young poplars was in the air.

Riabovitch, who in addition to the music was under the influence of the cognac he had drunk, leant against the window, smiling. He began to follow the movements of the women, and it seemed to him that the scent of rose and lilac and poplar did not come from the garden but from their faces and dresses.

Von Rabbek's son invited a tall, thin girl to dance, and took two or three turns round the room. Lobitko glided over the polished floor to the girl in lilac and whirled her away across the room. The dancing began . . . Riabovitch stood by the door among the non-dancing men and watched. He had never once danced in his life, nor had it ever fallen to his lot to put his arm around the waist of a respectable woman. The idea that a man in the sight of all should take a strange young girl by the waist and offer his shoulder for her arm to rest on was very pleasing to Riabovitch, but he could never imagine himself in the position of such a man. There had been a time when he had envied the courage and daring of his comrades, and his heart had sickened at the consciousness that he was shy and round-shouldered and colourless and that he had lynx-like mustachios, but with the years he became reconciled; as he now gazed at the dancing couples and at those talking in loud assured voices he no longer envied them, he was affected only by a feeling of sadness.

When the quadrille was about to begin young von Rabbek came up to the non-dancing men and invited a couple of the officers to a game of billiards. The officers followed him out of the drawing-room. Riabovitch, from want of something to do and a desire to participate in some way in the general bustle, went after them. They walked through the drawing-room, then along a narrow glass corridor and into another room, where three sleepy footmen jumped up hastily from a couch at their appearance, and, passing through a host of other rooms, they at last entered the billiard-room. The game began.

Riabovitch, who never played at anything but cards, stood by the table looking indifferently at the players, while they, coats unbuttoned, cues in hand, walked about joking and calling out incomprehensible words. The players took no notice of him, only now and again when someone accidentally hit him with an elbow or a cue they turned with a polite 'pardon!' The first game had scarcely finished when he grew tired of it, and it seemed to him that he was not wanted there and was in the way. Again he was drawn to the ballroom and went out.

On his way back he met with a little adventure. About halfway he observed that he was not going in the right direction. He remembered quite well that he should have passed through the room where there were three sleepy footmen, but he had gone through six rooms and the footmen seemed to have vanished. Seeing his mistake he went back a little way, and turning to the right entered a dimly-lighted room which he did not remember seeing on his way to the billiard-room; standing still for a moment, he resolutely opened the first door that met his gaze and found himself in a dark room. In front of him through the cracks in a door a bright light shone through, and from behind the door came the muffled strains of a sad melody. Here, as in the ballroom, the windows were wide open and there was a scent of poplar, lilac and rose . . .

Riabovitch stopped in perplexity. At this moment he heard a hurried footstep and the rustle of a dress, a woman's voice full of emotion whispered 'At last!' and two soft, fragrant arms, unmistakably a woman's, were put around his neck; a warm cheek was laid against his own, and at the same moment there was the sound of a kiss. But instantly the woman gave a faint cry and, it seemed to Riabovitch, jumped away from him in horror. He, too, nearly cried out and made a rush towards the bright crack in the door. . . .

When he returned to the ballroom his heart beat fast and his hands trembled so visibly that he hastily hid them behind his back. For the first few moments he was torn by shame and terror. It seemed to him that everyone in the room must know that he had just been embraced and kissed by a woman, and he cast an anxious glance around, but being convinced that all were dancing and chatting calmly as before, he abandoned himself to the enjoyment of the sensation experienced for the first time in his life. Something strange had happened to him . . . His neck, that had only just been encircled by two soft, fresh arms, seemed to him to be anointed with oil; on his cheek near the left ear, where the strange unknown had kissed him, was a pleasant sensation of cold as from peppermint drops, and the more he rubbed the spot the greater this sensation became; from the crown of his head to the soles of his feet he was filled with a new strange feeling that grew and grew . . . He wanted to dance, to talk, to run out into the garden, to laugh aloud . . . He had quite forgotten that he was round-shouldered and colourless, that his appearance 'was indefinite' (as a lady of his acquaintance had said in a conversation with another woman, a conversation he happened to have over-heard). When von Rabbek's wife passed him, he gave her such a broad, kindly smile that she stopped and looked at him in surprise.

'I do like your house!' he said, refixing his spectacles.

The general's wife smiled and remarked that the house had belonged to her father, then she went on to ask him if his parents were alive, and how long he had been in the service, and why he was so thin, and so on . . . After talking to him for a while she went on further, and Riabovitch began to smile still more broadly and kindly and to imagine that he was surrounded by the kindest of people. . . .

At supper Riabovitch ate and drank mechanically everything that was placed before him. He did not hear a word that was being said and tried to puzzle out his recent adventure. The adventure was both mysterious and romantic, but not difficult to explain. Some girl or a married woman, perhaps, had arranged to meet some man in that dark room, and being in a state of nervous excitement because she had waited a long time, she had mistaken Riabovitch for her hero, particularly as Riabovitch had stopped in uncertainty when he had entered the room, as though he, too, were expecting to meet someone . . . In this way Riabovitch accounted for the kiss he had received.

'But who is she?' he thought, gazing round at the faces of the women. 'She must be young, for old women do not arrange meetings with men. And she must be intellectual; I felt it in the rustle of her dress, in the scent about her, in her voice. . . .'

His gaze alighted on the girl in lilac and she seemed very attractive to him; she had beautiful shoulders and arms, an intelligent face, and a beautiful voice. Looking at her Riabovitch determined that she and none other should be his fair unknown . . . But she smiled in an artificial way and screwed up her long nose, which made her seem old; then he removed his gaze to the fair girl in the black dress. She was younger and simpler, had beautiful temples and a pretty manner of drinking out of her glass. Riabovitch now wanted her to be his unknown, but soon he found that her features were too flat, and turned his attention to her neighbour.

'One can't tell,' he thought musingly. 'If one could take the shoulders and arms of the girl in lilac and add the temples of the fair girl and the eyes of the one sitting on Lobitko's left, then . . .'

In imagination he modelled the form of the girl who had kissed him, a form that he desired but could not see at the table.

After supper the guests, satisfied and a little the worse for drink, thanked their hosts and took their leave. Once more the general and his wife apologised for not being able to put them up for the night.

'Very glad to have met you, gentlemen!' the general said, quite sincerely this time. (Departing guests are treated more frankly than arriving ones.) 'Very glad! I hope you will come and see us on your way back! Quite simply, you know. Which way are you going? Are you riding? If not, go down by the garden, it is much nearer.'

The officers went out into the garden. After the bright light and the noise it seemed to them very dark and still in the garden. They walked to the gate without speaking. They were half-drunk, merry and contented, but the darkness and stillness made them pensive for a moment. No doubt the same thought had occurred to them as to Riabovitch. Would they, like Rabbek, one day possess a big house, a family, a garden, and would they have the opportunity of entertaining guests, even insincerely, and of making them drunk and contented?

Coming out of the gate, they began to talk all at once and to laugh without any cause. They were now walking along the path that led down to the river and ran along the water's edge, winding round bushes and overhanging willows. The bank and the path were scarcely visible, and the opposite bank was completely enveloped in darkness. Here and there in the dark water were the reflections of stars, and only by the way they trembled and swam asunder could one tell that the river was flowing swiftly. The air was still. Sleepy woodcocks called on the opposite bank, and on a bush a nightingale, disregarding the officers, poured out its song. One of them stopped by the bush and shook it, but the nightingale continued to sing.

'What a brave beggar!' approving voices exclaimed. 'Here we are, standing near him, and he takes no notice of us, the rogue!'

Towards the end the path began to ascend, and by the church it led out on to the road. Here the officers, out of breath with their walk uphill, sat down to smoke. A dim red light appeared on the opposite bank, and from want of something to do they spent a long time in speculating whether it was a camp-fire, a light in a window, or something else ... Riabovitch also gazed at the light, and it seemed to him that it smiled and winked at him, as though it knew about the kiss.

Reaching his quarters, Riabovitch undressed quickly and went to bed. In the same hut were Lobitko and Lieutenant Mersliakov, the latter a quiet, taciturn fellow, who was held to be a cultured man, and who always read *The Messenger of Europe*, which review he carried about with him everywhere. Lobitko undressed and paced the room from end to end with a dissatisfied air, then he sent the orderly for beer. Mersliakov got into bed, at the head of which he placed a candle, then buried himself in the pages of the review.

'I wonder who she was?' Riabovitch thought, gazing at the grimy ceiling.

His neck still seemed to be anointed with oil, and a sensation of cold as of peppermint was still about his mouth. His imagination conjured up images of the shoulders and arms of the girl in lilac, the temples of the fair girl in black, her waist, garments, jewels. He tried to fix his attention on these images, but they danced before his eyes, appearing and disappearing. When, on shutting his eyes the images completely vanished, he could hear hasty footsteps, the rustle of a dress, the sound of a kiss, and a feeling of intense unreasoning joy took possession of him. As he abandoned himself to this feeling he heard the orderly return and say that no beer was to be had. Lobitko was much annoyed and again began to pace the room.

'Isn't he an idiot?' he said, stopping now by Riabovitch's bed, now by Mersliakov's. 'A man must be a dolt and a fool not to be able to get beer, what? The rascal!'

'Of course he can't get beer here,' Mersliakov remarked, without looking up from the pages of his journal.

'Why do you think so?' Lobitko persisted. 'I'll bet you anything I'll find some beer, and women too! I'll go this minute ... You can call me any names you like if I don't find them!'

He took a long time in dressing and pulling on his long boots, then he lighted a cigarette and went out without another word.

'Rabbek, Grabbek, Labbek,' he mumbled, stopping in the passage. 'I don't feel like going alone, damn it! Riabovitch, won't you come for a stroll, eh?'

Receiving no reply, he came back, undressed slowly, and went to bed. Mersliakov sighed, threw his journal aside, and blew out the candle.

'Yes,' Lobitko muttered, smoking a cigarette in the darkness.

Riabovitch pulled the bed-clothes over his head, and curling up began piecing together the disconnected images floating about in his brain, but he failed to obtain any result. He soon fell asleep, his last thought being that someone had caressed and made him happy. Some good, joyous thing had come into his life even though it was senseless. This thought did not leave him even in sleep.

When he awoke the feeling of oil on his neck and the sensation of cold as from peppermint around his lips had left him, but as yesterday a feeling of joy filled his heart. In ecstasy he gazed at the window-panes turned golden by the rising sun, and listened to the noise in the street without. A loud conversation was going on under his very window. His battery-commander, Lebedetsky, who had only just caught up the brigade, was talking to a sergeant at the top of his voice from force of habit, never speaking in any other tone of voice.

'And what else?' the commander cried.

'Golubushka was hurt when she was shod, your Honour; the surgeon applied some clay and vinegar. And last night, your Honour, Mechanic Artiemev was drunk, and the lieutenant ordered him to be put on the reserve gun-carriage.'

The sergeant informed him also that Karpov had forgotten the new lanyards for the friction-tubes and the pegs for the tents, and that the officers had spent the evening at General von Rabbek's. During the conversation Lebedetsky's red beard appeared at the window. His short-sighted eyes peered at the sleepy faces of the officers; he greeted them.

'Is everything all right?' he asked.

'The saddle-horse galled his withers with the new yoke,' Lobitko replied with a yawn.

The commander sighed, deliberated for a while, then said aloud:

'I was thinking of going to Alexandra Evgrafovna – I must pay her a visit. Good-bye. I will catch you up by the evening.'

In a quarter of an hour the brigade had started on its way. When they had passed von Rabbek's barns Riabovitch looked at the house. The blinds were still down. The inmates were doubtless asleep. And she, too, slept – the girl who had kissed Riabovitch yesterday. He tried to picture her sleeping. There was the wide-open window of her bedroom, the green branches peeping in, the fresh morning air, the scent of poplar, lilac and rose, the bed, a chair with the dress she had worn yesterday thrown over it, slippers, a watch on the table – all these objects he saw clearly and precisely, but the girl's features, her sweet dreamy smile, the very thing he most desired to see, slipped his imagination as quicksilver slips through the fingers. About half a verst further on he turned round; the yellow church, the house, the river and garden were bathed in light; the river looked beautiful with its bright green banks, reflections of the sky, and silver patches of sunlight. Once more Riabovitch looked at the village, and a feeling of sadness came over him, as though he were leaving something very near and dear to him behind.

On the road, only the familiar scenes, void of interest, met the eye. To the right were fields of young rye, and buckwheat and hopping rooks; in front, dust and the napes of human necks; behind, the same dust and faces. Ahead of the column marched four soldiers with guns – the vanguard. Next came the bandsmen. Vanguard and bandsmen, like mutes in a funeral procession, now and then ignoring the regulation intervals, marched too far ahead. Riabovitch with the fifth battery could see four batteries in front of him.

To a civilian, the marching brigade, long and cumbersome, presented a novel, interesting spectacle. It is hard to understand why a single gun needs so many men, or why so many strangely harnessed horses are needed to drag it, but to Riabovitch, who was familiar with all these things, it was extremely dull and uninteresting. He had learned years ago why a solid sergeant-major rides beside the officer in front of each battery and the drivers of leaders and wheelers behind them. Riabovitch knew why the near horses were called saddle-horses and the off horses led-horses, and he found it all intensely boring. On one of the wheelers rode a soldier, his back still covered with yesterday's dust and a clumsy ridiculous guard on his leg. Riabovitch knew the use of this guard and found it in no way ridiculous. The horsemen, every man of them, rode mechanically, with an occasional cry or flourish of the whip. The guns were not beautiful to look at. On the limbers were tarpaulin sacks full of oats, and the guns themselves, hung round with teapots, the soldiers' wallets and bags, looked like some harmless animals surrounded for some reason by horses and men. On the lee side of each gun, swinging their arms, marched six gunners, and behind came more leaders, wheelers and more guns, each as ugly and uninspiring as the one in front. Behind the second followed a third and then a fourth by the fourth an officer, and so on. There were six batteries in the brigade, and each battery had four guns. The cavalcade stretched about half a verst along the road. At the end came a train of wagons, near which, with head bent in thought, walked the donkey Ulagar, who had been brought over from Turkey by a battery commander.

Riabovitch gazed indifferently at the necks in front and the faces behind; another day he would have closed his eyes and tried to doze, but now he abandoned himself to his new and pleasant thoughts. When the brigade had first started he tried to convince himself that the incident of the kiss was only a funny little adventure that could not be taken seriously, but he soon waved logic aside and abandoned himself to his dreams . . . He imagined himself in the Rabbeks' drawing-room, now by the side of a girl resembling the one in lilac and the fair girl in black when he closed his eyes, by the side of a strange girl with vague, elusive features. In thought he spoke to her, caressed her, drew her to his breast. He imagined himself going to the wars and leaving her behind, then the return and the supper with his wife and children.

'To the brakes!' rang the command before the descent of

each hill. He too cried, 'To the brakes!' dreading each time that the cry would break the spell of his dream and bring him back to reality.

They passed a large country house. Riabovitch looked over the hedge into the garden. An avenue, long and straight as a rule, met the eye, strewn with yellow gravel and planted with young birches ... With the ecstasy of a dreamer he pictured tiny feminine feet walking along the yellow path, and unexpectedly the image of the girl who had kissed him rose before his mind, the girl he had been unable to visualise yesterday at supper. This image became fixed in his brain and never afterwards left him.

At midday a loud command was heard from the rear of the column:

'Attention! Eyes right! Officers!'

In a carriage drawn by a pair of white horses was the brigade general. He stopped by the second battery and called out something that no one understood. Several officers rode up, Riabovitch among them.

'Well, how goes it?' the general asked, blinking his reddened eyes. 'Are there any sick?'

Receiving a reply, the little general mused for a moment, then turned to one of the officers:

'The driver of your third gun wheeler has taken off his leg-guard and hung it on the limber, the blackguard. Punish him.' He raised his eyes to Riabovitch and continued, 'And the breechings of your harness are too long.'

After a few more tiresome remarks the general turned to Lobitko with a smile.

'Why so sad today, Lieutenant Lobitko?' he asked. 'Are you sighing for Madame Lopukhova, eh? Gentlemen, Lobitko is sighing for Madame Lopukhova!'

Madame Lopukhova was a tall, portly lady, well on the wrong side of forty. The general, who had a weakness for large women of any age, suspected his officers of a like taste. The officers smiled respectfully. The general, pleased with his amusing sally, laughed aloud, then touched the coachman's back and saluted. The carriage rolled away.

'Though it seems to me like the wildest of dreams, beyond the range of possibility, it is really a very commonplace thing,' Riabovitch mused, gazing at the cloud of dust raised by the general's carriage. 'It is very usual and happens to everyone . . . Take the general, for instance; he must have fallen in love; now he is married and has children of his own. Captain Bachter is also married and loved, no doubt, for all that he has an ugly neck and no waist; and Salmanov is a rough fellow, too much of the Tartar, yet he had a love affair that ended in marriage. I am just as other men, and sooner or later the same fate will befall me . . .'

And the thought that he was an ordinary man and that his life was ordinary rejoiced and encouraged him. He gave free rein to his imagination and pictured *her* and his future happiness as he would like it to be.

When the brigade reached its destination and the officers rested in the tents, Riabovitch, Mersliakov and Lobitko were seated at supper round a box. Mersliakov ate slowly, reading *The Messenger of Europe* lying on his knee. Lobitko talked incessantly and kept on filling his glass with beer, and Riabovitch, whose head was in a whirl with his long daydreams, drank silently. After the third glass he grew tipsy and weak; an uncontrollable desire came over him to tell his colleagues of his new emotions.

'A funny incident happened to me at those Rabbeks',' he began, trying to give an indifferent, disdainful tone to his voice. 'I went into the billiard-room, you know.' . . . And he related the tale of the kiss in detail and was surprised that it took so little time in the telling – not more than a minute at most. It seemed to him that the story of the kiss would have taken at least till the morning in the telling. Lobitko, who was a confirmed liar, and thus believed no one else, looked at Riabovitch with an incredulous smile. Mersliakov raised his brows, and without looking up from his journal said:

'A strange thing, to be sure! To throw herself on a man's neck without a word. The girl must be neurotic, I should think.'

'No doubt,' Riabovitch agreed.

'A similar incident once happened to me,' Lobitko began. 'I

was travelling to Kovna last year, second class. The carriage was packed with people; to sleep was impossible. I gave the conductor half a rouble and he took up my luggage and led me into a sleeping car. I lay down and covered myself with a blanket . . . It was quite dark, you know. Suddenly I felt someone touch me on the shoulder and breathe into my face. I put out my hand and felt an elbow . . . I opened my eyes, and would you believe it – there was a woman! Black eyes, lips as red as a fine salmon, nostrils breathing passion, a bosom like a buffer . . .'

'I can understand about the bosom,' Mersliakov interrupted him calmly, 'but how could you see the lips in the dark?'

Lobitko began to hedge and then to laugh at Mersliakov's lack of imagination. Riabovitch was offended; he walked away from the box, lay down and promised himself never to be communicative again.

The life of the camp began. Day followed day, each like every other. Riabovitch the whole time thought and felt and behaved like a man in love. Every morning, when the orderly brought his washing things and he poured the cold water over his head, he remembered that something sweet and precious had come into his life.

Sometimes, when his comrades began to talk of love and women, he drew nearer, listening, his face assuming the expression of a soldier hearing the tale of a battle in which he had fought. And on evenings when the officers, at the instigation of the setter, Lobitko, made Don Juan excursions into the village, Riabovitch, though he participated in them, was miserable and felt himself immeasurably to blame; in thought he asked forgiveness of *her* . . . In leisure hours, or on sleepless nights, when the desire usually came over him to recall his childhood, his father, mother, all that was near and dear to him, he invariably thought of Mestechko, the curious horse, Rabbek, his wife who looked like the Empress Eugénie, the dark room, the bright crack in the door . . .

On the 31 of August he returned from camp, not with the whole brigade, but with two batteries only; the whole way he was strangely excited, as though he were going home to his native place. Once more he longed to see the strange horse, the church, Rabbek's affected family, the dark room. An 'inner voice' that so often deceives those in love told him that he would see *her*. And he began to wonder how he would greet her, what he would say to her. Had she forgotten about the kiss? If the worst were to happen and he did not see her at all, he would, at any rate, walk through the dark room and remember. . . .

Towards the evening, the familiar church and white barns appeared on the horizon. Riabovitch's heart beat fast. He did not hear what the officer who rode near him was saying, he forgot everything, and with a great longing gazed at the river sparkling in the distance, at the roof of the house, at the dovecot and circling doves, lighted up by the setting sun.

They arrived at the church; he listened to the quartermaster's report, expecting every moment to see the horseman appear who would invite them to the general's to tea, but the quartermaster had finished, the officers hastened to the village, and still the horseman did not come . . .

'Rabbek will soon learn from the peasants that we are here and will send for us,' Riabovitch thought, entering the hut and failing to comprehend why his comrades had lighted the candles and why the orderlies were preparing the samovars.

He felt depressed. He lay down, then got up and looked out of the window to see if the horseman was coming. But no horseman was in sight. Once more he lay down, and unable to bear his anxiety, after a while he went out into the street and made his way to the church. The square by the church fence was dark and deserted. Three soldiers were standing together in silence at the crest of the hill. At sight of Riabovitch they started and gave the salute. He saluted in turn and began to descend the hill along the familiar path.

On the opposite bank the sky was a bright purple; the moon rose; two women, talking loudly, were pulling cabbage leaves in a kitchen-garden: beyond the kitchen-garden were the dark outlines of several huts . . . On this side it was the same as in May – there was the path, the bushes, the overhanging willows – only the song of the brave little nightingale was missing and the scent of poplar and young grass.

Riabovitch approached the garden and looked through the gate. It was dark and quiet within. The white trunks of the nearest birches were visible and a part of the avenue, the rest was a darkened mass. Riabovitch listened intently and peered into the darkness, but after half an hour of waiting and watching, and hearing no sound and seeing no light, he turned back.

He stopped by the river. Before him, gleaming in the darkness, was the general's bathing-hut and a sheet hanging on the rail of the little bridge. He went on to the bridge and without any reason put out his hand to touch the sheet . . . He gazed down into the water . . . The river flowed quickly and made a faint murmur by the stakes of the bathing-hut. The moon, large and red was reflected near the left bank; tiny waves floated across it, extending the reflection, breaking it to pieces, as thugh they wished to carry it away . . .

'How senseless! how senseless!' Riabovitch thought, gazing at the quickly flowing water. 'How senseless it all is!'

Now that he no longer expected anything, the story of the kiss, his impatience, his vague hopes and disillusionment appeared to him in a true light. It seemed no longer strange to him that the general's horseman had not appeared and that he would never meet the girl who had kissed him in mistake for someone else; on the contrary it would have been strange if he had met her. . . .

The water flew past him, whither and why no one knew. It had flown past in May. From a little stream it had poured into a great river, then into the sea; from the sea it had risen in mist, then come down in rain, and now perhaps the water flying past him was the very same he had seen in May. Why? Wherefore?

And the whole world and life itself seemed to Riabovitch to be one great, incomprehensible, senseless jest. He raised his eyes from the water and looked up at the sky; once more he remembered how fate, in the form of an unknown woman, had unexpectedly caressed him; he recalled his dreams and images of the summer, and his life appeared to him so poor, wretched and colourless. . . .

When he returned to his quarters, not one of his colleagues

was there. The orderly informed him that the officers had all gone to General 'Fontrabkin,' who had sent a horseman for them ... A feeling of joy for a moment sprang into Riabovitch's heart, but he instantly smothered it. As though to spite Fate, who had treated him so badly, he did not go to the general's, but went instead to bed.

Faust

BY E. CHIRIKOV

1864–1932

When Ivan Mihailovitch awoke everyone in the house was already up, and the sound of children's ringing voices was heard in the distance, the clatter of dishes, and the shrill call of the canary in the drawing-room, which sounded like a policeman's whistle. Ivan Mihailovitch did not want to get up – it was so hard to get out of bed, and dressing was such a trouble, so he lay in bed smoking cigarette after cigarette before he managed to summon sufficient courage to move. He usually got up feeling irritable and discontented, for Ivan Mihailovitch was not pleased with the order of a life that compelled him to hurry over his toilet and morning tea to rush off to his work whether he would or no.

'Go and see if Papa is awake,' he heard his wife's voice, and a little head as round as a ball was thrust in at the door.

'Are you up, Papa?'

'Yes, yes!' Ivan Mihailovitch replied with a grunt of annoyance, spluttering as he rinsed his mouth viciously.

At table he was sulky and morose, and sat as though engrossed in weighty thought, paying no heed to anyone. His wife, glancing at him, thought, 'He must have lost at the club again last night, and now does not know where to get the money.'

At ten o'clock Ivan Mihailovitch departed to his work at the bank, and at four he returned home tired, hungry and irritable still. At dinner he tucked his napkin into his collar and ate noisily, like a pig at a trough. His hunger satisfied, he softened, and blowing out his cheeks said facetiously:

'No more? . . . Now for a little snooze.' And he departed to his study, which was decorated with the horns of a stag and a gun that he never used. There, after coughing and spitting for a time, he began to snore, so loudly that the children were afraid to pass his door, and the nurse, in order to stop a fight or a quarrel would say to them threateningly. 'A bear is sleeping in there . . . You had better be good or I will let him out!'

Ivan Mihailovitch slept until eight o'clock, and when someone came to wake him he called out 'all right!' in an angry voice, and went on snoring. When at last he emerged from his study, morose, with swollen eyes, looking indeed like a bear, he began in a raucous voice:

'Why did no one wake me?'

'You were called and you said "all right." '

'All right! A sleepy man will say anything! Is the samovar ready?'

Then he went into the dining-room and sat down by the table with a newspaper, once more with an air as though engrossed in some profound, weighty thought. His wife, Ksenia Pavlovna, pouring out the tea, was not visible from behind the samovar, and his mother-in-law, Maria Petrovna, at the other end of the table was, as usual, darning the children's socks, a heel stretched over a spoon. Everyone was silent, except for an occasional laconic question and reply.

'More?'

'Yes!'

'No lemon again?'

'There it is under your nose!'

After tea Ivan Mihailovitch departed to his club for a game of cards, and after cards he had supper, to return home at two o'clock in the morning to find his wife asleep. Only Maria Petrovna was still about, hair dishevelled, in an old dressing-jacket; and she usually greeted him with a deep sigh. Ivan Mihailovitch knew the meaning of her mysterious sighs; they were the unspoken reproaches and censure of his conduct. Thus it was that when he removed his goloshes he said:

'No sighing, if you please!'

Ksenia Pavlovna never reproached her husband; she had grown used alike to his snoring and to his absence. It was only

Maria Petrovna who could not reconcile herself to these things.

'A fine husband, to be sure! All you see of him is his dressing-gown hanging on a peg!' she used to say.

'Don't Mamma . . . All husbands are like that . . .' Ksenia Pavlovna remonstrated, but her face grew sad and set in an intense melancholy. Pacing the drawing-room at dusk with hands behind her she would muse about something, humming to herself softly and plaintively:

'Beyond the far horizon is a blessed land. . . .'

Then she suddenly shook her head and went into the nursery to play at dolls with the children, or to tell them fairy-tales about sister Alenushka and brother Ivanushka. The eldest boy was like his father, that is, before the latter had taken to spitting and snoring and appearing before Ksenia Pavlovna in his shirt-sleeves. When watching the boy Ksenia Pavlovna was vaguely carried back in thought to the past, and the bedimmed visions of her bygone girlhood banished from her soul the feeling of emptiness, weariness, boredom and unappeased longing. . . .

'Mamma! Mammotchka! Now the story about Baba Yaga! Will you?'

'Very well. Once upon a time there lived a Baba Yaga; her bony leg . . .'

'Did she snore?' asked the little girl, her blue wide-open little eyes fixed on her mother intently.

Ksenia Pavlovna burst out laughing, and, seizing the child in her arms, kissed her passionately and forgot everything else in the world.

Twice a month they entertained. Their guests were all stolid, respectable and dull, having passed their lives in complete uniformity, in the deepest of ruts, smoothly, monotonously, without ever a mishap. They all liked to talk about the same things and act in the same way. At first they sat in the drawing-room and talked about their houses, their children's stomachs and the weather, and while Ksenia Pavlovna entertained them, her mother prepared the tea. Filling the best dishes with jam, she looked at the pots and said to herself:

'Last till the new fruit season, indeed! We shall be thankful if we have enough till Easter!'

And filling the sugar-basin, she looked into the sugar-bag, thinking aloud:

'Twenty pounds, to be sure! A pood would be barely enough!'

'Will you come to tea?' she invited the guests, coming to the door with a welcome smile on her face.

And the guests streamed into the drawing-room, buttoning their coats on the way. They seated themselves ponderously, chaffing those who happened on the corners of the table, saying that they would not marry for seven years, then came a clinking of spoons, sounds of 'merci !' or 'please!' and again they reverted to their houses, their children's stomachs or teeth, or to the rise in the cost of provisions. After tea there were the open card-tables in the drawing-room; candles and cards and chalk, all ready. Everyone was animated, then came a tiresome mood noticeable when people are compelled to do something they have no desire to do. Men and women seated themselves at the tables, and amidst the tobacco smoke the game began, and after arguments and disputes and mutual reproaches they suddenly began to laugh and seemed on the whole so thoroughly engrossed and contented that they might have been the happiest people in the world. They became like the maddest of fanatics and were annoyed when some person who happened not to be playing turned to them with an irrevelant remark. Ksenia Pavlovna did not play; her one care was to feed and entertain her guests. While they played she and her mother prepared the supper, bickering a little over the arrangements, yet in such a way that no one should hear them. When supper was announced the guests jumped up hurriedly, making a clatter with their chairs, and went laughing to the table, two or three perhaps, more interested in the game than the rest, remaining behind to finish a heated argument about the knave of spades, ready to forgo their supper to prove each other in the wrong . . . The host came and put his arms around their waists and led them away.

'Now for a glass,' Ivan Mihailovitch usually began.

Several glasses were drunk without any toasts, then they began to drink the health of Ksenia Pavlovna and the other ladies. Faces grew flushed, eyes grew merry, and from one end of the table to the other a hubbub arose.

'Peter Vasilievitch, will you please pass the caviare?'

'Nikolai Gregorivitch, will you please pass the herring?'

Jests followed about their wives, and stories and anecdotes which had been told many a time before.

Ivan Mihailovitch remarked with pride that he and his wife had married for love . . .

'We married for love . . . Indeed, I eloped with Ksenia Pavlovna. . . .'

'Really?'

'I remember it as though it had happened yesterday . . . I nearly shot myself! What do you think of that? We had arranged to meet in the garden. Theirs was a beautiful garden, only foolishly they sold it with the house . . . Well, I was waiting in the old summer-house . . . My heart beat so loudly that it sounded like the throbbing of a train, tuk, tuk, tuk!'

Ivan Mihailovitch related every detail and Ksenia Pavlovna, sitting a little apart from him, blushed faintly. She trembled and half closed her eyes.

'At last she drove up!'

'Walked up,' she corrected him unexpectedly, for every sentence, every detail in the narrative was dear to her.

'Walked up, drove up, what difference does it make?' Ivan Mihailovitch said irritably, annoyed at the interruption, and he finished his tale ignoring Ksenia Pavlovna's correction, and ignoring Ksenia Pavlovna herself, as though she and the woman of his story bore no relation to each other. . . .

Supper over, tea was served again. The guests tried to smother their yawns behind the palms of their hands or their table-napkins; they breathed deeply, looked at the clock and exchanged glances with their wives.

'It's time to go home,' the wives said, and there was a general leave-taking, the women kissing each other, the men hunting for goloshes and caps, the subject of further jokes.

When they had all gone, leaving the room full of tobacco

smoke and half-finished glasses of tea with cigarette ash in the saucers and the remains of the supper, a tranquil peace settled over the house, and Ksenia Pavlovna, throwing herself into a chair, fell into a silent apathetic state of indifference to her surroundings. She rested after the empty talk, the noise and the meals, feeling as though she had just been through some severe illness, or had escaped some awful punishment. Her mother, passing through the drawing-room, opened the window, saying, 'Like a barracks, to be sure!' then, taking the cigarette ends out of the flower-pots, her anger rose.

'I put two ash-trays to each table on purpose! Nothing will satisfy them but they must stick their cigarette ends in the flower-pots!'

And with a will she set to work clearing the tables and arranging the chairs. And Ivan Mihailovitch took off his coat, unbuttoned his waistcoat, and walked from room to room yawning and showing his decaying teeth.

'Folks are sleeping on the Volga and we, too, must to bed,' he muttered to himself.

And he went into his bedroom, undressed and stretched himself at full length on the comfortable broad iron bedstead with the silver knobs and spring mattress. He was floating in a sea of contentment and composed himself for the coming of his wife. He became annoyed that she was so long in coming.

'Bother the clearing up! Can't you leave it alone?' he called aloud and listened. 'What a row the children are making!'

From the nursery came the sound of a child crying and his wife's voice. It was useless waiting further; she would not come for a long time now. Ivan Mihailovitch pulled the bedclothes over his shoulders, curled up and turned his face to the wall.

Once or twice a month they went out visiting. The process was just the same – there was tea, talk of houses and children's stomachs, the green tables, the tobacco smoke, the arguments about the knave of spades, the supper, the vodka, the cheap wine, the caviare and salt herring, the inevitable cutlets and cucumber. And when they departed, the windows were no doubt opened after them and their hosts abandoned themselves to the peace and quietness that followed. . . .

Thus life went on day in, day out, dull and monotonous, colourless and wearisome like a grey, gloomy evening. 'Life is like the perpetual study of a cookery-book . . . the only variety in the days is that one day we have soup and cutlets and another borshch and cutlets,' Ksenia Pavlovna sometimes thought, and a wave of despair passed over her; she felt she must make some decision, must do something. But what could she do? And in answer to this question a sad smile flitted across her lips, wan and helpless, and the unbidden tears stood in her eyes. . . .

At such times a horrible depression came over her; she grew weary of everything and did not wish to see or to speak to anyone. It seemed to her that everyone talked of things they never thought about, and the things they thought about were carefully hidden from the rest of the world; that everyone laughed at things that were not funny, merely from a sense of kindness and politeness, and that everyone endeavoured to appear good and clever when in reality they were stupid, commonplace and insufferably dull. . . .

She sat by the window, her elbows resting on the sill, gazing into the street and watching the wearisome day fade away into the grey twilight. She recalled her girlhood and the days when life had seemed to her so big, with such endless stretches of horizon enveloped in a hazy blue mist, so interesting in its limitless variety, so mysterious and incomprehensible. All that mattered, all that she desired was in front of her, and her girlish heart stood still with fear and curiosity at the unknown future, and her soul was vaguely perturbed at the prospect of some happiness, the happiness perhaps of triumphant love . . .

But here was real life! The horizon ended on the other side of the street with a shop where they were always in debt, and the only poetry was the cookery-book. Day in, day out, people lived in constant boredom and empty gossip of houses and places, playing cards, bearing children and ever complaining – husbands against wives, wives against husbands. And there was no triumphant love, only triumphant commonplaceness, vulgarity and boredom . . . Everything that was interesting in life had happened in her girlhood, her happiness flitting by her

unheeded – a happiness that comes but once and never returns
. . .

It grew dark. Timid lights flickered in the street. A bell rang for vespers. The reverberating church bell aroused some vague perturbing sensation in the heart that was neither a resigned sadness over something that has vanished into eternity nor a reproach at the present life. 'The evening bell, the evening bell!' Ksenia Pavlovna whispered with a deep sigh. A white figure appeared in the dark room; it was Ivan Mihailovitch who had come out of his study in his shirt-sleeves. He stretched himself and said with a yawn:

'I have eaten well and slept well . . . What are you dreaming about?'

'Nothing. I was thinking. What a bore life is, Ivan Mihailovitch!'

'You've had three children and now find it boring!'

'How commonplace!'

'Depressed again, I see,' Ivan Mihailovitch said irritably, and walked away with a wave of the hand.

Ksenia Pavlovna smiled, then laughed, and her laughter turned to tears and ended in hysterics.

'What a nuisance!' grumbled Ivan Mihailovitch, and called aloud to the maid for water.

'Bring it cold, from the tap!'

'What is the matter? What have you done to her?' cried the mother, rushing in, the whites of her eyes gleaming in the darkness. Her whole attitude expressed a desire for revenge and a reckoning. 'What have you done to her?'

'Nothing whatever! I don't know what it means; I haven't the least idea! Your daughter is not a normal woman; she is quite abnormal!'

'Did you say anything to hurt her feelings?'

'Not in word or thought. I came into the room and she was sitting by the window, when suddenly, without rhyme or reason, she burst out laughing and then crying.' Ivan Mihailovitch shrugged his shoulders, and Maria Petrovna, whom in moments of irritation he called Baba Yaga, refused to believe him and demanded an explanation.

'Don't say that to me . . . Abnormal, indeed! Our family was always healthy and normal . . . What have you done to her?'

'Very well, let her be normal! So much the better!' Ivan Mihailovitch said maliciously and left the house. He went to his club, where he played cards, and to spite everyone staked high and lost.

Maria Petrovna meanwhile went about with a worried look, not able to comprehend what had taken place between them. Now and again she came up to Ksenia Pavlovna and began:

'You disagreed and quarrelled . . . But what about? Have you found out something about him?'

'No.'

'Did he offend you?'

'No.'

'It is vain for you to hide things from me . . . Murder will out . . . I know everything, my dear,' the mother said, changing her tone and attacking the subject from a different angle. 'He is jealous . . . You mustn't provoke him. . . .'

'Well, really! He is simply a fool, nothing more,' Ksenia Pavlovna interrupted, laughing through her tears. The mother became angry.

'When a wife talks like that about her husband nothing good can come of it!'

And she began to defend her son-in-law with all the eloquence she could command, making out that a better man than Ivan Mihailovitch did not exist.

'Look at others, now! There is Kapitalina Ivanovna's husband! The poor woman bears her troubles without a murmur and doesn't go about calling her husband a fool. You don't value what you've got, my dear! It won't be any use crying when you have lost it!'

And Maria Petrovna got no explanation from her daughter and wearied herself with speculations and surmises. She did not go to bed till her son-in-law's return, and sat on the drawing-room sofa thinking and wondering. 'Hm!' she said from time to time.

And Ivan Mihailovitch having supped and drunk, returned to his home, and the noise of his angry ring resounded throughout the quiet room and startled Maria Petrovna. 'I suppose he is drunk,' she thought, and opening the door, she did not sigh as usual, but said pleasantly:

'There is supper for you in the dining-room.'

Ivan Mihailovitch did not reply. He stalked from room to room with an air of protest, banging doors, coughing aloud, letting everyone know that he was master in his own house. To show his displeasure still more and assert his independence, Ivan Mihailovitch did not go to bed that night in the comfortable bed with the silver knobs, but lay down on the sofa in his study, beneath the stag's horns and the gun that he never used.

'At least take this pillow,' came the softened voice of Maria Petrovna through the opened door, as she thrust a white pillow into the room.

Her son-in-law was silent.

'You'll get a stiff neck like that.'

'Don't worry about my neck, please.'

Maria Petrovna threw the pillow on to a chair and shut the door. Ivan Mihailovitch had a will of his own; he did not take the pillow, but lay with his head on his fist, oppressed by the weight of his family troubles.

The house dog, Norma, always took Ivan Mihailovitch's side. When husband and wife quarrelled Norma would not remain with the women. With a paw he opened the door and went in to comfort his offended master. He walked up to the sofa and laid his head with the wet, dripping jaws on Ivan Mihailovitch's chest, looking at him with an air that seemed to say:

'What swine they are, to be sure! They don't appreciate you!'

Ivan Mihailovitch was inexpressibly grateful to Norma, and stroked him fondly and pulled his large ears. Again the study door was opened and Maria Petrovna called softly:

'Norma! Norma!'

Norma did not move. Ivan Mihailovitch, a hand on his neck, began to stroke him more violently.

Again the voice came softly:

'He may give you a flea . . . Norma, Norma!'

Ivan Mihailovitch jumped up and banged the door, and the melodious echo of a key turning in the lock put an end to Maria Petrovna's diplomatic attempts at a reconciliation.

'To sleep with the dog, indeed . . . That's the last straw,' she mumbled on the other side of the door.

Scenes such as these had a dramatic element in them, but there were others not dramatic at all, and these were repeated regularly on the twentieth of each month, when Ivan Mihailovitch received his salary and a settling followed with his numerous petty creditors. There was never enough money to cover everything, and it seemed to Ivan Mihailovitch there ought to have been enough. He railed at women in general, saying that while they wanted emancipation, they were not fit to conduct their own households. . . .

'Emancipation, indeed!' he said, taking out the notes from his pocket-book.

'What has emancipation to do with it?'

'The devil knows why they teach you geography and algebra and trigonometry! What use are they when you cannot make income and expenditure balance? Emancipation, indeed!'

'Perhaps they would balance if you didn't go so often to your club,' remarked Maria Petrovna.

'Where can I get the money? I can't make it. I am not a counterfeiter.'

Thus the three of them bickered and reproached each other, descending to such petty meannesses that they were afterwards heartily ashamed of themselves. After the twentieth of each month an apathy settled on the soul of Ksenia Pavlovna; the brightness went from her eyes and her movements became slow and heavy. At these times she seemed to grow old and haggard and careless of her appearance; from a pretty young woman she became like a bunch of withered flowers that someone had thrown out of a window.

Thus they passed their days, months, years, and when some friends asked them how they were, they replied:

'Oh, we have nothing to complain of, thank God!'

One had to get some recreation from this life occasionally,

and with Ivan Mihailovitch it took the form of getting drunk three times a year.

'It is necessary to shake yourself up occasionally, it does you good,' he would say on the day following these occasions.

Ksenia Pavlovna's idea of recreation was to go to a theatre but this so rarely happened in her life that a theatre became an event of the utmost importance. When she suggested that they should go to the theatre for a change, her husband always reminded her of a visit to the opera in St Petersburg, when they were first married, about nine years ago. 'Is it worth spoiling the impression of Figner and Savina?' he asked, and went away to his club to play cards.

However, when *Faust* was announced at the local theatre, without being asked, Ivan Mihailovitch booked stalls for himself and his wife.

'We are going to *Faust* this evening,' he said irritably, when he returned from his work and threw the two coloured tickets on the table.

'*Faust*?' Ksenia Pavlovna cried joyously, and her face lighted up with pleasure.

Happy and exulting, Ksenia Pavlovna began to dress early. Ivan Mihailovitch watched his wife as she dressed and arranged her hair, for when he appeared in public with her he liked her to look well. He wanted people to say when they saw her on his arm. 'A fine-looking woman that!'

Consequently, as a critic, Ivan Mihailovitch was severe. While Ksenia Pavlovna was dressing, he plagued her with his criticism.

'You have not curled your hair properly. It doesn't suit your face and makes you look like a Jewess!'

'I don't think so.'

'It's funny that women never know what suits them. And they never want to please their husbands.'

Ksenia Pavlovna herself wanted to look nice, but she had no belief in her husband's taste and little reliance on her own. The usual quarrel ensued, and they left the house cross with each other, with spoiled moods and heavy hearts. They set out to the theatre without any feeling of pleasure; they might have been forced to go there. As they walked out arm in arm, each desired to snatch the arm away. Ivan Mihailovitch called to an *isvoschick* angrily, as though he hated all the *isvoschicks* in the world. A sleigh drove up; Ivan Mihailovitch helped his wife into it and put his arm round her waist as he sat down beside her. They did not speak a word the whole way, Ivan Mihailovitch venting his ill-humour on the driver.

'Mind the ruts! Steady, you blockhead! Keep to the right! Whoa!'

And all the time Ivan Mihailovitch felt angry with the woman he was holding round the waist, which seemed to be loaded with hostility towards him and might explode at any moment like a bomb . . . The *isvoschick* smacked his lips and pulled his reins, hoping thereby to deceive the cross gentleman and make him believe that he was going at a smart pace, but Ivan Mihailovitch was not to be taken in.

'Do you think it's a funeral?' he asked, poking the *isvoschick* in the back. 'Funerals don't go to theatres. You don't give your horse enough to eat, you rascal!'

'What makes you think so?' the astonished *isvoschick* asked, turning round.

'How dare you answer back?'

The police, too, came in no less for Ivan Mihailovitch's displeasure. He usually managed to create a scene at the entrance of the theatre. To-night the constable responsible for order hurried the *isvoschicks* away as soon as they drove up, and Ksenia Pavlovna had hardly managed to put one foot to the ground when he cried:

'Move on! look sharp!'

'Where did you get your manners from, young man?' Ivan Mihailovitch turned to him furiously and threatened to report him to the chief-of-police, with whom he was on intimate terms. He offered his arm to Ksenia Pavlovna and stalked past the constable with an air as majestic as that of the chief-of-police himself.

The orchestra was playing the *Faust* overture.

They walked arm in arm down the lengthy carpeted gangway to their seats. Ivan Mihailovitch imagined that all eyes were turned on him; he tried to give a greater dignity to his gait, holding himself erect and throwing out his chest. Ksenia Pavlovna walked with her eyes to the ground as one condemned to death, her face impassive in shame and anguish. The lights went out. The curtain (with a design of a sea that looked like a sky and a sky that looked like a sea and some fantastic ruins and tropical vegetation) went up, and a traditional Faust in a brown dressing-gown and nightcap and a long white beard began to sing in a metallic tenor voice, stroking his beard:

'Vain! in vain do I call throughout my vigil weary. . . .'

At first Ksenia Pavlovna was not affected by the music or by the singing. She could see more than she could hear. When a flaming red Mephistopheles came on and announced that he had everything ready and plenty of money, Ksenia Pavlovna remembered that it would soon be the twentieth of the month, and that for two months past the butcher's bill had not been paid. . . .

'Emancipation,' the voice of Ivan Mihailovitch echoed in her brain, and when she left off thinking of the butcher and emancipation, Faust had already discarded his beard and dressing-gown and been transformed from an old man to a young and handsome one; the surprise at the sudden change brought the first smile to her face

'O youth, without measure be thy delight . . .'

Faust sang, stepping triumphantly towards the footlights and raising his arms. And Ksenia Pavlovna thought of Ivan Mihailovitch's age and their lost youth. She sighed and cast a stealthy glance at her husband; he was sitting deep down in his chair, with his hands folded over his stomach, his head a little to the side; so much complacency and bourgeois repectability was expressed in his clean-shaven face and dyed and waxed mustachios that Ksenia Pavlovna hastily looked away.

In the first interval they walked out into the *foyer* arm in arm, Ivan Mihailovitch disturbed by the thought that his wife's hair was not properly done, and that her face was not bright and gay like the faces of the other women there, whose eyes sparkled as they swished about in their silk skirts, talking and laughing with their happy ringing voices.

Having walked about a little they returned to their places in silence, as though they did not exist for one another ... Beneath the flood of light cast by the electric lights the women's garments shone and the hubbub of the many voices sounded like bees in a hive, but to Ksenia Pavlovna the movement and rustle, the brilliance and riot of colour seemed strange and remote, and the rows of human faces and the boxes that looked like bunches of flowers made her feel forlorn and lonely.

She did not look round at the audience, but sat with her hands resting limply on her lap, her eyes downcast, hoping that no chance acquaintance would disturb her silent mood with a 'How do you do?' or that Ivan Mihailovitch would not speak to her crossly on the subject of the constable or Figner. When the lights went out she felt a sense of relief, as though she suddenly found herself alone in the chamber of her girlhood.

As she looked at the stage she gradually became lost to the world of sound and abandoned herself to a vague spiritual mood which began to stir within her. She forgot her anger, she forgot the petty bickerings, the butcher, and the dull prose of life; her soul grew clear and tranquil; the ever-open wound had healed at last and ceased its gnawing pain ... In the third act Ksenia Pavlovna had soared away from her native little town, forgetting herself and the people about her in abandonment to the music, the moonlight and the contemplation of love and a happiness that grew and grew and became infinite and all-absorbing, though it was enveloped in sadness, soft and gentle as the moonlight; and the lovely girl on the stage, with the long golden plait, was begging for mercy at the feet of the youth with the ardour and simplicity of a child. There she was, bathed in moonlight, trembling with fear and joy, her head nestling against the handsome youth's shoulder ... There she was singing of her joy at the open window, telling the stars of her happiness, and the still night and the dreamy enchanted garden, and her song, pure and sacred as a prayer, rose to the starlit sky. ...

How dear it was, how intimate to those who had outlived such happiness! Ksenia Pavlovna herself had once been a girl with a golden plait, singing as joyously of her happiness to the stars and the silent garden, bathed in mysterious moonlight, and she too had trembled in joy and fear and begged for mercy. . . .

'Ha, ha, ha!' came the rolling laugh of Mephistopheles – such a ruthless, pitiless, mocking laugh – and the chord sounding in Ksenia Pavlovna's heart with a sweet sadness ceased instantly, leaving the sound of this laughter only, crushing and triumphant in its commonplace reality . . .

Her reveries and visions were rudely torn asunder. Ksenia Pavlovna lowered her eyes and pressed her lips firmly together. A smile flitted across her face – a strange, panic-stricken smile, and Ivan Mihailovitch, sitting up straight in his chair, said solemnly:

'Not a bad laugh, that.'

Ksenia Pavlovna glanced at her husband and gave a pitiful sigh . . . She had become reconciled to Ivan Mihailovitch, to his pompousness, to the hands crossed over his stomach . . . The latter no longer gave her a feeling of disgust . . . The man sitting beside her had once been her Faust, her dream of love was bound up with him. It may have been a mirage, a mistake, but a mistake that constituted her whole life, and was as irrevocable as youth itself.

The certain descended, the applause came like rain; the uproars of the gallery filled the whole house, the curtain with the design of a sea and ruins went up once more, and Faust, Margaret and Mephistopheles appeared hand in hand, smiling to the audience. Ksenia Pavlovna felt as though rudely awakened from a dream full of sweet, enchanting visions forgotten; the awakening annoyed her; painfully she tried to bring back the scattered visions . . . She did not want to see Margaret turned actress, eager for applause and flirting with that big monster, the audience, nor did she wish to see Mephistopheles, who put his hand over his heart in pleasure and gratitude, nor Faust, who now looked like a hairdresser, and wafted kisses to both sides of the house . . .

'Come, Vania!'

Ivan Mihailovitch gallantly offered his arm and they went out into the *foyer*. He ordered tea, and afterwards oranges.

'I am thirsty,' he explained, handing Ksenia Pavlovna an orange, and from that moment all hostile feelings between them ceased.

'Are they sour?'

'No, they are quite nice.'

Ksenia Pavlovna ate an orange and watched the men as they passed. 'They don't behave like this at home,' she thought. 'They are all going to their clubs. After all, my Vania is better than many of them here!'

'How did you like Margaret, Vania?'

'Not bad, though after Alma Foster, of course . . .'

'Have you heard Alma? I didn't know.'

'Don't you remember? We heard her together in St Petersburg.'

'Oh, it's so long ago. . . .'

'Of course, the opera itself is immortal . . . I have seen it a hundred times and could see it as many times more. Life is reflected as in a mirror . . . Yes . . . Do you remember . . . in the garden?' Ivan Mihailovitch concluded softly, leaning towards his wife.

A faint flush spread over Ksenia Pavlovna's features; her eyes, sad and dreamy, gazed musingly at the distance.

'It must have happened in a dream,' her lips whispered softly and her head trembled above her pretty bare neck.

Some friends came up and greeted them.

'How are you?'

'Oh, we have nothing to complain of, thank God. And you?'

'Quite well, thank you. How well you are looking, Ksenia Pavlovna! You get prettier and prettier.'

Ksenia Pavlovna blushed and a scarcely perceptible wave of pride and pleasure spread over her face, making it look charming.

'It is nice of you to say so. I think that I get plainer every day!' she replied, half closing her eyes and fanning herself coquettishly.

The men protested in chorus, and the women silently put their hands to their hair. Ivan Mihailovitch looked at his wife; she was really pretty, he thought, one of the prettiest women in the theatre. His face, too, assumed an air of pride.

'There is a portrait of her painted when we were engaged. Have you seen it?' he asked, twirling his moustache. 'It hangs above my writing-table. She used to have a plait twice as thick as that of Margaret's to-night.'

During the last act a change had come over Ivan Mihailovitch's soul. He imagined his wife undergoing the unhappy fate of Margaret and himself as Faust, and he began to pity Ksenia Pavlovna. The sombre prison walls, the grey stone floor, the straw, and the woman, abused, guilty, her reason gone, yet still so pure and holy, and the soft, gentle melodies, stirring vague recollections of past happiness – all caused Ivan Mihailovitch to draw deep breaths. He glanced at his wife, and observing the tears in her eyes felt that she was infinitely dear to him, and that he was immeasurably to blame in some way. . . .

Ivan Mihailovitch gazed in despair at the stage, listening to the soft music; it seemed to him that his own Ksenia had been cast into prison and was recalling their first meeting at the fair and how he had sung to her 'Amidst the noisy fair,' and how they had sat together in the dark garden, listening to the nightingales and gazing at the stars. . . .

They left the theatre with souls regenerated and filled with a sweet sadness. It seemed to them both that all the vulgarity, the petty commonplaces of life had gone, and that part of their former joy had come back . . . They flew home quickly in the light sleigh, squeaking over the well-trodden road; Ivan Mihailovitch held his wife tightly round the waist, as though he feared to lose her on the way. Ksenia Pavlovna hid her face in the soft collar of her coat, only her eyes shone out beneath her white cap, like two gleaming coals of fire. Ivan Mihailovitch wanted to kiss her, and forgetting everything, made an attempt to do so, but Ksenia Pavlovna, with laughing, half-closed eyes, gently shook her cap at him. . . .

Maria Petrovna and the samovar were waiting for them at home, the samovar boiling and bubbling in its majestic, shining splendour above the snow-white tablecloth. The brown rolls looked and smelt inviting, and the lightly boiled eggs only awaited a crack of the spoon. Maria Petrovna, yawning, floated out of the nursery in an old dressing jacket and said pleasantly:

'Come in, children. Would you like something to eat?'

Ivan Mihailovitch did not reply. He went into the dimly-lighted drawing-room, humming as he paced slowly up and down, '*Let me gaze on the form before me . . .*' stroking his head with the palm of his hand.

He returned to the dining-room, walked up to his wife and kissed her on the forehead, then went off again singing '*Let me gaze on the form before me. . . .*'

'Eat something first and do your gazing afterwards. The eggs will be getting cold,' Maria Petrovna said, glancing in at the door.

'Coming, coming!' Ivan Mihailovitch replied, annoyed, still pacing the room and humming, abandoning himself to his mood, to vague recollections and sweet regret of the past.

The three of them sat down to tea, talking in a friendly way, peace and tranquillity at heart. Ksenia Pavlovna had changed into a white dressing-gown with sleeves like wings, and put down her hair. Now and again she went into the nursery, where she fell on her knees by the children's beds and with motherly love and tenderness looked at her sleeping babes, at their bare little arms and sweet innocent faces. It seemed to her that they were little angels sleeping there, pure and gentle, and that their purity had carried the soul of Margaret to heaven. . . .

'You look like Margaret in prison,' Ivan Mihailovitch remarked, resting his elbow on the table and looking intently at his wife. Years seemed to have slipped; before him was the sweet girl with the golden plait whom he had wanted to love and worship always. . . .

As he looked at her, Ksenia Pavlovna lowered her eyes; she smiled; deep, deep down in the bottom of her heart, like a mountain echo, there sounded the broken melody of the unfinished song of her youth.

Ivan Mihailovitch, who usually had supper in his shirt-sleeves and braces, now did not want to take off his coat. In as far as he could he tried to give more grace to his movements and gestures; he was even more polite to Maria Petrovna.

'Butter?' he asked, forestalling her needs.

'For all the world like a visitor,' Maria Petrovna remarked with a contented smile, and taking the butter added 'Merci!'

'Good-night, my Margaret!' said Ivan Mihailovitch, and he looked long into his wife's eyes and kissed her hand and cheek.

'Sleep well, my Faust!' Ksenia Pavlovna jested, and kissed her husband contentedly on the lips.

Ivan Mihailovitch shook hands with Maria Petrovna when he bid her good-night, and went into the bedroom. A small lamp was burning beneath the ceiling, bathing the room in a blue, dreamy light, soft and soothing. How pleasant it looked! ... Ivan Mihailovitch undressed slowly, and removing his boots he sang in a soft falsetto voice:

'All hail, thou dwelling pure and lowly. . . .'

A Grand Slam

BY LEONID ANDREYEV
1871–1919

They played *vint*[1] three times a week – on Tuesday, Thursday
and Saturday. Sunday would have been a very convenient day
to play, but Sunday had to be kept open for all kinds of
accidents, such as a casual caller or a theatre, and was thus
considered the dullest day in the whole week. However, when
in the country during the summer they played on Sundays too.
The partnerships were arranged in this way: portly, irritable
Maslenikov played with Jacov Ivanovitch, while Evpraksia
Vasilievna played with her solemn brother, Propkopy
Vasilievitch. The arrangement had been made six years before,
and Evpraksia Vasilievna always insisted on its observance.
Playing against her brother presented not the remotest interest
either for her or for him, since the winnings of one would have
meant the losses of the other, and though from a gambling
point of view the play was insignificant, and neither of them
was in need of money, still, she could not understand the
pleasure of playing for the sake of the game alone, and was
always delighted when she won. The money she won at cards
was always kept separately in a money-box and it seemed
more precious and important to her than the big notes with
which she paid for their expensive flat and for housekeeping.

  They all met at Prokopy Vasilievitch's, for there was only
himself and his sister in their big flat (not mentioning the big
white tom-cat, who was always asleep in an armchair); and
they thus made sure of the quietness essential to their

---

[1] A game similar to auction bridge played in Russia before the latter became the
vogue.

occupation. Evpraksia Vasilievna's brother was a widower. He had lost his wife in the second year of their marriage, and spent two months in a mental nursing home after her death. Evpraksia Vasilievna herself was not married, though she had once been in love with a student. No one knew, and it seemed that she herself had forgotten, why it was that she had never married her student, but every year when the usual appeal was made on behalf of poor students she sent to the committee a carefully folded hundred-rouble note signed 'Anonymous.' In years she was the youngest of the players, being forty-three.

The eldest of the players, Maslenikov, was at first annoyed with the arrangement of the partnerships, since it meant that he always had to play with Jacov Ivanovitch – in other words, to give up his dream of a grand slam in no trumps. In every respect he and his partner were unsuited for each other. Jacov Ivanovitch was a withered little old man, silent and solemn, and even in summer he went about with coat and trousers lined with wadding. He always came at eight o'clock, not a minute earlier or later, and instantly took a small piece of chalk in his dry fingers, on one of which a large diamond ring moved about freely. The most dreadful thing about his partner, Maslenikov considered, was the fact that he never bid higher than four tricks, even when he had a good hand and the game was certain. It happened once that Jacov Ivanovitch began with the two and went on to the ace, taking every trick to the thirteenth. Maslenikov furiously threw down his cards on the table, and the little old man gathered them up quietly and scored the number of points necessary for four tricks.

'Why didn't you declare a grand slam?' cried Nikolai Dmitrievitch. (That was Maslenikov's name.)

'I never play higher than four,' the old man replied dryly, and added in explanation: 'You never know what may happen.'

And Nikolai Dmitrievitch could never convince him. He himself always played a bold game, and being unlucky in his hand, he invariably lost, but he never despaired, and kept on hoping to win the next time. By degrees they grew used to their position and ceased interfering with each other. Nikolai

Dmitrievitch ran risks; the old man quietly marked down their losses and declared four.

Thus they played summer and winter, spring and autumn. The crazy world, submissively bearing the burden of endless existence, now reddened with blood, now bathed in tears, was marking its course through space with the groans of the sick, the hungry and injured. A faint echo of this disturbing alien life was brought by Nikolai Dmitrievitch. Sometimes he came in late, when the rest were already seated at the table, the cards, like a pink fan, spread over its green surface.

Nikolai Dmitrievitch, red-cheeked, with the fresh air still about him, hastily took his seat opposite Jacov Ivanovitch, and, excusing himself, said:

'What a lot of people there are walking in the boulevards! They come and come without end. . . .'

Evpraksia Vasilievna considered it her duty as hostess to pay no heed to the peculiarities of her guests. Thus she was the only one to reply, while the little old man, silent and solemn, was preparing the chalk, and her brother was making arrangements about the tea.

'Yes, the weather must be fine. But hadn't we better begin?'

And they began. The lofty room grew still, every sound being deadened by upholstered furniture and heavy hangings. A maid moved noiselessly over the soft carpet, handing round glasses of strong tea; there was only the rustle of her starched skirt, the squeak of the chalk, the sigh of Nikolai Dmitrievitch, marking his first fine. His glass of tea was always weak and placed on a separate table, for he liked to drink it from the saucer.

In winter Nikolai Dmitrievitch would remark that in the morning there had been ten degrees of frost, which had now risen to twelve, and in the summer he would say:

'A company of people has just gone into the wood with baskets.'

Evpraksia Vasilievna would look up politely (in summer they played on the verandah), and though not a cloud was in sight and the tops of the firs shone golden, she would say:

'I wonder if it will rain?'

And the little old man, Jacov Ivanovitch, spread the cards solemnly, and taking out a two, decided that Nikolai Dmitrievitch was an incorrigibly frivolous man. Once Maslenikov greatly alarmed the rest. Every time he came he made a remark or two about Dreyfus. With an melancholy air he would say:

'The Dreyfus case is going badly.'

Or, on the other hand, he would laugh and declare that the unjust sentence would probably be revoked.

Later he took to bringing newspapers from which he read paragraphs, always about Dreyfus.

'Have you finished?' Jacov Ivanovitch asked dryly, but his partner did not hear him and went on reading the paragraphs that interested him. In this manner he one day led the rest into a dispute which nearly developed into a quarrel, for Evpraksia Vasilievna refused to acknowledge the order of legal proceedings and demanded that Dreyfus should be instantly released, while Jacov Ivanovitch and her brother maintained that it was at first necessary to go through certain formalities and then to release him. Jacov Ivanovitch was the first to recollect himself. Pointing to the table, he said:

'Isn't it time to begin?'

And they sat down to play, and no matter what Nikolai Dmitrievitch said about Dreyfus afterwards, he was met by a stolid silence.

Thus they played summer and winter, spring and autumn. Sometimes an incident of an amusing nature happened, such as that Evpraksia Vasilievna's brother forgot what his partner had said about her hand and did not take a single trick, when he had felt absolutely certain of five. Then Nikolai Dmitrievitch laughed aloud and exaggerated the importance of the loss, while the old man, smiling said:

'Had you declared four, you know, the money would have remained in your pocket.'

A tense excitement took possession of them all whenever Evpraksia Vasilievna made a high bid. She flushed red, lost her head, not knowing where to put the cards, and gazed at her silent brother entreatingly; while her opponents, with a chivalrous sympathy for her womanly helplessness, encouraged her with their condescending smiles, as they waited impatiently for the result. In general, however, they were serious and thoughtful when playing. To them the cards had long ceased to be mere lifeless matter, and every suit and every card in it had its own individuality, and lived its own particular life. There were suits they liked and suits they did not like, lucky suits and unlucky suits. The cards arranged themselves in infinite monotony, and this monotony was subject neither to analysis nor rule, and was at the same time right and proper. People desired to have their way, and did what they liked with them, while the cards did their own work as though possesed of individual will, taste, sympathy and caprice. Hearts often fell to Jacov Ivanovitch, while Evpraksia Vasilievna would constantly receive spades, though she hated spades. Sometimes the cards would be capricious and Jacov Ivanovitch did not know how to escape from spades, while Evpraksia Vasilievna, delighted with her hearts, bid high and lost. At such times the cards seemed to laugh. No particular suit ever fell to Nikolai Dmitrievitch for several times running, and his cards generally bore an air of hotel visitors who come and go and are indifferent as to the place where they shall lodge for the few days. For several evenings following sometimes he got nothing but twos and threes, coming to him with an insolent, mocking air. Nikolai Dmitrievitch was convinced that he could never bid a grand slam because the cards knew of his ambition and did not come to him out of sheer malice. And he affected a complete indifference to his declaration and tried to delay looking at his hand. But the cards were rarely deceived by his manner; they usually saw through this device, and when he opened his hand three sixes laughed out at him, and the king of spades, whom they had dragged in for company, gave him a solemn smile.

Evpraksia Vasilievna fathomed the mysterious qualities of the cards less than the rest; the old man, Jacov Ivanovitch, had long attained a severe, philosophic attitude, and was never surprised or grieved, possessing the invincible armour against fate in his rule of never playing higher than four. Only Nikolai

Dmitrievitch could never reconcile himself to the capricious character of the cards, their mockery and inconsistency. When going to bed he would imagine himself playing a grand slam in no trumps, and it seemd so simple and possible; one ace would come, then a king, then another ace. But when, full of hope, he sat down to play the following evening, the cursed sixes would be grinning at him once more. There was something fateful and malicious about it. And gradually a grand slam in no trumps became the dream and ambition of Nikolai Dmitrievitch's life.

Other events happened which had no relation to cards. Evpraksia Vasilievna's large white tom-cat died of old age, and with the landlord's permission was buried beneath a lime-tree in the garden. The Nikolai Dmitrievitch once disappeared for two whole weeks and the other three did not know what to think or what to do, since *vint* for three was contrary to their habits and considered dull. The cards, too, seemed to be conscious of it and arranged themselves in the strangest manner. When Nikolai Dmitrievitch appeared again his ruddy cheeks, so marked in contrast to his mass of grey hair, had grown pale, and altogether he seemed slighter and smaller of build. He said that his eldest son had been arrested for something and sent to St Petersburg. They were all surprised, since no one knew that Maslenikov had a son; no doubt he had told them at some time or another, but they had forgotten the fact. Not long after he disappeared for a second time, and on a Saturday too, when they played longer than on any other evening – and again they all learnt in wonder that he had long suffered from heart disease, and had had a bad attack on Saturday.

And once more they settled down, and their game became more serious and absorbing, for Nikolai Dmitrievitch now rarely created a diversion in the form of irrelevant conversation. There was only the rustle of the maid's starched skirt as the satin-backed cards slipped through their fingers, living their own mysterious, silent life, apart from the life of the people who played with them. To Nikolai Dmitrievitch they were as indifferent as ever, sometimes even malicious and mocking; there was something fatalistic about them.

On Thursday, the 26th November, an unusual change took place in the cards. The game had no sooner begun than Nikolai Dmitrievitch obtained a sequence and took not merely the five tricks he had declared, but made a small slam, as it turned out that Jacov Ivanovitch had an extra ace he had not wanted to show. Then for a time the usual sixes appeared again, but soon disappeared, giving place to full suits that came in strict order, as though each suit was eager to witness Nikolai Dmitrievitch's joy. He declared hand after hand, to the astonishment of all, even quiet little Jacov Ivanovitch. Nikolai Dmitrievitch's excitement communicated itself to the other players; the cards slipped quickly from his fat perspiring fingers with the wrinkles on the knuckles.

'You are in luck to-day,' said Evpraksia Vasilievna's brother solemnly; he had no faith in sudden good fortune; in his experience it was always followed by misfortune.

Evpraksia Vasilievna was pleased that Nikolai Dmitrievitch had good cards at last, and at her brother's words she spat three times to the side to counteract his prophecy of evil.

'Faugh! There is nothing unusual; the cards come and come, and I hope they will keep on coming.'

For a moment the cards seemed to be uncertain; a few twos appeared with a guilty air, and then again with greater rapidity came the aces, kings and queens. Nikolai Dmitrievitch had barely time to collect his cards and make his declaration; twice he made a false deal, and had to deal the cards over again. And he was lucky in every hand, though Jacov Ivanovitch maintained a stolid silence about his aces; the latter's astonishment had given place to disbelief in this rapid change of fortune, and once again he reminded his partner of his fixed rule of never playing higher than four.

Nikolai Dmitrievitch flushed and panted; he became angry with him. He no longer hesitated over his leads and bid high boldly, confident that he would draw what he wanted from the pack.

When, after solemn Prokopy Vasilievitch had dealt the

cards, Maslenikov uncovered his hand, his heart gave a bound and instantly sank. Darkness appeared before his eyes, and he swayed to and fro; his hand contained twelve tricks – clubs and hearts from the ace to the ten, and the ace and king of diamonds. If he drew the ace of spades, he would have a grand slam in no trumps.

'Two in no trumps,' he began, controlling his voice with difficulty.

'Three in spades,' replied Evpraksia Vasilievna, who was also very excited, having nearly all the spades from the king down.

'Four in hearts,' Jacov Ivanovitch said dryly.

Nikolai Dmitrievitch instantly declared a small slam, but Evpraksia Vasilievna, excited, would not give way, and though she knew quite well that it was hopeless, declared a grand slam in spades. Nikolai Dmitrievitch hesitated for a moment, and then in a somewhat triumphant tone, behind which he concealed his misgiving, pronounced slowly:

'A grand slam in no trumps!'

Nikolai Dmitrievitch was to play a grand slam in no trumps! All were amazed, and the hostess's brother even exclaimed 'Oh!'

Nikolai Dmitrievitch stretched out his hand to the pack, but he swayed and upset a candle. Evpraksia Vasilievna seized it, and Nikolai Dmitrievitch for a moment sat straight and motionless, laying his cards on the table, then he threw up his hands and slowly fell over to the left. When falling he upset a little table on which stood a saucer of tea, his body hitting against the leg.

When the doctor arrived he declared Nikolai Dmitrievitch to have died of heart failure, and to console the living he said a few words about the painlessness of such a death. The dead man was laid on a Turkish divan in the room where they had been playing and covered with a sheet; he looked gruesome and terrifying. One foot, turned inwards, remained uncovered and did not seem to belong to him, as though it were the foot of another man; on the sole of the boot, still quite black and new in the instep, a piece of chocolate paper adhered. The card-table stood as it had been left, the cards thrown down in disorder, backs downwards; only Nikolai Dmitrievitch's cards lay in a forlorn little heap as he had placed them.

Jacov Ivanovitch with short uncertain tread paced the room, trying not to look at the dead man, nor to step off the carpet on to the polished floor, where his heels made a loud intermittent clatter. Passing the table several times he stopped, and carefully taking up Nikolai Dmitrievitch's cards, he examined them, then arranging them in the same order as before he quietly put them back on the table. He then examined the pack; there was the ace of spades, the very card Nikolai Dmitrievitch had needed for his grand slam. Pacing up and down a few more times, Jacov Ivanovitch went into the next room, where he buttoned his wadding-lined coat still closer about him. He wept bitterly, for he pitied the dead man. Closing his eyes he tried to recall Nikolai Dmitrievitch's face as it had been when he was alive, laughing over his winnings. He was particularly moved when he recalled Nikolai Dmitrievitch's vanity, and his desire to play a grand slam in no trumps. All the events of the evening passed before him, beginning with the five tricks in diamonds the dead man had played and ending with the continuous flow of lucky cards which in itself foreboded evil. And now Nikolai Dmitrievitch was dead – dead, just when he could have played a grand slam.

An idea, terrifying in its simplicity, struck the emaciated little body of Jacov Ivanovitch, causing him to leap from his chair. Peering round as though the thought had not come to him of its own accord, but had been whispered by someone into his ear, he said aloud:

'But he will never know that the ace was in the pack, and that his hand contained a certain grand slam. Never! Never!'

And it seemed to Jacov Ivanovitch that he had not understood until this moment what death really meant. And now he understood, and the thing he saw plainly was senseless, awful, irrevocable. He would never know! Were Jacov Ivanovitch to cry it into his very ear and hold the cards before his very eyes, Nikolai Dmitrievitch would not hear him and would not know, because Nikolai Dmitrievitch was no more. One more movement, one more second of life and Nikolai Dmitrievitch would have seen the ace and known that he had a grand slam, but now all was over and he did not know and never would know.

'Nev-er, nev-er,' Jacov Ivanovitch said slowly to convince himself that such a word existed and had meaning.

The word existed and had meaning, but the meaning was so strange and so bitter that Jacov Ivanovitch again fell into a chair and wept helplessly. He pitied Nikolai Dmitrievitch in that he would never know, and he pitied himself and everyone, since this senseless, cruel thing would happen to him and to everyone alike. He wept – and in thought he played Nikolai Dmitrievitch's hand, taking trick after trick to the thirteenth, and thinking how much they would have scored, and that this too Nikolai Dmitrievitch would never know. This was the first and last time he had ignored his fixed rule of four, and had played a grand slam in no trumps for friendship's sake.

'Is that you, Jacov Ivanovitch?' asked Evpraksia Vasilievna, entering. She sank into a chair beside him and burst into tears. 'How awful! How awful!'

They both looked at each other and wept silently, conscious that in the next room, on the divan, was a dead man's body, cold, heavy and silent.

'Have you sent word to his people?' asked Jacov Ivanovitch, blowing his nose violently.

'Yes, my brother and Annushka have gone, but I don't know how they will find his home, for we haven't got his address.'

'Isn't he living in the same place as last year?' Jacov Ivanovitch asked absent-mindedly.

'No, he had moved. Annushka says that he used to take an *isvoschick* somewhere to the Novensky Boulevard.'

'They will find out through the police,' the little old man comforted her. 'I believe he has a wife, hasn't he?'

Evpraksia Vasilievna gazed pensively at Jacov Ivanovitch and made no reply. It seemed to him that in her eyes he saw reflected the very thought that had just come to him. Once more he blew his nose, put the handkerchief into the pocket of his wadding-lined coat and said, raising his eye-brows questioningly above his reddened eyes:

'And where shall we get a fourth now?'

But Evpraksia Vasilievna, engrossed in thoughts of a domestic nature, did not hear him. After a short pause she asked:

'Are you still living in the same place, Jacov Ivanovitch?'

The Swamp

BY A. KUPRIN

1870–1938

The summer evening was fading, the forest retiring to rest. A pregnant stillness reigned around. The tops of the great pines were still tinged with the delicate rose of the after-glow, but below it grew dark and damp. The warm, dry odour of resin became fainter, giving place to a heavy smell of smoke, wafted the livelong day from some distant forest fire. Quickly and silently the southern night descended over the earth. The birds ceased their song with the setting of the sun, only the woodpecker's sleepy, lazy call still reverberated throughout the thicket.

Jmakin, a surveyor, and Nikolai Nikolaevitch, a student, the son of Madame Serdukov, a widow with a small estate, were returning from their work. It was too far and too late to go back to Serdukova, so they resolved to spend the night in the forest with the keeper Stepan. The narrow path wound in and out among the trees, completely lost to view a step or two ahead. The surveyor, gaunt and tall, walked bent, with hanging head, in the swinging gait of a man accustomed to long walks. The plump, short-legged little student could scarcely keep up with him; his white cap had fallen to the nape of his neck, his reddish tousled hair fell over his forehead, his pince-nez sat crooked on his wet nose. His feet now slipped over the carpet of last year's leaves, now struck against the projecting roots in his path. The surveyor saw his difficulty but would not slacken his pace. He was tired, cross and hungry, and the student's difficulties gave him a certain malicious pleasure.

Jmakin had been engaged by Madame Serdukov to make a

simple plan of the sparse pieces of woodland, trampled by cattle and felled by peasants, that belonged to her. Nikolai Nikolaevitch, her son, of his own accord had offered to help him. As an assistant the young man was attentive and diligent, and by nature he was companionable – bright, easy-going, frank and kindly, though still possessed of certain childish qualities, observable in his rather naïve precipitance and enthusiasm. The surveyor was a man well known throughout the district as a drunkard and in consequence found it hard to obtain work and was badly paid when he obtained it.

During the day he managed to keep up a show of friendly intercourse with young Serdukov, but at night, tired with the long tramp and hoarse with the day's shouting, he became very irritable. And it seemed to him then that the young student's interest in the work and his gossip with the peasants at their halting-places was merely pretended, and that his mother had sent him with a secret injunction to see that the surveyor did not drink while at his work. And the fact that the student was sufficiently intelligent to have mastered all the intricacies of astrolabe surveying in a single week created a feeling of envy and jealousy in Jmakin, who had failed three times in his own examination. And Nikolai Nikolaevitch's irrepressible talkativeness irritated the old man, and so did his fresh, robust youthfulness, his tidiness, his attractive deferential politeness. But most of all was Jmakin tormented by the consciousness of his own sorry old age, his roughness, his bruised heart, his impotent, unjust malice.

The nearer it grew to the end of the day's surveying, the ruder and more querulous grew the surveyor. He gallingly exaggerated Nikolai Nikolaivitch's every mistake and inter-rupted him at every step. But the student possessed such a fund of youthfulness and inexhaustible good-nature that he seemed incapable of taking offence. He apologised for his mistakes with a touching readiness, and to Jmakin's stiff reprimands he replied with a ringing laugh that echoed long among the trees. As though failing to notice the surveyor's gloomy mood, he showered him with questions and jokes, with the jolly, clumsy, importunate good-nature in which a lively young puppy teases an old dog.

The surveyor walked silently with downcast eyes. Nikolai Nikolaevitch tried to keep by his side, but as he knocked against trees and stumbled against roots he frequently fell behind and had to catch his companion up at a run. Notwithstanding his panting condition he spoke loudly and excitedly, with animated gesticulations and unexpected exclamations, his voice reverberating throughout the sleeping wood.

'I have not lived in the country long, Egor Ivanovitch,' he said, trying to give a penetrating tone to his voice, and pressing his hands over his heart convincingly; 'and I agree, I fully agree with you in that I do not know the country, but in all I have seen until now there is so much that is touching and profound and beautiful . . . Of course,, you will say that I am young and impetuous . . . I am prepared to grant you that, but as a level-headed, practical man I want you to look at the life of the people from a philosophic point of view . . .'

The surveyor gave a contemptuous shrug of the shoulder and a wry, caustic smile, but held his peace.

'Just think, dear Egor Ivanitch, what deep historic antiquity there is in all the usages of country life. A plough, a harrow, a cottage, a cart – who invented them? No one. Acquired of the whole human race. Two thousand years ago these things were exactly the same as they are now. In the same way, too, men sowed and ploughed and built. Two thousand years ago! But when, in what devilishly distant age did this cyclopic husbandry come into being? We dare not even think of it, dear Egor Ivanitch. Here we stumble against the endless, countless centuries. We know nothing at all. How and when did man come to make the first cart? How many hundreds and thousands of years did it take to accomplish this creative work? The devil knows!' the student exclaimed suddenly at the top of his voice, pulling his cap quickly over his eyes. 'I don't know, and no one knows . . . It doesn't matter what you take – clothes, utensils, a shoe, a spade, a spinning wheel, a sieve – but generation on generation of millions of people successively racked their brains to obtain them. The people have their own medicine, their own poetry, their own worldly wisdom, their own beautiful language; but for all that, I will have you notice, not a single name has been handed down, not a single author! It may be little and poor in comparison with battleships and telescopes, but, believe me, a pitchfork moves and inspires me infinitely more!'

'Tu-ru-ru, tu-lu-lu,' Jmakin sang in a falsetto voice, with a motion of the hand as though turning a barrel-organ. 'The machine is set going. I wonder you're not tired of it! Day after day the same thing.'

'No, Egor Ivanovitch, listen,' the student went on hastily. 'No matter where a peasant turns his attention, no matter what he looks at, around him everywhere is old truth, hoary and wise. Everything is enlightened by the experience of his forefathers, all is simple, clear and practical. And what is of far more importance, there is absolutely no question of the usefulness of his labour. Take a doctor, a judge, a writer – there is much in these professions that is contestable and illusive. Take a pedagogue, a general, a civil servant, a priest . . .'

'Please don't touch upon religion,' Jmakin said solemnly.

'I didn't mean it in that sense, Egor Ivanitch,' Serdukov said with an impatient wave of the hand. 'Take a barrister, an artist, a musician, if you like. I have nothing to say against these worthy people. But each must have asked himself at least once in his life whether his profession was as essential to humanity as it appeared to be. A peasant's life is wonderfully harmonious and clear. If you sow in the spring, you are fed in the winter. If you feed your horse, he will support you in return. What could be simpler or more certain? And this same practical sage is torn from his intelligible life and thrust by the scruff of his neck into the arms of civilisation. 'By the power of article so and so, and the findings of the Court of Appeal for number so and so, the peasant Ivan Sidorov has offended against the law of private property on a field running through so and so, and is condemned,' and so on and so on. Ivan Sidorov replies quite reasonably. "Your Highness, our grandfather and great-grandfather ploughed by that willow of which there is only a stump now." But then the surveyor Egor Ivanitch Jmakin appears on the scene.'

'Please don't drag me in,' Jmakin interrupted in a huff.

'Well, let us say the surveyor Serdukov, if that will please you better. 'Line A B,' he announces, 'ending Ivan Sidorov's property according to the compass, runs south-east forty degrees thirty minutes – that is to say, Ivan Sidorov and his grandfather and great-grandfather have tilled land that did not belong to them.' And Ivan Sidorov is put into jail, quite justly according to all the articles of the penal code, but the poor man understands nothing and only sits blinking his eyes. What does he know of your compass in forty degrees when with his mother's milk he has sucked in the conviction that the land is no man's, but belongs to God?'

'Why do you fling all this at me?' Jmakin asked gloomily.

'Or take another point – Ivan Sidorov is driven into the army,' Serdukov continued enthusiastically, not hearing the surveyor's remark. "Attention! Eyes right! Dress by the right! Attention!" he is taught by the sergeant. I, too, have served my country for a couple of months, and am ready to believe that for military service all these contrivances are necessary, but for a peasant it is nothing but the sheerest nonsense. Say what you like, but you can't expect a man torn from a simple, intelligible life to take you at your word and believe that all these tricks are really necessary and have any sense and reason behind them. And of course he looks at you as a ram does at a new gate.'

'Isn't it enough for to-day, Nikolai Nikolaevitch?' the surveyor asked. 'To tell you the truth, I am tired of this talk. You want to figure as something or other, but there is no sense or logic in what you say. Is it a kind of Don Juan you want to make of yourself? Why all this talk? I really can't understand.'

Making a circuit round a bush the student caught the solemn surveyor up at a trot.

'You said this morning, if you remember, that the peasant was stupid, lazy, brutal. You expressed yourself with a certain hatred and were consequently less just than you would like to have been. But don't you understand, dear Egor Ivanovitch, that the peasant lives in a different dimension from us. With difficulty he has attained the third dimension when we already begin to think about the fourth. How can you say the peasant is stupid? You have only to listen to him talking about the weather, about his horse, the hay-making. It is wonderful. Every word is simple, significant, expressive and fitting . . . But you hear the same peasant tell you a tale about how he had been to town and gone to the theatre and what a nice time he had had in a public-house, where a barrel-organ was playing. What vulgar expressions, what ridiculously corrupted words he makes use of! It is horrible to hear him!' the student burst out, appealing to space and throwing out his arms as though the wood were full of people listening to him. 'I grant that the peasant is poor, rough, dirty, but give him time to rest. The constant strain has rent him; he is rent socially and historically. Feed him, cure him, teach him to read and write, but do not crush him with your fourth dimension. I am firmly convinced that until you enlighten the people, all your findings of the Court of Appeal, your compasses, notaries, servitudes will be dead words to him like your fourth dimension!'

Jmakin stopped suddenly and turned to the student.

'Nikolai Nikolaevitch, I must ask you to stop!' he exclaimed in a plaintive voice, like that of an old woman. 'You've talked so much that my patience has reached its limit. I can't listen any longer, and I don't want to listen! To all appearances you are a man of common sense, yet you do not understand a thing so simple. You have opportunities of airing your views at home or among your own friends. I'm not your friend. You are what you are and I am what I am, and I don't want these conversations. I have a perfect right . . .'

Nikolai Nikolaevitch looked askance at Jmakin over the top of his pince-nez. The surveyor had an unusual face – narrow, long and sharp in front, but broad and flat at a side view – a face without a front, so to speak, and a dismal, crestfallen nose. And in the clear, soft twilight the student saw reflected in his face such an expression of boredom and hatred of life that his heart was torn with pity, and with a sudden penetration he realised with a painful clearness all the pettiness, the

limitations, the senseless ill-nature that filled the poor unfortunate man's lonely soul.

'Don't be angry, Egor Ivanovitch,' he said in a conciliatory,
confused tone. 'I meant no offence. You are very irritable.'

'Irritable, irritable,' Jmakin repeated in a senselessly
malicious tone. 'Time I was irritable. I don't like these talks, I
tell you . . . And what sort of a companion can I be to you? You
are a man of culture, an aristocrat, and what am I? A grey,
shadowy being, nothing more.'

The student, disillusioned, held his peace. He always grew
sad when he came upon roughness and injustice. He lagged
behind the surveyor and walked silently, looking at his back.
And even the man's back, bent, narrow and stiff, expressed
without words his senseless, wretched life, the rude buffets
dealt him by fate, his obstinate, vicious self-conceit . . .

It grew quite dark in the wood, but the eyes, accustomed to
the gradual change from light to darkness, could distinguish
the vague fantastic forms of the trees. Not a sound nor a
movement was heard: the air was laden with the sweet smell of
grass, wafted from the distant fields.

The path inclined downwards. At a bend a damp cold, as
from a deep underground cellar, struck the student in the face.

'Tread carefully, there's a swamp here,' Jmakin said
abruptly without turning round.

Nikolai Nikolaevitch then noticed that his step was sound-
less as though he were treading on a soft carpet. To the right
and left were tangled low-growing bushes, around which,
clutching at the branches, stretching and quivering, floated
white, broken clouds of mist. A strange sound suddenly
echoed through the wood; prolonged and low and har-
moniously sad, it seemed to come out of the very earth. The
student stopped in terror.

'What is that?' he asked in a trembling voice.

'A bittern,' the surveyor replied curtly. 'Let us walk quickly,
there is a dam here.'

Nothing was now visible. To the right and left the mist hung
like a heavy white curtain. The student felt its moist, clinging
touch against his face. In front of him was a dark, moving

speck – the surveyor's back, walking ahead. The path was invisible, but on either side of it one felt the swamp, and rising from it was a strong smell of decaying water-weed and damp mushrooms. The dam was soft and springy to the feet and at every step the slime oozed out of it.

The surveyor stopped: Serdukov hit his face against his back.

'Mind, you'll slip!' Jmakin grumbled. 'You had better wait while I call the keeper. You've only to breathe and you'll go down in that cursed quagmire.'

He put his hands against his mouth and gave a prolonged cry: 'Stepa-an!'

Carried away into the soft mist, the voice sounded faint and toneless, as though saturated by the damp gases of the swamp.

'Damn! You don't know where to tread!' the surveyor grumbled, clenching his teeth viciously. 'I suppose we shall have to crawl on all-fours. Stepa-an!' he cried again in an irritable, plaintive voice.

'Stepan!' the student called in a quick, hollow bass.

They called in turn for a long time, until, some distance away, a formless patch of yellow light appeared through the mist. It did not seem to be coming towards them, but turned to the right and left.

'Is that you, Stepan?' the surveyor called.

'Gop-gop!' a muffled voice seemed to come from the distance. 'Is it Egor Ivanovitch?'

The dim patch of light grew nearer and spread, shining yellow through the mist; a huge shadow fell across the illuminated space, and a little man loomed out of the darkness with a tin lantern in his hand.

'So it is,' the keeper said, raising the lantern on high. 'And who is that with you? Not Master Serdukov?'

'Good evening, Nikolai Nikolaevitch. I suppose you will stay the night? You are quite welcome. I wondered who it might be calling, but I took my gun with me in case of need.'

The yellow light cast by the lantern made Stepan's face stand out in sharp relief against the darkness. It was completely overgrown with fair hair, curly and soft – beard, whiskers and brows. His blue little eyes only peeped out of the dense mass, and the rings of tiny wrinkles surrounding them gave his face the expression of a kindly, weary, smiling child.

'Let us go,' he said, and vanished into the mist as he turned. The large yellow patch of light cast by his lantern quivered low over the earth, lighting up a small piece of the path.

'Still shivering, Stepan?' Jmakin asked, following behind the keeper.

'Yes, Egor Ivanitch,' Stepan's voice replied from the distance. 'During the day it is not so bad, but when night comes on the shivering begins. But we've got used to it, Egor Ivanitch.'

'Is Maria any better?'

'No, I'm sorry to say not. The wife and children are all very bad. The baby is still sound, thank God, but of course he will get it, too, in time. And your little godson we took to Nikolsky last week . . . This makes the third we have buried . . . Let me light your way, Egor Ivanitch. You must go carefully here.'

The keeper's hut, as Nikolai Nikolaevitch observed, was built on stakes, leaving a space of about five feet between the floor and the ground. Some crooked steps led to the door. Stepan raised the lantern above his head to light the way, and the student, when passing him, noticed that he was shivering all over and huddling into the collar of his grey uniform.

From the open door issued the warm, putrid smell common to a peasant's dwelling, mingled with the sour odour of tanned leather coats and baked bread. The surveyor was the first to enter, stooping low beneath the lintel of the door.

'Good-evening, mistress!' he greeted Stepan's wife with a frank kindliness.

A tall, gaunt woman, standing by the open stove, turned slightly in his direction, bowed morosely and silently, without looking at him, then continued rummaging on the hearth. Stepan's hut was big and dirty; the cold and bareness made it seem like a deserted human dwelling-place. Along the whole length of the timber walls, meeting in the corner facing the door, stretched narrow tall benches, uncomfortable alike for sitting or lying on. Many blackened images hung in the corner, and to the right and left of them, pasted to the walls, were familiar popular wood-cuts, such as 'The Last Judgement,' picturing numerous green demons and white angels with sheep-like faces, 'The Parable of the Rich Man and Lazarus,' 'The Ladder of Human Life,' 'A Russian Merry-making.' In the corner opposite to it was a stove, which occupied nearly a third of the hut. Two little children's heads hung over from the top of it, with hair as white and bleached by the sun as one finds only among children brought up in the country. Against the back wall stood a broad double bed with red print bed-curtains. A little ten-year-old girl was sitting on it, her feet dangling. She was rocking a creaking cradle, and her large bright eyes gazed at the new-comers in terror.

In the corner beneath the images was a large bare table, and above it, suspended from the ceiling on a metal hook, hung a wretched lamp with a grimy chimney. The student sat down by the table, and instantly a feeling of great depression came over him; he seemed to have been sitting in that spot for many, many hours in forced idleness. The smell of paraffin from the lamp aroused in his mind some vague bygone sensation. Was it a dream or a recollection? When and where had it come to him? He seemed to be sitting in a bare, arched, echoing room that looked like a corridor; there was a strong smell of paraffin from a lamp, and from the wall, drop by drop, the water trickled noisily on to the iron hearth-plate; and Serdukov's soul was filled with a feeling of intense depression.

'Will you get the samovar ready for us, Stepan, and beat up an egg?' Jmakin asked.

'In a moment, Egor Ivanitch, in a moment,' Stepan replied hastily.

'Maria,' he turned to his wife in uncertainty, 'won't you get the samovar ready? The gentlemen would like some tea.'

'All right, I heard what they said,' Maria replied crossly.

She went out into the passage. The surveyor crossed himself before the image and sat down by the table. Stepan sat down at some distance from them on the very edge of the bench near the door, where stood a bucket of water.

'And I kept on wondering who it could be calling,' he began

good-naturedly ' "Can it be our forester?" I thought. "But what would he be wanting at night? He couldn't find his way here." He's a strange gentleman, to be sure. He expects us all to behave like soldiers. It gives him great pleasure. You go out with your gun and report, "Your Highness, in my round everything was as it should be at the Chernatinsky house in the wood . . ." For all that he is just a man. The fact that he ruins the girls, of course, is no business of ours . . .'

He ceased. Maria was heard noisily throwing the charcoal into the samovar in the passage, and the children on the stove breathed heavily. The cradle continued its monotonous plaintive creak. Serdukov gazed more attentively at the face of the little girl on the bed, and was struck by its feverish beauty and the rarity of its expression. Notwithstanding the slight swelling of the cheeks, the features were soft and delicate, like a drawing on a piece of fine transparent china; the beautiful large eyes stood out unnaturally bright, gazing with a dreamy naïve wonder, like the eyes of the women in pre-Raphaelite pictures.

'What is your name, my beauty?' the student asked kindly.

The child covered her face with her hands and hid quickly behind the curtains.

'She is shy,' Stepan exclaimed. 'What are you afraid of, you silly little thing?' He gave an awkward, good-natured smile, that caused the whole of his face to disappear into his beard, making it look like a hedgehog. 'Her name is Varia. Don't be frightened, you foolish child; the gentleman will not hurt you,' he added, trying to comfort the child.

'Is she sick, too?' Nikolai Nikolaevitch asked.

'What?' Stepan queried. The bushy hair on his face parted, and once more his kindly, weary eyes gazed out. 'Did you ask if she was sick? We are all of us sick. The wife and the children there on the stove – all of us. We buried the third on Tuesday. The place is damp, you know; that is the main cause. We shiver and shiver and the end comes in time.'

'Why don't you take something for it?' the student asked with a shake of the head. 'Come round to our place and I will give you some quinine.'

'Thank you, Nikolai Nikolaevitch, may God reward you. We've tried to take things many times, but nothing ever comes of it.' Stepan threw out his arms hopelessly. 'We have buried three of them . . . It is damp here from the swamp, and the air is heavy and stagnant.'

'Why don't you move to some other place?'

'What? To another place, did you say?' Again Stepan repeated the question. It seemed to cost him an effort to fix his attention on what was being said to him; he had to shake off his drowsiness at every word. 'Of course it would be better to move, sir; but still, someone must live here. The house is a big one, and they can't do without a keeper here. If not we, then others must live here. Before I came the keeper Galaktion lived here; a sober man he was, and independent . . . First he buried his two children, then his wife, and then he died himself. It doesn't seem to matter where you live. Our Father in Heaven is wise; He knows best where we should live and what we should do.'

Maria came in with the samovar, opening and shutting the door with her elbow.

'A nice thing, indeed, to sit yourself down like that!' she flew at Stepan. 'You might have got the cups ready at least!'

She dumped the samovar on the table furiously. Her face, prematurely old, was haggard and grey; on her cheeks, beneath the network of tiny wrinkles, were two spots of flaming red; the eyes glistened unnaturally. With an equally angry gesture she threw the cups, saucers and bread on the table.

Serdukov would not take any tea. He was confused, perplexed and overwhelmed by all that he had seen and heard that day. The surveyor's senseless, ill-natured malice, Stepan's gentle humility before a remorseless, mysterious fate, his wife's silent anger, the sight of the children dying one by one from the swamp fever – all combined an overwhelming depression; the poignant, helpless kind we experience when looking into the intelligent eyes of a sick dog or the sad eyes of an idiot, or when we hear or read about the sufferings, oppressions and betrayals suffered by innocent men and women.

The surveyor drank cup after cup of tea, greedily eating the bread, which he bit off from a huge chunk in large mouthfuls; and while he ate, the sinews moved on his cheek-bones like a mass of strings; his eyes, dull and indifferent, stared straight before him, like the eyes of an animal. After long persuasion Stepan out of the whole family agreed to take a cup of tea. He drank it long and noisily, blowing at the saucer and taking nibbles at his piece of sugar. When he had finished, he crossed himself, turned the cup upside down, and carefully put back the remaining piece of sugar into a fly-blown tin.

The time dragged slowly and painfully. Serdukov wondered how many more long dull evenings would be seen in that hut, forlorn as a lonely little island in a sea of damp, poisonous mist. The dying samovar suddenly began to hum a thin, plaintive tune, an echo of the general hopelessness and despair. The cradle ceased its creaking, only now and again at regular intervals a cricket sang its monotonous, soporific song. The little girl on the bed dropped her hands between her knees and sat staring at the lamplight pensively, as one entranced. Her big, unearthly-looking eyes opened still wider; the head leant over to one side in passive, unconscious grace. What was she thinking of, what did she feel, looking thus intently at the light? Now and again her thin little arms stretched out in weary lassitude, and at these moments her eyes lighted up with a strange, inexpressible smile, subtle, gentle and expectant, as though the stillness and darkness of the night held a sweet promise for her, unknown to the rest. And a disturbing, almost superstitious thought entered the student's brain; the family seemed to him to be in the clutch of the mysterious power of disease. Looking at the child's unnaturally bright eyes, he wondered whether ordinary everyday life existed for her. Slowly and indifferently the day would arrive with its usual cares, disturbing noises and bustle and tiresome light; the evening would come, and fixing her eyes on the lamp-light she would sit waiting in weary impatience for the night, when the spirit of incurable disease, enervating the feeble little body, would take possession of her little brain, and wrap it in wild, sweet and painful dreams . . .

Somewhere, long ago, Serdukov had seen a picture by a well-known artist entitled 'Malaria.' On the edge of a swamp, by the water, covered with water-lilies, lay a little girl, tossing wildly in her sleep. And from out of the swamp, the folds of her garments disappearing into the mist, rose the thin, ghost-like figure of a woman with big wild eyes, who was drawing slowly, slowly nearer to the child. Serdukov suddenly recalled this forgotten picture, and was seized by a sudden mystic terror, as though a cold brush had been passed down his back.

'In America they sit and sit, then go to bed,' the surveyor remarked, rising from his chair. 'Will you get our beds ready, Maria?'

Everyone stood up. The little girl clutched her head in her hands and stretched out on the bed. She half closed her eyes, and a glad, dreamy smile played about her mouth. Yawning and stretching herself, Maria went out and bought in two armfuls of hay. The cross expression had left her face, her eyes were softer; a curious expression of weary impatient expectancy was reflectd in them.

While she was pulling out the benches and arranging the hay, Nikolai Nikolaevitch went on to the doorstep. Around him nothing was visible except the dense, grey, damp mist, and the steps on which he was standing seemed to be floating in it like a boat in the sea. When he went indoors again his face, hair and clothes were wet and cold, saturated by the penetrating mist of the swamp.

The student and surveyor lay down on the bench, heads beneath the ikons and legs stretched out. Stepan fixed up a bed on the floor by the stove. He put out the lamp and for a long time was heard whispering a prayer; then he lay down. Maria walked up to the bed, treading noiselessly with bare feet. The hut grew still; only the cricket sang its monotonous, soporific song, and the flies beat against the window-pains, humming persistently in endless, wearisome complaint.

Despite his exhaustion Serdukov could not sleep. He lay on his back with wide-open eyes listening to cautious sounds that assume such strange proportions on dark sleepless nights. The surveyor dropped off instantly, breathing through his open mouth, his breath seeming to break through a thin membrane in his throat with a gurgling sound. The little girl in bed with her mother muttered some indistinct words; the children on the stove breathed quickly and heavily, as though trying to blow away the burning, feverish heat from their lips. Stepan moaned quietly with each breath.

'Mamma, some water!' a sleepy child's voice asked fractiously. Maria obediently jumped out of bed and pattered barefooted across the room to the bucket. The student heard the water trickle into the iron jug, and heard the child drink it greedily in large gulps, stopping now and then to take breath. Again all was still. Monotonously the gurgling sound issued from the surveyor's throat, and the children's breaths came quick and sharp like puffing little steam-engines. The eldest girl awoke and sat up in bed; she tried to say something, but her lips could not frame the words; her teeth were chattering violently. 'C-c-old,' she managed to pronounce at last. Sighing and whispering tender words, Maria wrapped a coat around the child, but for a long time the student heard her teeth chattering in the darkness. In vain did Serdukov employ all the familiar methods of sending himself to sleep. He counted to a hundred and more, repeated all the poems he knew by heart and the *jus* from the *Pandects*; he tried to visualise a bright spot, and the undulating surface of the sea, but it was all to no purpose. Around him sick feverish breasts breathed heavily, and in the close, stuffy darkness he seemed to feel the mysterious invisible presence of the evil bloodthirsty spirit that had settled in the keeper's hut.

The baby by the bed began to cry. The mother touched the cradle, and battling with her sleep she began an old plaintive lullaby, to the accompaniment of the creaking cords:

> 'Ah-ah-ah-a!
> Good people all are sleeping,
> And animals too . . .'

Drawn out and depressing the half-tones of the sad, soporific song sounded in the darkness, and something of the dim, distant ages was heard in its rude naïve melody. Just in such a way must the cave-men have sung at the dawn of human life, far back beyond the ken of history. Weighed down by the terrors of the night and their hopelessness they must have sat by their caves on the seashore around the first fire, gazing into the mysterious flames, their arms round their gaunt knees, rocking to and fro in measure to the sad, doleful melody.

The student started from an unexpected knock at the window above his head. Stepan got up from the floor. For a long time, as though regretting his lost sleep, he stood on the same spot moving his lips and scratching his breast and head. Then pulling himself together, he went up to the window, flattened his face against the pane, and called into the darkness, 'Who is there?'

A muffled sound came from the other side of the window.

'In Kislinska?' Stepan asked the invisible person. 'Yes, I hear. All right, you can go, God be with you. I'll come at once.'

'What is the matter, Stepan?' the student asked anxiously.

Stepan fumbled by the stove seeking the matches.

'Oh, dear . . . I've got to go; I must,' he said regretfully. 'There's nothing to be done. A fire has broken out in the Kislinsky house, and the forester has ordered all the keepers to be called. . . . The agent has just been here.'

With sighs, yawns and groans Stepan lighted the lamp and dressed. When he went out into the passage Maria slipped lightly from the bed and went to shut the door after him. A cold draught, like some putrid, poisonous breath, rushed into the warm room.

'Take a lantern with you,' Maria was heard to say behind the door.

'What is the use? You lose your way still more with a lantern,' Stepan replied in a calm hollow voice that seemed to come from beneath the floor.

With chin resting on the sill Serdukov glued his face to the window. Without was the dark night and the grey mist. A cold keen draught streamed through the cracks in the window-frame. The quick, hurried footsteps of Stepan were audible beneath the window, but the man himself was no longer seen, swallowed up in the mist and the night. Without question, without complaint, racked by fever, he had risen in the dead of night and gone out into the damp mist, into the awful, mysterious stillness. There was something incomprehensible about it to the student. He recalled the path he had trodden last evening – the white curtains of mist on either side of the dam, the soft, squashy soil beneath his feet, the low, prolonged cry of the bittern – and, like a child, a sensation of fear came over him. What strange, incredible creatures came to life in the night in the big dense bottomless bog? What hideous snaky things squirmed and wriggled among the reeds and the gnarled branches of the willows? And alone, gently submissive to his fate, without a touch of fear in his heart, Stepan was now wending his way across the swamp, shivering from the cold and damp and the fever that racked him – the same fever that had carried three of his children to their graves and would probably take away the rest. And this simple-hearted man with the hedgehog beard and kindly, weary eyes was an incomprehensible mystery to Serdukov.

The student fell into a light sleep. Pale, shadowy forms and faces passed before him. 'This is only a dream; these are only apparitions,' he said to himself, knowing that he was asleep. In sad, dim visions again he lived through the impressions of the day – the surveying in the fragrant pinewood beneath the baking sun, the narrow path, the mist on either side of the dam, Stepan's hut, Stepan himself and his wife and children. And Serdukov dreamt, too, that passionately, with a pain in his heart, he said to the surveyor: 'To what end is this life?' the hot tears standing in his eyes. 'What good does this pitiful human vegetation do to anyone? What sense is there in the sickness and death of poor innocent children whose blood is being drained by the vampire of the swamp? What account, what justification can fate give of their sufferings? But the surveyor puckered his brows in anger and turned away his face. He had long grown weary of philosophic speculations. And Stepan stood by with a kindly, condescending smile. He shook his head gently in seeming pity for the headstrong youth who could not realise that human life was abjectly poor and contrary and that it mattered not where one died – on the battle-field, in foreign lands, in one's bed at home or of the swamp fever.

And when he awoke it seemed to Serdukov that he had not been asleep at all, only thinking intently and disconnectedly of these things. Outside the dawn was breaking. The mist still hung thick and heavy as at night, but it had turned from grey to snow-white and trembled in places like a heavy curtain about to rise.

A wild, passionate desire suddenly came upon Serdukov to see the sun and to breathe the fresh, pure air of a summer's morn. He dressed quickly and went out. A dense wave of damp mist beat against his mouth, causing him to cough. Bending low to distinguish the path, Serdukov ran quickly across the dam and began to ascend. The mist settled on his face, saturating his mustachios and eyelashes; he felt it on his lips, but with each step breathing grew less difficult. At last, as though climbing out of a deep, damp abyss, he reached the top of a sandy hill. His breath stopped in a wave of unutterable joy. The mist lay an endless shimmering white plain at his feet, but above him was the blue sky, and the fragrant green boughs whispered to each other and the sun's golden rays rejoiced in triumph and victory.

In The Steppes

BY MAXIM GORKY

1868–1932

We had left Perekop in the worst of moods, hungry as wolves and hating the whole world. For twelve whole hours we had vainly employed all our efforts and ingenuity to steal or to earn something, and when we were at last convinced that neither the one nor the other was possible, we decided to go on farther. Where? Just farther.

The decision was unanimous and communicated one to the other, but we were ready, too, in every respect, to travel farther along that path of life we had long followed; this decision was arrived at silently; it was not voiced by any of us, but was visibly reflected in the angry beam of our hungry eyes.

There were three of us. We had known one another for some time, having stumbled across each other in a public-house in Kherson on the banks of the Dniepr. One of us had been a soldier in a railway battalion and then a workman in one of the railways on the Vistula in Poland; he was a red-haired, sinewy man; he could speak German and possessed a detailed knowledge of prison life.

Men of our kind do not like to talk of their past, having always some more or less valid reason for not doing so, hence we believed what each said as a matter of course; that is, we believed outwardly – inwardly each had but a poor belief in himself.

When our comrade, a dry little man with thin sceptically compressed lips, informed us that he had been a student in the Moscow University, the soldier and I took it for granted that he had. At bottom, it was all the same to us whether he had been a student, a thief or a police-spy; the only thing that mattered was that when we met him he was our equal, in that he was hungry, enjoyed the special attention of the police, was suspiciously treated by the peasants in the villages, and hated the one and the other with the impotent hatred of a hunted, hungry animal, and dreamed of universal vengeance against everyone – in a word, his position among the kings of nature and the lords of life, and his mood, made him a bird of our feather.

Misfortune is the best of cement for making the most opposite of characters stick together, and we all felt that we had a right to regard ourselves as unfortunate.

The third was myself. In my innate modesty, which I have evinced since my earliest days, I will say nothing about my virtues; and having no desire to appear naïve, I will likewise be silent about my vices. Suffice it for a clue to my character to say that I have always regarded myself as better than others and continue to do so to-day.

Thus, we had left Perekop and went on farther. Our aim for that day was to strike one of the shepherds in the steppe; one could always beg a piece of bread from a shepherd; shepherds rarely refused to give to passing tramps.

I was walking beside the soldier, the 'student' followed in the rear. On his shoulders hung something that had once resembled a jacket; on his head, which was sharp-pointed, angular and closely-cropped, rested the remains of a broad-brimmed hat; grey trousers with variegated patches encased his thin legs; tied to his feet with some string made out of the lining of his suit were the soles of some boots he had picked up on the road, which implements he called sandals. He walked in silence, raising much dust, his small green eyes shining brightly. The soldier wore a red fustian shirt, which, to use his own expression, he had 'acquired with his own hands' in Kherson; over the shirt he wore a warm padded waistcoat; a military cap of an indefinite hue was 'tilted over the right brow,' according to army instruction; wide, rough trousers flapped about his legs; his feet were bare.

I, too, was barefoot.

We walked on. Around us on all sides with a magnificent

gesture stretched the steppe; canopied with the sultry blue dome of a cloudless summer sky, it lay round and black like a great dish. The grey dusty road cut across it in a broad line and burned out feet. Here and there were stubble tracts of cut corn, which bore a strange resemblance to the unshaven cheeks of the soldier.

The latter was singing as we walked, in a hoarse bass voice, 'And Thy holy sabbath we praise and glorify . . .'

When he was in the army he used to fulfil an office in the battalion church in the nature of chanter, and consequently he had an abundant knowledge of hymns and church music, a knowledge which he misused every time our conversation lagged.

Against the horizon in front of us forms of gentle line towered up, soft of hue, blending from purple to pale pink. 'Those must be the Crimean mountains,' said the 'student' hoarsely.

'Mountains?' exclaimed the soldier. 'Too soon to be seeing them, my friend! That's a cloud . . . Simply a cloud. And what a cloud! Like cranberry-jelly and milk.'

I observed that it would be agreeable if the cloud were really of jelly, which instantly aroused our hunger, the scourge of our days.

'Hell!' cursed the soldier, as he spat. 'Not a living soul to be met. No one . . . There's nothing to do but suck your paws like the bears in winter.'

'I told you that we ought to have made for the inhabited parts,' said the 'student,' with a desire to improve the occasion.

'You told us!' the soldier rejoined. 'It's your place to tell us, as you're educated. But where are the inhabited parts? The devil knows!'

The student said nothing, but compressed his lips. The sun sank and the clouds on the horizon danced in a myriad of indescribable hues. There was a smell of earth and of salt, and this dry and savoury smell made our appetites the keener. The pain gnawed at our stomachs, a strange, unpleasant sensation; the sap seemed to be oozing slowly from all the muscles of the body; they were drying up and losing their living suppleness. A parched, stinging sensation filled the cavity of the mouth and the throat, the brain was muddled and small dark objects danced before the eyes; sometimes these took the form of steaming chunks of meat, or of hunks of milk-bread; memory supplied these 'ghosts of the past, dumb ghosts,' with their natural odours, and then it seemed as if a knife were veritably turned in the stomach.

Still, we walked on, discussing our sensations and keeping a sharp look out on all sides for signs of sheep, or listening for the loud squeaking of a Tartar cart carrying fruit to the Armenian market.

But the steppe was solitary and silent.

On the eve of this hard day the three of us had eaten four pounds of rye bread and five melons, and had walked some forty versts – expenditure not commensurate with income – and having fallen asleep in the market-place of Perekop we had been awakened by our hunger.

The 'student,' in justice be it said, had advised us not to go to sleep, but to work during the night . . . As projects for the outrage of private property are not mentioned in polite society. I will say no more about it. My desire was to be just, it is against my interest to be vulgar. I know that in our highly civilised days people are becoming more and more tender-hearted, and that when one seizes a neighbour by the throat with the object of strangling him, it is done with every possible kindness and the decorum appropriate to the occasion. The experience of my own throat has made me notice this progress in morality, so that I am able with a pleasant feeling of confidence to assert that everything in this world is developing and progressing. The progress may particularly be seen in the annual increase in the number of prisons, public-houses, and brothels . . .

And so, swallowing our hungry saliva, and endeavouring by friendly conversation to still the pain in our stomachs, we walked across the deserted and silent steppe, walked towards the red glow of the sunset, filled with a vague kind of hope. In front of us the sun was sinking gently into the soft clouds, profusely painted with its rays, and behind us, on either side, the blue darkness which rose from the steppe to the sky narrowed the unfriendly horizon around us.

'Collect some stuff for a fire, brothers,' said the soldier, picking up a piece of wood. 'We've got to spend the night in the steppe, and there's a dew on. Anything will do, dried dung, twigs.'

We separated to both sides of the road, and commenced to collect dry grass and any combustible material. Every time it became necesary to bend to the ground, the whole body was filled with a desire to fall on it, to lie still and to eat it, black and rich, to eat and eat, until one could eat no more, and then to sleep. What mattered it if it meant to sleep for ever, so long as one could eat and feel the warm, thick mess slowly descending from the mouth down the parched gullet to the hungry, gnawing stomach, hot with desire for something to digest.

'If only we could find a root or something,' the soldier sighed. 'There are roots you can eat . . .'

But the black ploughed earth contained no roots. The southern night descended swiftly; the last rays of the sun were barely extinguished when the stars were shining in the dark blue sky and the shadows around us merged closer and closer together, shutting out the infinite flatness of the steppe.

'Brother,' the 'student' whispered, 'there's a man lying to the left of us.'

'A man?' the soldier asked doubtfully. 'Why should he be lying there?'

'Go and ask. He's probably got some bread if he can spread himself out in the steppe,' the 'student' ventured. The soldier looked in the direction indicated and, spitting resolutely, said, 'Let us go to him.'

Only the sharp green eyes of the 'student' could have seen a man in the black heap some fifty sajens to the left of the road. We walked towards him, stepping quickly over the clods of ploughed earth, our newly awakened hope for food quickening the pangs of our hunger. We were quite close to him, but the man did not move.

'Perhaps it isn't a man.' 'The soldier gloomily expressed the thought of all.

But our doubt was scattered that very instant. The heap on the ground suddenly moved, rose up, and we could see that it was a real, living man, kneeling, his hand outstretched towards us.

'Stop, or I'll shoot!' he said in hoarse, trembling voice.

A sharp click rent the turgid air.

We stopped as at a word of command, and for some seconds we were silent, overcome by the pleasant greeting.

'Well, I never! The villain!' the soldier muttered expressively.

'Um! Travelling with a revolver,' the 'student' said thoughtfully, 'must be a fish rich in caviare.'

'Hi!' shouted the soldier; he had evidently decided on some course.

The man did not change his posture, and did not speak.

'Hi, you! We won't harm you . . . Give us some bread . . . We are starving. Give us bread, brother, for Christ's sake! Be damned to you!'

The last words were uttered under his breath.

The man was silent.

'Can't you hear?' the soldier asked, trembling with rage and despair. 'Give us some bread. We won't come near you. Throw it to us.'

'All right,' said the man abruptly.

Had he said 'my dear brothers,' and put into those words the most sacred and purest of feeling, they would not have roused us more or made us more human than that hoarsely spoken and abrupt 'All right.'

'Don't be afraid of us, good man,' said the soldier kindly, with an ingratiating smile on his lips, though the man could not see the smile, being at a distance from us of at least twenty paces.

'We are peaceful folk. We are on our way from Russia to Kuban. We've lost our money and eaten everything we've got. It's two days since we've had a meal.'

'Wait,' said the man, flourishing his arm in the air. A black lump flew out and dropped near us on the ploughed earth. The 'student,' fell upon it.

'Wait, here's more and more. That's all. I haven't any more.'

When the 'student' had collected these original gifts, they were found to consist of about four pounds of stale black bread, covered with earth. The latter circumstance did not trouble us in the least, the former pleased us greatly, for stale bread is much more satisfying than new, containing less moisture. 'There . . . and there . . . and there,' the soldier gave us each our portions. 'They are not equal. I must take a pinch more of yours, scholar, or there won't be enough for him.'

The 'student' obediently submitted to the loss of a fraction of an ounce of bread. I took the morsel and put it into my mouth, and commenced to chew it. I chewed it slowly, scarcely able to restrain the convulsive movement of my jaws, which were ready to chew stone. I had a keen sense of pleasure to feel the spasm in my gullet and satisfy it gradually, bit by bit. Warm, inexpressibly and indescribably sweet the bread penetrated mouthful by mouthful into the burning stomach and seemed instantly to be turned to blood and brain. Joy, a strange, peaceful, vivifying joy glowed in the heart in the measure in which the stomach was filled; the general condition was one of somnolence. I forgot the chronic hunger of these cursed days, I forgot my comrades, who were immersed in the enjoyment of sensations similar to my own. But when I threw the last crumbs into my mouth with the palm of my hand, I began to feel a deadly hunger.

'The devil's probably got some more, and I dare say he's got some meat, too,' mumbled the soldier, sitting on the ground and rubbing his stomach.

'To be sure he has. The bread smelt of meat. I'm certain he's got more bread,' the 'student' added under his breath. 'If it weren't for that revolver . . .'

'Who is he, eh?'

'Our brother Isaac, evidently.'

'The dog!' the soldier concluded.

We were sitting close together, looking askance in the direction where our benefactor sat with the revolver. No sound of life escaped him.

The night gathered its dark forces around us. A dead silence reigned in the steppe; we could hear each others' breathing. Now and again came the melancholy cry of a marmot. The stars, the living flowers of heaven, were shining above us. . . . We were hungry.

I will say with pride that I was no better and no worse than my casual comrades of that rather strange night. I suggested that we should go over to the man. We need do him no harm, but we could eat up all his food. If he shoots, let him. Out of the three only one of us might possibly be hit, and that was very unlikely, and if any one were hit the wound might not be fatal.

'Come,' said the soldier, jumping to his feet.

And we went, almost at a run, the 'student' keeping behind us.

'Comrade!' the soldier called reproachfully.

A hoarse mumbling met us, the click of a catch, a flash, and a sharp report rang out.

'Missed!' the soldier exclaimed joyously, reaching the man at a bound. 'Now, you devil, now you'll get it.'

The 'student' threw himself on the man's wallet. The 'devil' rolled over on his back and began to moan, shielding himself with his hands.

What the devil!' exclaimed the soldier in his bewilderment. He had already raised his foot to kick the man. 'He must have hit himself. Hi! you! Have you shot yourself?'

'Here's meat, pasties, and bread, lots of it, brothers,' said the 'student' exultantly.

'Oh, die and be damned . . . Come and eat, friends!' the soldier cried.

I took the revolver from the man's hand. He had ceased to moan, and was lying quite still. The chamber contained one more bullet.

Again we were eating, eating in silence. The man, too, lay silent, without so much as moving a limb. We paid not the slightest heed to him.

'Have you really done this all for the bread, brothers?' a trembling, hoarse voice asked suddenly.

We all started. The 'student' even choked and coughed, bending down to the ground.

The soldier cursed as he chewed a mouthful of food.

'You soul of a dog, may you burst like a rotten log! Did you think we wanted to skin you? What good would your skin be to us? You damned silly mug! Arms himself and shoots at people, the devil!'

As he was eating during all this, the invective was robbed of its force.

'Wait till we've done eating, we'll settle with you!' the 'student' said threateningly.

At this the stillness of the night was broken by a wailing and sobbing that frightened us.

'Brothers . . . how was I to know? I fired because I was frightened. I'm on my way from New Athens . . . to the Smolensky province. . . . Oh, Lord! The fever's got hold of me . . . It comes on when the sun sets. Miserable wretch that I am . . . It was because of the fever that I left Athens . . . I did carpentering there . . . I am a carpenter by trade . . . I've got a wife at home and two little girls. I haven't seen them for four years . . . Brothers . . . eat everything.'

'We'll do that without your asking,' the 'student' said.

'Oh, God, had I only known that you were kind-hearted, quiet folk . . . You don't think I'd have fired? But what would you have, brothers, in the steppe at night . . . Am I to blame?'

He was crying as he spoke, or more correctly, emitting a trembling, frightened, wailing sound.

'There he goes whining now,' the soldier said contemptuously.

'He's probably got some money on him,' suggested the 'student.'

The soldier half closed his eyes, looked at him, and laughed.

'You're a good one at guessing . . . Come, let us light a fire and go to sleep.'

'And what about him?' the 'student' inquired.

'Let him go to the devil. You don't want to roast him, eh?'

'He deserves it.' The 'student' shook his sharp-pointed head.

We went to fetch the materials we had collected, which we had dropped when the carpenter had stopped us by his menacing cry. We brought them over, and were soon sitting by a fire. It burned gently in the still night, lighting up the small space in which we sat. We felt sleepy, but could have supped all over again.

'Brothers!' called the the carpenter. He was lying about three paces from us, and now and then it seemed to me that I could hear him whispering.

'Well?' asked the soldier.

'Can I come to you . . . to the fire? I am dying . . . My bones are all aching . . . Oh, God, I shall never get home.'

'Crawl over here,' the 'student' said.

Slowly, as though fearing to lose a hand or a leg, the carpenter moved over the ground to the fire. He was a tall man, terribly emaciated. His clothing hung about him with a horrible looseness, and his large, troubled eyes reflected the pain that he suffered. His distorted face was haggard, and, even by the light of the fire, the colour of it was yellowish, earthy, and dead. He was trembling all over; we felt a scornful pity for him. Stretching out his long, thin arms to the fire, he rubbed his bony fingers, the joints bending slowly and feebly. When all is said and done he was a disgusting sight to look at.

'Why do you travel in this condition and on foot? Mean, eh?' the soldier asked sullenly.

'They advised me not to go . . . they said . . . by the water . . . but to come through Crimea . . . because of the air . . . they said. . . . And now, brothers . . . I can't go on . . . I'm dying! I shall die alone in the steppe . . . The birds will peck at me and no one will recognise me . . . My wife . . . my little girls, are expecting me . . . I wrote to them . . . And my bones will be washed by the rains of the steppe . . . Lord, Lord!'

He howled like a wounded wolf.

'Oh, hell!' exclaimed the soldier, enraged, and jumping to his feet. 'Stop your whining! Leave us in peace! Dying are you? Well, get on with it, and don't make so much row about it! You won't be missed.'

'Give him a knock on the head,' the 'student' suggested.

'Let us go to sleep,' I said. 'And as for you, if you want to stop by the fire, you mustn't whine.'

'Do you hear?' the soldier said angrily. 'Mind you do what he says. You think we're going to pity you and nurse you because you threw us a piece of bread and fired at us! To hell with you! Others would . . . Phu!'

The soldier ceased, and stretched himself out on the ground. The 'student' was already lying down. I, too, lay down. The terrified carpenter, shrinking into a heap, moved over to the fire and stared into it silently. I was lying to the right of him and could hear the chattering of his teeth. The 'student' was lying to the left, curled up and apparently asleep. The soldier was lying face upwards, his hands under his head, looking up at the sky.

'What a night, to be sure! What a lot of stars! It looks like heat.' After a time he turned to me. 'What a sky! Looks more like a blanket than a sky. I do like this wandering life, friend. . . . It may be a cold and hungry life, but it's free . . . No one to lord it over you . . . You are your own master . . . If you want to bite your own head off, no one can say you nay . . . How good! The hunger of these days made me vicious . . . but here I am now, looking up at the sky . . . The stars are winking at me. They seem to say, 'Never mind, Lakatin, go over the earth, learn, but don't give in to anyone.' . . . Ha! . . . How comfortable the heart feels! And how are you, carpenter? You mustn't be angry with me, and there's no need to fear anything. . . . If we have eaten up your bread, what does it matter? You had bread and we hadn't, so we ate yours . . . And you go and shoot bullets at us like a savage. You made me very angry, and if you hadn't fallen down, I'd have given it to you for your impudence. And as for the bread, you'll be getting to Perekop tomorrow, you can buy some there . . . You've got money, I know . . . How long have you had the fever?'

For a long time I could hear the droning of the soldier's deep voice and the trembling voice of the carpenter. The dark, almost black night descended lower and lower over the earth; the chest was filled with fragrant, juicy air. The fire emitted an even light and a vivifying warmth. The eyes closed, and through the drowsiness a soothing, purifying influence was borne.

'Get up! Quick! Let us go!'

With a feeling of apprehension I jumped to my feet, assisted by the soldier, who was tugging me up from the ground by my sleeve.

'Come, quick march!'

His face was grave and troubled. I looked about me. The sun was rising and its rosy rays fell on the still, blue face of the carpenter. His mouth was open; the eyes were bulging out of their sockets and stared with a glassy stare, expressive of horror. The clothing at his chest was torn; his posture was unnatural and convulsed.

'Seen enough? Come on, I say.' The soldier tugged at my arm.

'Is he dead?' I asked, shuddering with the keenness of the morning air.

'I should say so. If I were to strangle you, you'd be dead, wouldn't you?' the soldier explained.

'Did . . . the "student"?' I cried.

'Who else? You, perhaps? Or I? There's a scholar for you . . . Did him in nicely and left his comrades in the lurch. If I'd only known this yesterday, I'd have killed that "student" myself. I'd have killed him with a blow. One punch on the temple and one blackguard less in the world. Do you realise what he's done? We must be gone from here so that not a human eye sees us in the steppe. Understand? They'll discover the carpenter today, strangled and robbed. They'll be on the look-out for the like of us. They'll ask where we've come from . . . where we've slept. And they'll catch us . . . But here's that revolver of his in my bosom! What a kettle of fish!'

'Throw it away,' I cautioned him.

'Why?' he asked thoughtfully. 'It's a thing of value . . . They mightn't catch us, after all. . . . No, I shan't throw it away. It's worth three roubles. And it's got another bullet in it. I wonder how much money he robbed him of, the dirty devil!'

'So much for the carpenter's little daughters,' I said.

'Daughters? What daughters? Oh, his ... Well, they'll grow up, and as it isn't us they'll marry, we needn't bother about them ... Come on, brother, quick ... Where shall we go?'

'I don't know. It makes no difference.'

'And I don't know, and I know that it makes no difference. Let's go to the right. The sea must be there.'

I turned back. A long way from us in the steppe a black hill towered up, and above it the sun was shining.

'Looking to see if he's come to life? Don't you fear, they won't catch us. A clever chap that scholar of ours was. Managed the thing well. A nice comrade, to be sure ... Left us well in the soup. Eh, brother, folk are getting more vicious. Year after year they get more and more vicious.' The soldier spoke sadly.

The steppe, silent and solitary and bathed in the bright morning sunshine, unfolded before us, merging at the horizon with the sky. It was light with a gentle, kindly light; all dark and unjust deeds seemed impossible in that great expanse of uninterrupted plain with a blue dome for a sky.

'I'm hungry, brother,' observed my comrade, rolling a cigarette from cheap tobacco.

'What shall we eat and where?'

'It's a problem.'

With this the teller of the story, a man lying in the bed next to mine in a hospital, concluded, saying, 'That is all. The soldier and I became great friends. We walked together as far as the Kara region. He was a kindly fellow, experienced, and a typical tramp. I had a great respect for him. We were together as far as Asia Minor and then we lost sight of each other ...'

'Do you ever remember the carpenter?' I asked.

'As you have seen, or rather, as you have heard.'

'No more?'

He laughed.

'What do you expect me to feel about him? I wasn't to blame for what happened to him, any more than you are to blame for what happened to me ... No one is to blame for anything, because we are all alike – beasts.'

The White Mother

BY THEODOR SOLOGUB

1863–1937

I

Easter was drawing near. Esper Konstantinovitch Saksaulov was in a worried, weary mood. It began, seemingly, from the moment when at the Gorodishchevs' he was asked, 'Where are you spending the festival?'

Saksaulov for some reason delayed his reply.

The hostess, a stout, short-sighted, bustling lady, said, 'Come to us.'

Saksaulov was annoyed. Was it with the girl, who, at her mother's words, glanced at him quickly and instantly withdrew her gaze as she continued her conversation with the young assistant professor?

Saksaulov was eligible in the eyes of mothers of grown-up daughters, and this fact irritated him. He regarded himself as an old bachelor, and he was only thirty-seven. He replied curtly: 'Thank you. I always spend this night at home.'

The girl glanced at him, smiled, and said, 'With whom?'

'Alone,' Saksaulov replied, with a slight surprise in his voice.

'What a misanthrope!' said Madame Gorodishchev with a sour smile.

Saksaulov liked his freedom. There were occasions when he wondered how at one time he had nearly come to marry. He was now used to his small flat, furnished in severe style, used to his own valet, the aged, sedate Fedot, and to his no less aged wife, Christine, who cooked his dinner – and was throughly convinced that he did not marry because he wished to remain

181

true to his first love. In reality his heart had grown cold from indifference resulting from his solitary, aimless life. He had independent means, his father and mother were long since dead, and of near relations he had none. He lived an assured, tranquil life, was attached to some department, intimately acquainted with contemporary literature and art, and took an Epicurean pleasure in the good things of life, while life itself seemed to him empty and meaningless. Were it not for a solitary bright and pure dream that came to him sometimes, he would have grown quite cold, as so many other men have done.

II

His first and only love, that had ended before it had blossomed, in the evening sometimes made him dream sad sweet dreams. Five years ago he had met the young girl who had produced such a lasting impression on him. Pale, delicate, with slender waist, blue-eyed, fair-haired, she had seemed to him an almost celestial creature, a product of air and mist, accidentally cast by fate for a short span into the city din. Her movements were slow; her clear, tender voice sounded soft, like the murmur of a stream rippling gently over stones.

Saksaulov — was it by accident or design? — always saw her in a white dress. The impression of white became to him inseparable from his thought of her. Even her name, Tamara, seemed to him always white, like the snow on the mountain tops. He began to visit Tamara's parents. On more than one occasion had he resolved to speak those words to her that bind the fate of one human being with that of another. But she always eluded him; fear and anguish were reflected in her eyes. Of what was she afraid? Saksaulov saw in her face the signs of girlish love; her eyes lit up when he appeared, and a faint blush spread over her cheeks.

But on one never-to-be-forgotten evening she listened to him. The time was early spring. It was not long since the river had broken up and the trees had clothed themselves in a soft green gown. In a flat in town Tamara and Saksaulov sat by the open window facing the Neva. Without troubling himself about what to say and how to say it, he spoke sweet, for her terrifying, words. She turned pale, smiled absently, and got up. Her delicate hand trembled on the carved back of the chair.

'Tomorrow,' Tamara said softly, and went out.

Saksaulov, with a tense expectancy, sat for a long time staring at the door that had hidden Tamara. His head was in a whirl. A sprig of white lilac caught his eye; he took it and went away without bidding good-bye to his hosts.

At night he could not sleep. He stood by the window staring into the dark street that grew lighter towards the morning, smiling and toying with the sprig of white lilac. When it grew light he saw that the floor of the room was littered with petals of white lilac. This struck him as naïve and ridiculous. He took a bath, which made him feel as though he had almost regained his composure, and went to Tamara.

He was told that she was ill, she had caught a chill somewhere. And Saksaulov never saw her again. In two weeks she was dead. He did not go to her funeral. Her death left him almost unshaken. Already he could not tell whether he had loved her or if it were merely a brief passing fascination.

Sometimes in the evening he would dream of her; then her image began to fade. Saksaulov had no portrait of Tamara. It was only after several years had gone by, during last spring, that he was reminded of Tamara by a sprig of white lilac in the window of a restaurant, sadly out of place amidst the rich food. And from that day he again liked to think of Tamara in the evenings. Sometimes when he dozed off, he dreamt that she had come and sat down opposite him and looked at him with a fixed, caressing gaze, seeming to want something. It oppressed and hurt him sometimes to feel Tamara's expectant gaze.

Now as he left the Gorodishchevs, he thought apprehensively:

'She will come to give me the Easter greeting.'

The fear and loneliness were so oppressive that he thought: 'Why shouldn't I marry? I need not be alone then on holy mystic nights.'

Valeria Michailovna – the Gorodishchev girl – came into his

mind. She was not beautiful, but she always dressed well. It seemed to Saksaulov that she liked him and would not refuse him if he proposed.

In the street the noise and crowd distracted his attention; his thoughts of the Gorodishchev girl became tinged with the usual cynicism. Moreover, could he be untrue to Tamara's memory for anyone? The whole world seemed to him so petty and commonplace that he longed for Tamara – and Tamara only – to come and give him the Easter greeting.

'But,' he reflected, 'she will again fix on me that expectant gaze. Pure, gentle Tamara, what does she want? Will her soft lips kiss mine?'

III

With tormenting thoughts of Tamara, Saksaulov wandered about the streets, peering into the faces of the passers-by; the coarse faces of the men and women disgusted him. He reflected that there was no one with whom he would care to exchange the Easter greeting with any pleasure or love. There would be many kisses on the first day – coarse lips, tangled beards, an odour of wine.

If one had to kiss anyone at all it should be a child. The faces of children became pleasing to Saksaulov.

He walked about for a long time; he grew tired and went into a churchyard off the noisy street. A pale boy, sitting on a seat, glanced up at Saksaulov apprehensively and then sat on motionless, staring straight in front of him. His blue eyes were sad and caressing, like Tamara's. He was so tiny that his feet were not long enough to dangle, but projected straight in front of the seat. Saksaulov sat down beside him and regarded him with a sympathetic curiosity. There was something about this lonely little boy that stirred sweet memories. To look at he was the most ordinary child; in torn, ragged clothes, a white fur cap on his fair little head, and dirty, worn boots on his feet.

For a long time he sat on the seat, then he got up and began to cry pitifully. He ran out of the gate and along the street, stopped, set off in the opposite direction and stopped again. It was clear that he did not know which way to go. He cried softly to himself, the big tears dropping down his cheeks. A crowd gathered. A policeman came up. The boy was asked where he lived.

'Gluikhov House,' he lisped in the manner of very young children.

'In what street?' the policeman asked.

But the boy did not know the street, and only repeated, 'Gluikhov House.'

The policeman, a jolly young fellow, reflected for a moment, and decided that there was no such house in the immediate neighbourhood.

'Whom do you live with?' asked a gloomy-looking workman; 'have you got a father?'

'I haven't got a father,' the boy replied, looking at the crowd with tearful eyes.

'Got no father! Dear, dear,' the workman said solemnly, shaking his head. 'Have you got a mother?'

'Yes, I have a mother,' the boy replied.

'What is her name?'

'Mother,' the boy replied, then reflecting for a moment added, 'Black Mother.'

'Black? Is that her name?' the gloomy workman asked.

'First I had a white mother and now I have a black mother,' the boy explained.

'Well, my boy, we shall never make head or tail of you,' the policeman said decisively. 'I had better take you to the police-station. They can find out where you live on the telephone.'

He went up to a gate and rang. At this moment a porter, catching sight of the policeman, came out with a broom in his hand. The policeman told him to take the boy to the police-station, but the boy bethought himself and cried, 'Let me go; I will find the way myself!'

Was he frightened by the porter's broom, or had he indeed remembered something? At any rate, he ran away so quickly that Saksaulov nearly lost sight of him. Soon, however, the boy slackened his pace. He went up the street, running from one side to the other, trying in vain to find the house he lived in.

Saksaulov followed him silently. He did not know how to speak to children.

At last the boy became tired. He stopped by a lamp-post and leant against it. The tears glistened in his eyes.

'Well, my boy,' Saksaulov began, 'can't you find the house?'

The boy looked at him with his sad, gentle eyes, and suddenly Saksaulov realised what had made him follow the boy so persistently.

In the gaze and mien of the little wanderer there was something very like Tamara.

'What is your name, my dear?' Saksaulov asked gently.

'Lesha,' the boy replied.

'Do you live with your mother, Lesha?'

'Yes, with mother – but she is a black mother; I used to have a white mother.'

Saksaulov thought that by black mother he must mean a nun.

'How did you get lost?'

'I walked with mother, and we walked and walked. She told me to sit down and wait, and then she went away. And I got frightened.'

'Who is your mother?'

'My mother? She is black and angry.'

'What does she do?'

The boy thought a while.

'She drinks coffee,' he said.

'What else does she do?'

'She quarrels with the lodgers,' Lesha replied after a pause.

'And where is your white mother?'

'She was carried away. She was put into a coffin and carried away. And father was carried away, too.'

The boy pointed into the distance somewhere and burst into tears.

'What can I do with him?' Saksaulov thought.

Then suddenly the boy began to run again. After having run round a few street-corners he slackened his pace. Saksaulov caught him up a second time. The boy's face expressed a strange mixture of fear and joy.

'Here is the Gluikhov House,' he said to Saksaulov, as he pointed to a big, five-storied, ugly building.

At this moment there appeared at the gates of the Gluikhov House a black-haired, black-eyed woman in a black dress, on her head a black kerchief with white spots. The boy shrank back in fear.

'Mother!' he whispered.

His step-mother looked at him in astonishment.

'How did you get here, you rascal?' she cried. 'I told you to stop on the seat, didn't I?'

She would have struck him, but observing a gentleman of solemn dignified mien who seemed to be watching them, she lowered her voice.

'Can't you be left for half an hour without running away? I've tired myself out looking for you, you rascal!'

She snatched the boy's little hand in her big one and dragged him within the gate.

Saksaulov made a note of the street and went home.

IV

Saksaulov liked to listen to Fedot's sound judgments. When he reached home he told him about the boy Lesha.

'She had left him on purpose,' Fedot announced. 'What a wicked woman, to take the boy so far from home!'

'What made her do it?' Saksaulov asked.

'One can't tell. Silly woman — no doubt she thought the boy would wander about the streets until someone or other would pick him up. What can you expect from a step-mother? What use is the child to her?'

'But the police would have found her,' Saksaulov said incredulously.

'Perhaps; but she may be leaving the town altogether, and how could they find her then?'

Saksaulov smiled. 'Really,' he thought, 'Fedot should have been an examining magistrate.'

However, sitting near the lamp with a book, he dozed off. In his dreams he saw Tamara — gentle and white — she came and sat beside him. Her face was wonderfully like Lesha's. She gazed at him incessantly, persistently, seeming to expect something. It was oppressive for Saksaulov to see her bright, pleading eyes and not to know what it was that she wanted. He got up quickly and walked over to the chair where Tamara appeared to be sitting. Standing before her he implored aloud:

'What do you want? Tell me.'

But she was no longer there.

'It was only a dream,' Saksaulov thought sadly.

V

Coming out of the Academy exhibition on the following day, Saksaulov met the Gorodishchevs.

He told the girl about Lesha.

'Poor boy!' Valeria Michailovna said softly: 'his stepmother simply wants to get rid of him.'

'That is by no means certain,' Saksaulov replied, annoyed that both Fedot and the girl should take such a tragic view of a simple incident.

'It is quite obvious. The boy has no father and lives with his step-mother. She finds him a nuisance. If she can't get rid of him decently she will cast him off altogether.'

'You take too gloomy a view,' said Saksaulov with a smile.

'Why don't you adopt him?' Valeria Michailovna suggested.

'I?' Saksaulov asked in surprise.

'You live alone,' she persisted; 'you have no one belonging to you. Do a good deed at Easter. You will have someone with whom to exchange the greeting, at any rate.'

'But what could I do with a child, Valeria Michailovna?'

'Get a nurse for it. Fate seems to have sent the child to you.'

Saksaulov looked at the flushed, animated face of the girl in wonder, and with an unconscious gentleness.

When Tamara again appeared to him in his dreams that evening it seemed to him that he knew what she wanted. And in the stillness of his room the words seemed to ring softly: 'Do as she has told you.'

Saksaulov got up rejoicing, and passed his hand over his sleepy eyes. He caught sight of a sprig of white lilac on the table. Where had it come from? Had Tamara left it in token of her will?

And suddenly it occurred to him that by marrying the Gorodishchev girl and adopting Lesha he would fulfil Tamara's wish. Gladly he breathed in the fragrant perfume of the lilac.

He recollected that he had bought the flower himself that day, but instantly thought, 'It makes no difference that I bought it myself. There is an omen in the fact that I wished to buy it and then forgot that I had bought it.'

VI

In the morning he set out to find Lesha. The boy met him at the gate and showed him where he lived. Lesha's mother was drinking coffee and quarrelling with her red-nosed lodger. This is what Saksaulov was able to learn about Lesha.

His mother had died when he was three years old. His father had married this dark woman and had also died within the year. The dark woman, Irena Ivanovna, had a year-old child of her own. She was about to marry again. The wedding was to take place in a few days, and immediately afterwards they were to go into the 'provinces.' Lesha was a stranger to her and in her way.

'Give him to me,' Saksaulov suggested.

'With pleasure,' Irena Ivanovna said with malicious joy. Then after a pause added, 'Only you must pay me for his clothes.'

And thus Lesha was installed in Saksaulov's home. The Gorodishchev girl helped him to find a nurse and with the other details in connection with Lesha's instalment at the flat. For this purpose she had to visit Saksaulov's home. Occupied thus she seemed quite a different being to Saksaulov. The door of her heart seemed to have opened to him. Her eyes became tender and radiant. Altogether she was permeated with the same gentleness that had emanated from Tamara.

VII

Lesha's stories of his white mother touched Fedot and his wife. On Passion Saturday, when putting him to bed, they hung a white sugar egg at the end of his bed.

'This is from your white mother,' Christine said. 'But you mustn't touch it, dear, until the Lord has risen and the bells are ringing.'

Lesha lay down obediently. For a long time he stared at the lovely egg, then fell asleep.

And Saksaulov on this evening sat at home alone. About midnight an uncontrollable feeling of drowsiness closed his eyes and he was glad, because soon he would see Tamara. And she came, clothed in white, radiant, bringing with her the joyful distant sound of church bells. With a gentle smile she bent over him, and – utterable joy! – Saksaulov felt a gentle touch on his lips. A gentle voice pronounced softly, 'Christ has risen!'

Without opening his eyes Saksaulov stretched out his arms and embraced a tender slim body. This was Lesha, who had climbed on to his knee to give him the Easter greeting.

The church bells had wakened the boy. He had seized the white egg and run in to Saksaulov.

Saksaulov awoke. Lesha laughed and held up his white egg.

'White Mother has sent it,' he lisped; 'I will give it you and you must give it to Auntie Valeria.'

'Very well, dear, I will do as you say,' Saksaulov replied.

He put Lesha to bed and then went to Valeria Michailovna with Lesha's white egg, a present from the white mother. But it seemed to Saksaulov at the moment to be a present from Tamara.

TOBAGO

Leeward Beaches   Stonehaven
                                   Back Bay (? robberies /
                                             naturists)
Englishmen Bay ✓   Bloody Bay

Carletur   Parlatuvier (survey
(nice but watch out)   poor ish)
; (Fisherman (s) to eat)

Northside Rd → Leeward Beaches

    King Peters Bay (Morrah) Mount Dillon view

Windward Beaches

    Kings Bay & Kings Bay Cafe (views)
         ('changing room)

Fishing / Boat
    Holly Williams 639 0485 (Carletur)

Places   Golden Dove } to eat
  ∑   Shamon + Phoebes   + Pirates Bay ✗✗✗
Charlotteville (Fishy Village) + Man War Beach
Speyside (Jemmas to eat)

Ocean Edge Rum Shop overlook Stonehaven
                                        Bay
         good beer @ sundown